where
we
fall

OTHER TITLES BY ROCHELLE B. WEINSTEIN

What We Leave Behind

The Mourning After

where
we
fall

ROCHELLE B. WEINSTEIN

LAKE UNION
PUBLISHING

Text copyright © 2016 Rochelle B. Weinstein
All rights reserved.

Published by Lake Union Publishing, Seattle

www.apub.com

Amazon, the Amazon logo, and Lake Union Publishing are trademarks of Amazon.com, Inc., or its affiliates.

ISBN-13: 9781612184432
ISBN-10: 161218443X

Cover design by Lindsey Andrews

Printed in the United States of America

For Steven, Jordan, and Brandon.
Because of you, my heart is full.
And in memory of my beloved mother,
Ruth Gratz Berger

SPRING 1997

ABBY

Imagining things any other way would be impossible. It's always been the three of us. Lauren. Ryan. Me. And *this*. This crazy, beautiful seam that fastens us together. I am flattened across the oversized boulders, soaking in the sun; Ryan and Lauren are steadying the inner tube against the water that shoots and winds down the rocks. Their toes sink beneath the frigid water, and Ryan calls in my direction: "C'mon, Abs, the clouds are moving in. You've got to take a run by yourself. Just once. Before we graduate. You'll love it."

"No," I say. "I can't. You know I can't."

"There's nothing to be afraid of," Lauren says. "We've done it a million times together. Try it solo. We'll tape you!"

I stand up and grab my video camera while my best friends nuzzle each other. Ryan kisses her head, and I feel the shiver of his lips down my legs when I walk. "Let's go down the three of us. Like we always do." Relenting, he positions himself along the tube, waving us to sit down. Lauren falls into his lap, and I wedge myself nearby. The plastic is not made to hold three people, but they have never left me out.

The natural slide is about fifty feet long, and the bouncy ride on the rugged rocks makes it feel longer. We are fused together—friendship and more—bound by arms and legs. The camera captures us coasting down the falls, where we blend and flow. It's exhilarating and daring, like us.

We are falling into one another, screaming all the way down, clasping on to one another for support. I point the lens toward the sky. The view is fast and fleeting, though it hinges on memory.

The drop at the end of the run meets us in a rush of crystal rapids. The first touch shocks as we land in the pond below and come apart. I raise the camera above my head to keep it from the water below. Lauren breaks the surface first. Then Ryan. Then me. Our faces are pinched in red, and our hair sculpted down our backs. The surprise dissolves and we laugh. Ryan grabs Lauren from behind while I jump on his back and straddle my legs around his waist. His hand reaches for hers, and he guides us to the warm rocks nearby.

The three of us. Perfectly happy.

Imagining things any other way would be impossible.

FALL 2014

CHAPTER ONE

ABBY

I am stirred awake by the demons that bothered me throughout the night. The crumpled sheets strangle my ankles, though they might as well be around my neck. My eyes adjust to the thick custard of dawn and fix on the bedroom I share with Ryan. The space beside me is empty, though I don't need to fan my fingers across the sheets to know this. His absence taunts me, much like the clock beside my bed. I wish the bright light of 6:07 away. Ryan is out for his morning run, before heading to the high school for his first class. The window is open, and a whiff of brisk autumn air fills the room. It should rouse me from the bottomless depths of sleep, but it does not. I am a prisoner in my bed. Much like I am in my mind.

Lately, it has been harder and harder to push through the thoughts.

If only they encompassed the trials of raising a teenager, the kinks in a marriage, the weathering that time has on our minds and our bodies. At thirty-eight, my flat stomach feels more dimpled to the touch. Gravity has taken over my lean arms and legs. Ryan would tell me, "You get better each year," without even glancing at me. That's Ryan's way.

It's one of the things that makes me loathe him at times, the artificial, insincere praise. But that's the least of our problems.

Last night, we slipped into bed, aware of the gentle quiet of our daughter Juliana's absence. The calm swathed us in a forgotten time, one when we had the whole house to ourselves and making love stemmed from raw, untainted desire rather than obligation. The expectation added to the pressure and pulled us apart. His cool foot grazing mine beneath the sheets felt more like an intruding guest than seduction. His solid arms weaved around my waist, yearning for something I could not give him. I long ago stopped feeling sorry for my inability to be the wife he deserves.

Our bedroom is a pillowy white with faint splashes of ivory. It emanates light and breeziness, but when I step over the threshold at night, darkness cloaks my shoulders and burrows into my chest. Nobody can understand. I barely understand it myself. There are horrible thoughts that trespass in my brain, imposters lurking, preying on my weaknesses. It takes all of my strength to annihilate them without doing further damage to the tender parts.

I have known battles with external forces—heated debates with loved ones, bad habits that need breaking, a loss not easily accepted—foes that are logical, though immeasurable. Those struggles made sense to me. What I can't understand is the feud that now dwells in my head, the two opposing sides that are dueling.

The door swings open to our bedroom, and in walks Ryan.

Ryan is beautiful to look at. Not because he has faultless features on a chiseled face—he has neither. It is his imperfections that make him just right. The hazel-green of his eyes coaxes and charms. One of his eyebrows is slightly thinner than the other, the result of stitches a few years back, and his thick, dark hair is matted in sweat with slick strands of gray. His skin sprouts a day-old shadow, and his lips are neither sensual nor demanding, but rather pursed and serious. His youthfulness disguises his thirty-eight years, and when he stands on the sidelines, coaching high school football, he appears more the kids' age than his own.

He leans over the bed and kisses the top of my head. His smell engulfs me, and our eyes meet. In his stare, I always hear what he's not saying. His voice bears the rhythm of a Southern drawl. "How you doin', sweetie?" he asks. "Have you heard from Jules? When's she coming home?"

When my inner voice starts poking away at my common sense, I get mean. "I told you already."

He backs away, recognizing immediately it's going to be one of those days.

Ryan's no stranger to bouts of depression. He's been dragging me off the floor for years. He's watched me sleep for days straight, withering into something more skeletal than human. He has begged me to return to therapy, but therapy doesn't work, not when my brain isn't working. "And medication?" he would plead. "Stay on it; don't go off it once you're feeling better." But I did go off it, and we tiptoed around the quicksand, trying not to sink through.

"What are you doing today?" He questions me while I study him from a safe distance. He is dressed in damp navy athletic shorts and the school's football T-shirt. The sleeves fit snugly around his arms; his wedding band stares at me. He is always tan, my husband, from days spent outdoors and on the field. Plus, he is generally happy. That can make anyone light up from within. The question means that he is worried and wants me to get out of bed. He does not wish for my insidious sorrow to unravel.

Before I can answer, an awful thought bursts into my brain, setting the kindling ablaze. I am lying in bed, safely hidden under the covers, though I am far from safe. I have to move. I have to escape.

"What's wrong?" he asks, as my bare feet hit the dark wooden floor, and I knock past him.

The bathroom door is a mere couple of steps away, but the effort to get there makes it feel farther. The walls are closing in around me. I lunge forward for the doorknob and push my weight through.

"Abby!" he yells.

There is an indescribable force that wills me to keep moving. It is at once a safety measure and an unstoppable energy that pushes me toward an unspeakable hell. The vanity mirror reflects my tangled dark hair and swollen eyes, and I don't recognize the person staring back.

"Abby!" he yells again, banging on the door that I have locked.

"Go away, Ryan," I beg, while my fingers crush the wadded-up picture and stuff it into the pocket of my pants. It was in a drawer of Ryan's, one I never bothered to look through. Their arms are around each other. Ryan is someone other than my husband.

"What the hell's going on?" he screams. "I'll break this door down, Abby! I will. Open up. Let me in."

"No," I shout back. "Just leave." I have collapsed to the floor and grabbed my knees to my chest. When he continues to pound on the door and demand that I open it, I place my hands over my ears and rock back and forth. The cotton pajama bottoms and flimsy tank top are no defense for the cold air that coats my body in a frosty layer of fright. Thoughts are bouncing around my head, terrifying and comforting me at the same time. I am at their mercy, submerged in doubt. This doubt guides me to the back of the bottom cabinet, where we hide dangerous things. I take them out, fingering them, rubbing my palms across their warnings before setting them beside me on the floor.

"Abby, you're scaring me."

"It's never going to work," I whimper, tears pooling around my eyes. "It was never meant to be."

"What are you talking about? You're not making any sense. Honey, just let me in. Talk to me."

The doorknob is jiggling, and I am torn between wanting him to break the door down and needing him to vanish. To my right, by the Jacuzzi tub, a glass cabinet holds tiny framed photos of Juliana as a baby, a picture of Ryan and me at the field, the two of us in front of Looking Glass Falls. My mind swirls with menacing thoughts when I crawl over to the case, grab hold of the glass frame, and throw it against the mirror. My face splinters into pieces before my eyes. And then there is black.

CHAPTER TWO

ABBY

I awake in a hospital bed in Charlotte's CMC-Mercy with a throbbing headache. Ryan later tells me that when he broke down the door, the hit to my head knocked me unconscious. He found me lying beside a bag of razor blades and some pills. They weren't Tylenol or Advil either. They were the stronger kind, capsules we've used when one of us can't sleep, and when Ryan broke his wrist at practice. The doctors had searched my body for evidence of damage, but there was none.

Unless you count the picture they found rolled in a ball in the pajama pocket.

It sits next to my bed atop the wooden furniture piece they call a nightstand. Their faces are crinkled and bent so Ryan's nose looks frighteningly large, despite someone's efforts to smooth the photo out. I don't like the way they are smiling at me so I turn the picture facedown.

"I thought you were dead," he whispers to me from his seat beside my bed. He is cupping my hands in his, and he is trying to conceal tears.

Ryan rarely cries. The only things that can move him to weakness are seeing his wife in a hospital bed with a mild concussion and the endless stream of questions that must be bouncing around in his head . . . like why is there a picture of him and Lauren, the one he kept hidden in his drawer, sitting next to me in this awful room?

Despite my condition, I feel remarkably calm.

"Were you planning to take those pills?" he asks. "Were you going to hurt yourself?"

"It's not what you think," I whisper.

"I don't know what to think anymore," he replies, his head drooping downward, his eyes opening and closing with an effort that tells me he is having a hard time with this, with me. Usually he is much stronger. Usually he picks up the pieces and puts us back together, and no one ever notices the scratches.

Then I turn the picture back around so he can see what he has done to me.

I can tell by his eyes and the way he lowers his head that he saw it there by my bed.

"How did you get that?"

"Why are you still holding on to it?" I fire back.

But then the shot of adrenaline is replaced with the icy cold liquid filling my veins and I don't hear his answer.

Frightful images race through my mind, voiceless weapons that strike unseen, but with palpable destruction. There are a thousand miles between a thought and an action, but try telling that to someone imprisoned by her unwanted fears: Obsessions. Phobias. Plane crashes. Lizards. Swallowing pills. Hurting one's own child. The preoccupation with bizarre ideas blares in my ears without making a sound. They are invasive, sneaky, and more powerful than physical touch. They are the thoughts that have plagued me for years.

"Ma, it's me."

I hear my daughter's voice through the fog of dense memory.

"Mama, can you hear me?"

My eyes open, and there is Juliana, our baby girl. She is standing over me with her choppy bangs shielding her fear-filled eyes. Her palm is wrestling with my fingers, which are controlled by an IV spouting a cocktail of Ativan and ibuprofen. "Juliana." I smile up at her. It is only her name that I whisper through dried lips; it tells her I am happy to see her.

"Is it true?" she asks. "They said you had pills . . ."

"No, honey, it's not what you think."

"Are things really that bad?"

My beautiful Juliana. The green of her eyes darts around the room. This is what I've done to her. Once she was the reason for the momentary calm between my rising storms. For her, I could buck up. For her, I could quiet the madness in my head. Until I couldn't anymore.

"Where's Daddy?" she asks, her eyes pleading.

I grab her hand. "He's here. He went to speak to the doctor."

"They said it was an emergency! They took me off the bus!"

As a small child, Juliana would ask why I was holed up in the dark for days. Ryan was gifted at interference and explained that I was sick with the flu, or fighting a cold, and then he would fling her on his shoulders and distract her with tales from the football field and promises to bring her to the next day's practice. As she got older, her wisdom surpassed her years and Ryan's answers provoked more questions. We decided to be straightforward with our child and tell her that I was depressed.

The violent, obsessive, uncontrollable urges were one aspect of my neuroses. That they turned me into a sad, hopeless person was another. After a thought would attack and penetrate, I felt stained and soiled. I could muster the strength to chip away at the frightening images that disarmed my mind, but their residual gook remained.

Juliana grasps my fingers tighter. "What are we going to do?"

As the only child—the domestic glue for bickering parents— Juliana has always taken on the role of the grown-up. She is the fixer, the unifier, the one who regrettably believes she can repair the damage and make wrong into right. Children like this mistakenly think they have the power to control any situation—which makes for altruistic teenagers, and ultimately very disappointed adults.

"You need help," she whispers. "Like real help."

Throughout my life, Juliana and Ryan witnessed the subtle entry and hastened departure of four different therapists. Each one pledged that with time and a commitment to healing, I could live a "normal" life. And while I would settle into the glowing promise of therapy and the life-changing medicines they threw my way, the light would return to the sky and brighten my fading universe. I responded extremely well and rather quickly to the boosters that were resetting my broken circuitry. Once I returned to "normal," though, I would abruptly stop taking the colorful pills. Then I would immerse myself in redecorating the house or shopping online or tending to Juliana's never-ending list of teenage demands. I would miss an appointment here or there. It would turn into more, until soon it would be months and hours of unreturned phone calls from Dale, Irene, Babs, and Lois, the band of therapists.

Ryan never noticed I wasn't keeping my appointments. As long as things were calm in his house when he walked in the door after practice— meaning I was dressed, a meal was prepared for dinner, and I wasn't hanging from the rafters—he could exhale. Ryan isn't one for therapy and self-reflection. He has a depth about him, but traversing his wife's psyche makes him queasy.

"Are you listening to me?"

I am. Sort of. What she is saying does not need to be said. I know by the wistful look in her eyes what she wants from me. If only I wouldn't have amnesia when I'd start to feel better. If only the ugly times hugged me a little deeper and harder as a reminder that I'd be suctioned through the cloud again if I didn't stay on my meds. Besides, I am thinking of other things. Like how Ryan and I used to talk *to* each other and not *at* each other.

Then Juliana begins to cry. "What's going to happen to you?"

Her question with its string of innuendo jerks me upright.

"Jules, I wasn't going to hurt myself. I would never do that to you."

I have never attempted suicide. What I am exacting on myself through my mind's fury is a continuous, wobbly threat. The fear leaves me in a constant state of alert, my body fighting a force that it has not seen or touched. By way of inner battle and allowing my thoughts to control me, I am slowly, painfully killing myself. I never told the quartet of therapists about my thoughts. I never told anyone.

Juliana's gaze forces me to answer. I can't tell her I was protecting myself, that I had the razor blades and the pills in my hands to throw them in the garbage. Self-preservation involves exposure to the things I fear most. It's a twisted test, a chance to show these objects that I am stronger.

"Do you want to die? Do you want to leave us?"

"No! *No!*" I repeat again. Though how can I explain to her, to anyone, these awful thoughts without sounding like I have a severe psychological imbalance?

The noise of the door breaks the silence. Juliana does not know what to say to me. This wasn't like the time when she was five and found me curled up in a ball on the bathroom floor with one of her dolls in my arms. She thought it was *cute* that I wanted to comfort the Powerpuff Girl with the stomachache.

Ryan pokes his head through the doorway, and thanks to his appearance, Juliana releases my fingers and meets his embrace. Ryan has always been Juliana's beacon. Their bond is unusual and strong, utterly enviable. In my absences, Ryan has become a single parent, a doting father, with nothing but pure and simple love for his daughter. My eyes follow her as she glides toward his voice. He has that way about him. Ryan can pluck the greatness from those closest to him: his teammates, his students, his daughter. Only not his wife.

CHAPTER THREE

JULIANA

Before I got the call about my mama, I was actually beginning to enjoy myself on the class trip. We were days into our trek through the Pisgah National Forest, where we were expected to commune with nature and live a no-Wi-Fi existence while searching for a surge of cell service. It wasn't easy trading in my favorite sneakers for hiking boots, but I had enjoyed the quiet more than I would admit to the others. Lately, my head had been jumbled with noise, and the peacefulness of the mountains had drained thoughts of E.J. and my mom from my muddled mind.

Dr. Tait, our chaperone for the week, had filmed our experience, shoving portable microphones in our faces with prompts that recorded what we had learned on the trip. When it was my turn, he asked me to share something about myself, something beyond my being almost seventeen and in the eleventh grade at Poplar Grove High School.

He was the only one who didn't laugh when I said I had a new appreciation for my bed, so he pushed me harder. "Tell us something personal, something you shared with the group this week."

I thought about the trust I had found in my classmates, and theirs in me, while tackling steep climbs and moving through our fear. "We're different people than when we arrived. We've had to rely on one another for support in dangerous situations. It didn't matter if the person holding out her hand was the girl I sat next to in history and ignored repeatedly day after day."

The kids around me were nodding their heads.

"That's what I got out of this trip. We're all different. We all came here carrying our *things*. Only I didn't feel any of those differences when I was plunging down the side of a mountain with Brook, over there, as my safety net. Or when I needed Wendy to help me start the fire so we could eat a proper meal.

"My daddy always says about his team, 'You don't need to be best friends, but you have to respect each other.'" The kids gathered around me, and I broke away from the camera to add the last part. "I don't imagine all of us will become best friends at school, but I can tell you this: you all have my respect."

Everyone had applauded and cheered for me. Even Dr. Tait. My best friends, Sophie, Nicole, and Marlee, all rallied around me while Dr. Tait snapped a picture of us on Mount Mitchell. It is the photograph on my phone I'm sharing with Daddy now. The parting gift for having to leave the trip early. Marlee with her blonde hair, aqua eyes, and a haughty smile. Nicole and Sophie, the fraternal twins who have identical chestnut hair and playful indigo eyes. I am a mixture of my counterparts—dirty blonde and green-eyed. "Marlee got so tall," he says. "She towers over you girls."

Daddy and I are thrust into our private world while Mama sits quietly by, half-awake and dreamlike. "The mountains were so beautiful, Daddy. You were right. The leaves are already changing up there. That smell you always talked about . . ."

"Fraser fir and pine," he says, with a trace of something sad in his voice I don't recognize.

"I don't like to admit when you're right."

"I know"—he laughs, coming back to life and putting his arm around me—"and I'm used to it, but honey, being up there was good for you. My best days were on mountains and by lakes, inhaling the clean air. It clears your head and grounds you. Anything seems possible." He hesitates before adding, "I'm sorry you had to leave the trip early."

Even his arm around me can't fix what's wrong. I glance at the photo of myself—me with the tentative smile, me staring out at the mountain range behind Dr. Tait's burly body, holding everything in. E.J. would call it my resting bitch face, a not-so-charming phrase he thinks is funny. *Who are you?* I ask the photo.

I'm wearing E.J.'s football sweatshirt. It's gray and roomy with bold navy letters across the front that spell out "Giants Football." I reach for the hood resting between my shoulders and pull it over my head as a shield. I smell E.J. in the folds of the cushy cotton, and I bury my hands in the deep pockets.

"You okay, honey?" he whispers. "I know this is hard for you."

"Daddy," I say, looking up at him, "you have no idea," and I know he thinks I'm talking about Mama, and that's what I want him to think, but it's so much more than that.

This is where it gets difficult for me. This is where the pain becomes less emotional and far more physical. The lingering ache in my backside shoots down my legs when I sit. It creates a kaleidoscope of feelings and sensations I simply must endure.

I know he didn't mean to hurt me.

I know E.J. never, in a million years, thought that his actions would result in my falling down a flight of stairs in the back stairwell of his school.

Accidents don't happen to girls like me.

Daddy takes the empty seat beside me. I close my eyes and rest my head against him. I see E.J., and I trace his face in my mind's eye. His scent brings him close to me; the pain pushes him away.

"Your mama's going to get the help she needs," he says, the two of us looking on as she fights to stay awake. "I promise. I won't let anything happen to you."

I nod, and he asks if I've heard from E.J.

"Of course," I lie.

"I bet you can't wait to see him."

I'm a mixture of feelings when it comes to E.J. "You're leaving Mama to go to the game?" I ask, though I don't know where the question comes from, the need to protect her from anything. Daddy is the one who needs saving.

"It's the other way around," he tells me, reminding me of the fact that Mama, despite all her craziness, never once missed one of Daddy's games. Oddly enough, she's his good-luck charm. I wish I could say she were the same for me. Mama and I clash like two animals on a hunt, circling around each other. Fighting with her, disagreeing with her, mocking her—these are the ways I block out how bad it feels to have a mama who's "limited." That's what Daddy calls it.

When I was a kid, and we'd be curled up in my bed reading a bedtime story, I'd ask, "Is Mama coming?" At first, the answer was "She's sleeping," or "She's resting," but as I got older and the absences were noticeably inexcusable, we talked about limitations. He'd come into my room with his "lights out" face, always with a kiss on the top of my head. By then I had stopped asking. "People have limits, Juliana. It doesn't make them bad or wrong." I knew he was talking about Mama, even if he mingled the things he'd say with other subjects, like boys or the kids at school.

I could accept that Mama was different. What I couldn't accept was the way it made me feel inside.

His voice plucks me from memory. "I'm going to be taking off soon," he says. "Can you stay here a little longer?"

I shrug. "Do I have to? I hate hospitals."

If we were a different kind of family, he would have pushed me harder.

But Daddy knows Mama's moods are fickle. Backing off is a means to safeguard my own sanity.

"Can't I go with you to the field? I don't want to go alone," I say, reminding him that my friends are all on the class trip. "I won't bother you or E.J. I promise."

Mama's voice whispers from the bed, "You two go on." Her voice is gravelly but insistent. "No sense babysitting me in here. I'll be all right. Me and my monitors will be just fine."

Daddy gets up first. I know I must follow. He takes Mama's hands into his and we stare down at her in the bed. The tubes and lights make her look scary. She could use a comb through her hair. "Go on," she says. "It'll make me nuts knowing you're here and I'm helpless to do anything."

"You're wrong," Daddy insists. "You're not helpless, Abby. You've gotta fight this, whatever it is. No more pretending it's going to just go away on its own."

My frustration has reached its boiling point. My eyes bore into hers when I say, "I agree with Daddy. Mama, it's time. Don't you think?"

"I'm okay," she says, stealing her eyes away from mine and turning them toward the ceiling. "I can do this on my own."

"That hasn't worked for you in a long time," says Daddy. He sighs, and a frown creeps across his face. His eyes look tired; his body is hunched over and beaten. "We love you, Abs, but something's gotta give. We'll be here for you. You won't go through this alone."

A sadness clouds Mama's features and she presses her lips together. She knows we're right, and instead of giving in, she pulls herself together and tells Daddy he'd better hurry up or he'll be late.

Her refusal deflates him. I can see it all over his face. He thinks that if he holds her gaze long enough she'll reconsider. I wish she didn't fight it so hard. He leans over and kisses her on the cheek and insists I do the same. One happy family.

Then he takes my hand and leads me out of the room.

CHAPTER FOUR

RYAN

"Coach, what's your strategy for tonight's game? How do you plan on using your young quarterback?"

This is my least favorite part of the job—the interviews. Having the number-one football team in the state has its perks, but as someone who thrives on the field and away from prying eyes, I am testy and short.

We are joined in a corner of the field by sports reporters from all over the area. These are the gentlemen who will ensure that my boys get in front of top college scouts. Everyone is here to see the state champs. Small towns breed large football hearts.

"Our quarterback's been training hard all summer. Hopefully we can get him some time in the pocket, and he can make some good decisions."

"What about Evan James? The word on the street is he's been distracted at practice. Any chance you sit him out tonight?"

"No. Next question."

"Coach, the team's coming off a close game last week. Anything you can say about the current state of your players' minds? Your state of mind?"

My assistant coach, Wayne Harrow, jumps in, seeing how the line of questioning will only provoke me. The older man grabs hold of the mic and dispels the interrogation with a loyalty that has characterized our years together. "We're here to play football. Pine Ridge is prepped and ready. We'll play as we always have . . . to win. Now, thank you. This interview is over."

The reporters drift off, and Wayne and I are left alone on the field.

He comes right out and asks me how I'm holding up. I consider pretending that he's concerned about my controversial running back and our team's mental prowess. Instead, I eye the man I know well and say, "Not so good, my friend. Not so good."

"How's she doing?"

If only I could have a nickel for every time Wayne has asked me that question. He is the assistant coach, but his wisdom and experience make him more of a father figure. The foibles of my wife have been subject to scrutiny and disdain. But empathy and sympathy wore off when the despair Abby wreaked on our home crept on to our crisp, green field.

Selfish. Wayne could pry my eyes open with that single word, but I had a difficult time labeling someone I loved who was so deeply troubled. It seemed unfair and cruel.

We take our seats in the bleachers alongside the field, where I am always overcome with pride. Wayne towers over me with his thick body and spray of gray hair. The man has the largest hands I've ever seen.

"When are they releasing her from the hospital?"

"Tomorrow. They want to watch her overnight."

"You all right with that?"

I shrug. Coaches and players have built dynasties around superstition and crazy rituals to ensure victory. Despite Abby's fickle mind, she has never once missed a game. As doomed as she seems at times, her presence on the sidelines always feels right.

"How long are you going to let this go on, son?"

The innuendo isn't an innuendo anymore when it's been asked a dozen times.

"I can't leave her, Wayne. I can't leave her like this. We promised to take care of each other. She's sick. I won't abandon her."

"What about you?" he asks. "What about the promises she made to you?"

It doesn't feel right to think about me at a time like this.

The players begin to arrive at the field for our pregame meeting, and Wayne excuses himself, telling me to take my time while he gets them started. With forty-two boys, there are numerous game-day superstitions, which are stupid only if they don't work. Eating green gummy bears and praying on the thirteenth row in the bleachers are among them. I'm watching Evan James warm up. I know precisely what he has eaten today. I know the color of his undershirt, and I know that he will not say so much as a word to the other players on the field until the kickoff. This is how he conditions himself before a game.

This is where I belong—this field, this house. In a world that has handed me some tough losses, this is where I learned of victory. Here is where it all makes sense. I love my wife. And though things haven't come easy, nothing worth having ever does. She bore me Juliana, my greatest blessing, and I will always be grateful for that.

Abby is a woman of shifting temperaments. When she is lying motionless in bed, I am reminded of our beginning, when she needed me and I could take care of her. When she is depressed, her emptiness makes her nicer. Her tangled and tortured mind bargains with her: if she is kind to others, maybe she will slip out of the dark.

Those nights when we lay in bed, I rubbed her shoulders and ran my fingers through her long, dark hair, and she would speak of how

God was punishing her. Her bronzed face would burrow into my arms, like a needy child. "What did I do to deserve this, Ryan?" she would ask. "Why is this happening to me?"

I never had the right answers for Abby. I am a man who thinks in statistics and strategy. Like a coach, I tried to draw Abby out. But Abby didn't want to come out. Not when there was so much wrong inside of her. And when she emerged from the dark episodes, she was someone entirely unrecognizable. We were unrecognizable to each other.

It's impossible to think of Abby lying in that hospital bed without that photo staring up at me. I block out her name and other parts. I don't want to remember how it felt to roll the word off my tongue, to whisper it into her ear. But I can still see her smile. Her fiery red hair. The girl who brought Abby into my life.

I push the thoughts of her away until the sheer will of my resistance flings them back. Like the picture I had held on to. It was the only one of us I didn't throw out. We are laughing at the camera, at a future we thought was ours. I stopped looking at it years ago, but I always knew it was there. Seeing her smile there on the nightstand in Abby's hospital room had shoved me into the past. Her name was staying with me longer than I could stand.

"Coach!"

The kids are stepping onto the field. I watch the tangle of limbs and legs cross the grass. Some of them are wearing their superstitions—bandanas, a certain color undershirt—and there's Jerry Goihman eating from his bag of Haribo gummy bears. We are a cluster of men who believe that engaging in senseless gestures can predict our performance and our future.

I watch my boys warming up and think about the words of wisdom I will share with them. I could talk about loss, but I won't. Not today. Today I will remind them how important it is to stay focused.

"C'mon in, boys," I say, signaling to the team.

The temperature has dropped a few degrees, though I don't feel the chill against my skin. I look up to the fifty-yard line and count five rows up to the spot reserved for Abby. It's not a formalized spot, but for the past dozen or more years, the crowd has respected that proprietary seat in Coach's palace. This is my kingdom, the field my shrine, and my girl in her designated seat is something I have come to rely upon.

Shutting out her absence, I am focused and in control. I stand before my team and say the words they need to guide them through the next forty-eight minutes. Though I am not a religious man, a coach's words are gospel. They can impact and incite, or deflate. It's both what I say and how I say it. The kids know my mood through the arc of my sentences, the tone of my voice. They know me well, and I, them. Despite what's going on at home, I need to parlay my words into the role of actor. I do this for the boys because they depend on me.

The team huddles around me. Wayne joins my side. The crowd has grown and spills out onto the field. ESPNU is on the sidelines waiting to film the game for national television. The noise is loud; the band plays the same song again and again, but spirit laces through the chords and makes it less annoying. I survey the boys. They are padded up and look larger and scarier than some of the college teams. My boys are black, white, but mostly poor. Colson Pepper was arrested for shoplifting at the Food Lion when he tried to sneak a twenty-five-pound turkey out underneath his girlfriend's dress; Tate Williams has been in and out of several foster homes; Braylon Jones is failing eighty percent of his classes. A few have beaten the odds and excelled in school. A few have had less chaotic upbringings, but they are few and far between.

This is important, because my team has risen from the ashes. I have watched the morale and confidence strip from their faces as the city around them lost faith and hope. They were *expected* to fail. They were *expected* to lose. It took us years to get inside their heads and to break through some of their most guarded exteriors. To some of them, Coach Harrow and I are the only people they can count on, the only ones who say they'll show up, and then do. When you build a team, it is easy to get caught up in the trappings of physical talent. No one can coach without it. But a team that wins championships is one with heart. And that comes with trust and a mental acuity that trumps bodily muscle. I am proud of these boys. They have overcome tough circumstances in ways most never will. Now it is up to me to inspire them. They will rely on my steadiness and rationale to make sense of their imperfect worlds. Together, on the field, is where we become unified as one. We are all the same. And we have one common goal on Friday night: to win.

"Coach Holden," comes the gruff voice from behind me. Sheriff Buford knows better than to bother me on the field while I'm meeting with my boys. "Coach Holden," he says again. I survey my players, looking for the one who looks away.

I am just about to move these boys into playing mode. It is a shift that will block out the noise and get them to concentrate on the task ahead. We are playing West Meck, and they are good, but never as good as us.

All eyes are on me. Except E.J.'s.

"Coach Holden, my apologies, sir," Buford says, as he takes off his hat. We don't shake hands. This is not a friendly visit. "We need to talk to one of your players." How many times have I sat in Sheriff Buford's office bailing out one of my kids?

"Now, Sheriff?"

"I'm sorry, Coach. You know I'd never disrupt y'all out here unless we had no choice." Sheriff Buford puts his hat back on, changes his mind, and takes it off again. He's in uniform, so the crowds have quieted down and all eyes are on the field. The ESPNU crew respectfully turns away from us. This is not the distraction my boys need. Seeing a cop throws them off balance and zaps that energy that was about to fuel them through four quarters.

Buford, a thick man with spiky dark hair, eyes me with cautious disregard. He finds my star player and says, "E.J. Whittaker, we need to ask you some questions."

And like Usain Bolt, E.J. is off and running.

Men are not equipped to be out of control. And football players build careers around control. I am powerless watching my boys grapple with what they've just witnessed. Buford sprints after E.J., but he doesn't stand a chance against this kid's unnatural speed. E.J. is across the field and over the fence before any of us even blink. A few of the boys holler at him to stop; the others are too shocked to speak. The ripple effect of what they've all witnessed spreads without mercy across our field. My boys are sluggish and hunched at the shoulders, their faces spooked and disbelieving.

"Daddy! Daddy!" come the shouts of my Juliana. E.J. is already long past the crowd of spectators and gawkers who opened up a space in the crowd for him to whip through.

"Ryan, go after him," says Wayne, shifting from coach to friend.

"Daddy! Please!" Juliana is crying and screaming and pulling on my shirt.

I have to grab her elbows and shake her to get her to calm down.

"You promised you would always watch out for him. You have to help him."

"Jules, look at me. Look in my eyes."

She stops crying, and the streaks on her face are filled with dread. Everything she shared with E.J. is dripping down her face.

"I'll take care of this. I promise you."

She begins to sob again as my words wrap around her, and she releases her fears into the air. Her daddy will collect them and put them somewhere safe.

"They'll hurt him, Daddy. He has nobody!"

We both know E.J.'s mother Ruby is working her second job of the day, and likely has no idea her son may have just committed a major offense.

"We'll figure this out."

Juliana nods and wipes her nose. She hugs me hard this time, harder than she ever has in front of my players.

By now, the boys are on one knee, the standard position when one of their own is down. They are praying, silently and desperately. I can feel their collective worry strumming around me. Sirens blare in the distance.

I draw strength from somewhere deep within and rouse my team with the thundering clap of my hands. "Boys, we have forty-eight minutes. You focus on those minutes. Nothing more. Nothing less. You find the fighter in you and you pull him out. The full forty-eight. Now get out there and hustle."

Concentrating on the game is tough. The question *Should I or shouldn't I go after E.J.?* is pulling at me. But now is not the time to abandon my boys with a league title coming up the pipe. *Stupid, E.J.*, I think. I set the thought aside and do what I do best. And for a short while, I don't think about anything but football. My wife is convalescing in the hospital, my star player is on the run, and my daughter is alone and frightened. Yet I coach my boys to a win, despite it being a tough match-up. I am proud of my young men and tell them so.

Many coaches will tell you their players learn the most from loss— that it builds character and resiliency. And there are those who say you'll learn more by watching an athlete win. How he reacts to his opponents, how he gloats or talks smack or shakes hands with integrity. These responses speak a lot about character. And without character, you can never be a successful ball player. I'm not sure what tonight's win means. My boys hold their heads high, though their hearts are with their brother E.J.

"Daddy?" She is standing there, my teenage daughter with a child's frightened face.

The last of the boys has departed the locker room, and I am sitting on a faded bench. Her eyes remind me of the day she was born, their light green searching for answers, unable to calibrate.

"Jules," I say, as she folds her crumpled body onto my lap. I bury my face in her hair, a rare moment when she allows me some affection. I will take it. I will latch on to it, ingesting all the parts of her that have escaped me in the years she pried herself away.

"I'm scared," she tells me. I'm not sure if she is referring to her mama or her boyfriend. When she whispers, "I'm sorry," I know at once it is E.J. who has pushed Jules's mother from the forefront and absorbed her worry.

Jules has been apologizing to me for months for falling for a member of my team. It was a strict rule in our home and on my field, and so the quintessential forbidden fruit. Their growing infatuation defied my refusals, and before long, even I came to understand and enjoy the refreshing affection of their relationship. Sure I was worried about E.J.'s background and how the fringes of his life would mingle with hers, but what Juliana lacks in grades, she makes up for in sensibility. The girl has a strong, capable head on her shoulders. Perhaps that comes from living with a woman who is so entirely unsure of herself. Jules knew early on who she was and exactly what she wanted.

E.J. swept into her life when neither of us was looking. He promised her things that scared and excited her. Here was a boy who doubled her in size, was flawed and imperfect, but managed to fit deep within her soul. I know Jules had struggled with the pressure to conform, to be like other girls her age. And with a mother who couldn't give her what she needed, it wasn't always easy for her to find her smile. But my girl changed when she was around E.J. I knew this when I watched them together. I had never seen her happier.

She is hunched over on my lap, and I wish I could reach inside her and fix all that's broken. Though it's a breezy fall night, she still smells like summer, and I brush her hair away from her face and feel the smooth texture of her skin against my fingers. I am not sure when she stopped being my little girl. One day she was squirming in my arms while I rocked her to sleep, and now she is almost a woman who astounds me with the magnitude of all she holds in her heart. She is heavier than I remember, and it has nothing to do with Cheetos and midnight pizza with her friends. My daughter is filled with the burdens of those she has chosen to love.

I tell her I need to go. She sits upright, burying herself into my shoulder, and her long lashes are covered in tears. I try not to focus on her sadness as she begs me to please go find E.J., mouthing his name in perfect synchronicity with the drops sliding down her cheeks. "He needs you more than she does," she says, though how she understands this at such a young age amazes me. Abby and I, we may not have been the perfect match, our story not quite ripped from the pages of a favorite fairy tale, but we did do something right by our daughter.

"Jules, I will. I'll go to the station and talk to Buford." I steal a glance at my watch and wonder whether I should ask her to go to her mother, or better yet, tell her to go home and get some rest. No matter how old your kids are, it's impossible to stop protecting them. I know she won't sleep. I know she'll wait to hear from me and from E.J. Only then will her world turn upright again.

There is an urgency gnawing at me, and I feel it permeating Juliana as well. "Daddy, he's not answering his phone. What if he's hurt?" And I know all the possible scenarios, but not until she holds me a little less close will I let her go. She's got to be worried about her mother, but that's harder for her to express. Worrying about E.J. protects her from the troubles of her own home; she sinks into his world rather comfortably.

She softens, and I feel her grasp loosen on my jacket. Part of me wants to stay with her and forbid her from ever crossing into adulthood. I could keep her insulated in our cocoon, where she would always remain my little girl. But since I can't, I will give her what she wants and what she can count on: my word. Something she hasn't always been able to get from those around her.

It is in that moment of oneness with my child that I notice the bruise across her lower back. She stands and reaches for her jacket, turns away from me, and tosses the quilted fabric around her shoulders. The movement is so fluid, I almost miss it. She raises her arms, and I am staring at the ugly shades of purple and black. Reaching for her waist, I hear myself shout, "Juliana, what is that?" But what I'm thinking is, *What the hell?*

The way my daughter retreats is a wordless response I despise. "Juliana?"

She descends deeper into the jacket, and her hands pull down her shirt, though the damage is already done. She frees strands of her dark golden hair from beneath the collar, and it falls like fur across her shoulders. I want to grab it and scream.

"Who did this to you?" The revelation sickens me. "Did he do this to you?"

Juliana is not quite my height, but when she has something to say I swear I am looking straight into her eyes. "How could you? How could you blame E.J.?" She is shrieking now, and this time the sympathy washes out of me. It is replaced with venom. It is so vile, I think I might throw up right there on the locker-room floor. Juliana whimpers, and I count to ten, a deflection that affords me time to consider the possibility that I'm wrong.

E.J.'s locker is behind us, and Juliana stomps over the pile of towels the boys left on the floor and makes her way over to its door. She opens it and quickly slams it shut. Then she proceeds to slam it open and closed again, until all the pain has receded in the gray metal. I watch her, even though I want to go to her and make her stop.

"He didn't mean it!" she shouts at me.

I try to be objective. I try to be her father. E.J., for all his troubles, has never shown violent tendencies. His gentle side contradicts his ferocity on the field. Only now I can't help but imagine my fingers around his throat.

"It was an accident, Daddy. Please, please, we'll talk about it later. He needs you."

"I may kill him," I say to her flushed cheeks.

"You have to believe me. He didn't mean for this to happen. E.J. would never hurt me. Just go to him. I'm begging you, Daddy. Please!"

Never before have I been more conflicted than in that moment. I want to destroy the boy who holds my little girl's heart. Her resolve cuts into me.

"Please," she says. "I'll tell you everything. First, you have to find him. I would never ask you to help someone who hurts me. You've gotta believe me."

And I love her so much that I turn from her and do as she asks.

CHAPTER FIVE

ABBY

I have never missed one of Ryan's games. Despite our differences and my state of mind, I show up. The players and coaches have a host of amulets, and I am his. But today, when he stamped me with his hasty look before clearing the hospital room with Juliana, he made it known that he was prepared to play this one without me.

Watching them exit, hand in hand, left me sad and relieved. I hated having them see me like this, although, at the same time, it was nice not to be scrutinized. When Ryan and Juliana are in each other's presence, I am an outsider, watching my life through someone else's eyes. Juliana once used to adore me the way she now worships her father. My inadequacies pushed her away, and it is something I have not been able to change, but I've tried. If only I could jump inside someone else's skin and replace my missing parts with better, stronger ones for her. It is hard not to hate yourself when you are convinced you are the cause of the suffering of those around you.

The nurse brings me dinner, and I shudder at the sight. I push the tray away without even pulling off the plastic wrap that's meant to keep it fresh and edible, but it looks otherwise. The hospital room is unfriendly and cold. I look around and see the window, and my first thought is, *How high?* And the next, *What if I jump?* But the drugs have kicked in, and even when I play these masochistic tricks with myself, I fail to elicit a reaction, because I'm not in charge right now; Mr. Ativan is.

The medicine, combined with boredom, puts me to sleep. When I open my eyes, I am startled to find Babs standing over me. My eyes clamp shut, and I open them again. I must be dreaming. But she's still there.

"Babs?"

Babs was therapist number three, and she holds the record for all my helpers. Six years we were together, though I haven't seen her in about four. I can't imagine why she's here.

"They told me you refused to eat dinner. You're really pushing this suicide thing."

Babs is a delightfully mean little person. She is five feet nothing with bleached blonde hair cropped close to her head. Unlike most psychologists in their ivory towers, Babs practices out of a dump in downtown Charlotte. It's not a great neighborhood, but Babs is tough and no one bothers to mess with her in her spandex workout gear. So why did I choose her once? She is far from our home and inner circles, and no one would catch me visiting her. There would be no chance of taking a seat in her run-down office and running into the PTA president.

It's hard to turn from the bright, satiny pants outlining the abnormally trim figure of a seventy-year-old grandmother. I can't get over how she keeps herself so fit.

"Abigail."

Babs always called me Abigail despite my efforts to interject Abby into every one of our conversations. I believe one of her granddaughters shares the name, and it's familiar to her, or maybe she is letting me know who's boss in her prickly militant style.

"Abigail," she repeats while I stare at how the years have hardly changed her. "What on earth is going on? Ryan called me. I was his *last resort*. Thanks for that, by the way. You know I'm retired now? But I got a soft spot for ya, kid."

Her appearance is jarring. Her eyes show new wrinkles, and I try not to stare. I am touched that she's come all this way, though I don't know how to express it. If I speak, my gratitude might reduce me to a puddle of tears. I remember vividly the sessions in her office when Juliana was a toddler, telling her how hard being a mom was, all the while my thoughts a looping reel of *What if I leave her in the car? What if I hurt her?* No matter what I had heard about the health-care system taking care of the mentally ill, I knew that if I told Babs my crazy thoughts, I would never see my family again.

"You never showed suicidal tendencies, Abigail. You didn't exhibit any of the signs or behavior. This *has* to be a mistake. I will take this as a personal affront if I failed you."

Instead of placating or pitying me, Babs makes this about her capability. And as soon as the words tumble from the tight skin of her chin and neck, she grabs my hand and yells, "I will not watch you lie in this bed and throw your life away, young lady. You've got a man who loves you, a daughter who needs you, and this—this *stunt*—is just unacceptable!"

The harshness of her words means she cares, and it revives me. "I never wanted to die," I tell her.

"I know. You were always my biggest hypochondriac. Tell me what happened."

Babs refuses to take my silence as an answer. All those years of workouts have made her physical strength proportionate to her cerebral prowess. She walks to the adjacent wall and grabs a chair that I am pretty sure had been nailed down to the floor and drops it next to my bed. Then she begins to rub my shoulder, and it actually feels nice.

"I thought therapists aren't supposed to touch their patients."

"You're dying. I'm allowed to touch you."

"I'm not dying, Babs."

"You're wrong, Abigail. You are dying. You may not be aware of it, but what you're doing to yourself and not *for* yourself is destroying you and everyone around you."

"Why do you bother?" I ask, shamelessly enjoying the way she's fixing my hair.

"My patients matter to me."

"I haven't been your patient in a long time."

"You're forgetting how much progress you made with me, Abigail. You were on your way."

This is the moment in the conversation when I am happy to allow the tranquilizers and stabilizers to carry me away from her overbearing voice, to disassociate. I don't need to be reminded of how happy I can be and how our lives can go back to temporary "normal." I don't want temporary. I want permanent.

"You have to want it badly enough. You. Not me. Not Coach. Not Juliana. You, my dear, are bullheaded. I've told you over and over when you make a commitment to heal yourself it's a long-term commitment. The worst time to leave therapy is when you're feeling better." She rolls her eyes, as though I have broken the cardinal rule of psychiatry. I am Freud's worst nightmare.

Memories of happier times always riddle me with guilt and hopelessness. When you are in the throes of emotional crises, depressive lockdown, it's impossible to imagine ever feeling good again. The vignettes are both a tease and a slap in the face.

"Do you remember when you first came to see me?" she asks.

"I was forced."

"You showed up at my doorstep. I thought the wind would knock you right off my stoop."

"That wasn't a stoop. It was more like a tired rug."

"I know you're hurting when you get like this, Abigail. Maybe others are scared of your sharp tongue. I'm not. I see right through it. That day you came to me, I asked you what was going on, why you were seeking help. Do you remember?

"You said, 'I don't feel a part of this world. Mine is fuzzy and dark. My lifeline is Amazon. The app has saved me from ever having to leave the house. And when I do have to leave, I stand in strange rooms and strategize the exits. My food tastes like metal. My body is freezing cold, then burning hot. I cry. I get back into bed. Nothing feels good anymore.'"

The hair on my arms stands up straight. "How do you remember that?"

"I pay special attention to those most in need."

She drops a folder in front of me with pages of her swirly handwriting. Flipping through the papers, I read our history. Dates that marked our exchanges and the highs and lows of my mixed-up life. There were stories I shared about Ryan and our temperamental sparring matches. There were pages on Juliana, how I hid my depression for so long, and the guilt I felt when she caught me napping midday. Looking up from the pile, I say to Babs, "There's a lot more to this story."

"Sure there is, Abigail. I made that very clear when you traipsed out of my office. I knew you weren't coming back, even before you did."

The folder rests between us, and I feel another surge of cool run through the IV. She stares me in the eyes and says, "Ryan wouldn't back down until I came here. He's a persistent one, that man. He loves you."

"It's more complicated than that." A growl escapes my belly.

The doctor pushes through the doorway, followed by someone I have never seen before. She screams of authority, and her silvery hair and bright red suit intimidate me.

Babs scoots over to let the two through, making no effort to leave.

After the introductions, I learn that the woman is from a clinic in western North Carolina. "Cold Creek" is emblazoned across the cover of a brochure she holds.

I am horrified. "You want to lock me up?"

All eyes turn to Babs, as though her presence will steer the group away from a battle with me.

At once I begin to protest. That the doctors think I'm crazy enough to hurt myself further validates the torment I feel inside. I am crazy. This just proves it.

"Listen to me, Abigail . . ."

"Stop calling me that!" I shriek at Babs, hating the name and its connection to my childhood in a lonely, scary house. "It's Abby. Why do you insist on calling me that stupid name?"

"Abigail . . ."

I glare at her.

"Think about it. Here lies an opportunity for you to get to the bottom of this."

I stare at Babs with fear and disdain. "Was this your idea all along? Did he put you up to it?"

"Get off your ass and get the help you need. You're ruining that young girl. You're breaking a piece of her every time you refuse help. And that husband of yours, it ain't right. You can't keep putting him through this."

"What time is it?" I ask, needing to shield myself from what I don't want to hear.

The trained eyes all turn my way. "Almost nine," says the doctor.

The idea of being locked up sends me into a fit of the shakes. I squirm in the bed, searching for the remote. "How did I miss the game?"

The doctor reaches for the wire that connects to the dangling remote, which has fallen to the floor. I take it in my trembling hands and thumb the power button several times before getting it right. My brain has turned off their stares. I think only of how it's the special teams who have their games televised on ESPNU, and how I would be there for Ryan even from this dingy bed.

"You're going to snuff us out with those boys dressed in girly tights?" asks Babs.

I flip through the channels, zapping away their voices, ignoring their pleas.

"We're not forcing you," preaches the important-looking lady whose fingernails match her suit and lips. Her name escapes me, but I'm not very good at remembering names right now. She says, "This would be voluntary. You haven't put anyone in the family at risk, but whenever there is a case of a possible attempt . . . we are urged to come down and talk to the patient."

Her words force me to respond: "I've told you. I wasn't trying to kill myself."

Even though I wasn't, what if they were able to read my thoughts? Sidestepping the things I feared only heightened their severity and gave them a power that brought me to my knees. This is the weight I have carried within me for what feels like a thousand years. And living in fear is exhausting.

Babs reaches for the brochure and plops it in my free hand. Serenity speaks from the page, a cascade of waterfalls meant to soothe and entice. And for a millisecond, it does. I consider my life, how it has all come to this. Random thoughts pop into my head: *Juliana has been getting ready for school without me for years; Ryan has his team to keep him busy; the two of them love their alone time together. How bad do I have to get to finally make a change? The world thinks I'm crazy anyway. Why not make it official?*

I close my eyes and see myself under the falls, the refreshing water pouring down my body, untangling my hair, cleaning parts of me that are stained. I wonder if I would have Internet access and if Zappos delivers there.

Red Suit Lady musters up some empathy and suggests I read through the material and consider what would be in my best interest.

"It's like a wheel, Abigail," says Babs. "You're the axle. Without you, that wheel just ain't moving."

"I get the point, Babs."

"You control the household. You understand that?"

From somewhere far within, I howl: "I don't want to control the household! I don't want to be forced to make decisions!"

The television screen comes alive, and Ryan's voice interrupts the terseness of my words. The game is over. He's giving his postgame speech. I can't tell if they've won or lost, but I know my husband is distracted.

"We've had some rough patches—all teams do. What makes us different? When we step onto that field, we are no longer individuals. Whether you're the best receiver in the country or the worst. Stats are numbers and they're worth nothing on their own. We're better together, we're fighters, and we're here to finish one job. And that's to win state. Good night, folks."

Ryan's peering through a camera lens, but I feel his eyes closing in on me. He's talking to me when he says, "We're better together." Those words crawl up and down my body; I can't make them go away. If I were one of his players, I might have been kicked off the team long ago. Unsportsmanlike behavior. Lack of commitment. A quitter. I don't want to be a quitter.

"You have a lot of fight left in you, Abigail," says Babs. "Don't give up. Don't ever give up."

I'm thinking about all these things while the picture of Ryan and Lauren watches me from a corner of the room. They expect me to do the right thing, their eyes like a caption I can't erase. *We're better together,* he had said, while Babs's lecture plays over in my mind. Her concern reminds me of a mother protecting her child, which is how my thoughts come to rest on my own. My Juliana. My love for her overwhelms me at times.

Babs is playing with my hair again. Slowly, I feel my head slipping into her fingertips. I don't have the strength to fight Babs when her presence cushions me. She knows, and her fingers find my hand, and she unfurls it from the tight knot it is fisted in. Hers are warm and comfortable. Babs is right. She's always been right, though I've been too weak to listen. Here's my chance to make it up to my daughter. I may never fix what's broken in my marriage, but I will do this for my girl. I will give her what my own mother couldn't give me.

"Okay, I'll go."

CHAPTER SIX

JULIANA

None of us slept last night. Or maybe Mama did, seeing how she was in the hospital and munching on happy pills. Daddy left the field after the win and headed straight to find E.J., both of us serial dialing an unreachable voice. Daddy knew where to look and who to ask, but no one had information. When that failed, he marched over to the police station and demanded answers from Buford. I waited by the phone for him to call, and by two in the morning, Daddy was rolling his truck into our driveway.

Running through the door and down the brick steps, I collide with him on the narrow path leading to the garage. "Sorry, baby, my phone battery died." I am too tired to argue, and he can tell I am worried sick. "E.J.'s missing," he says.

"What do you mean, missing? They didn't find him?"

I follow him through the doorway, where he drops his keys in a bowl on the table and his jacket falls to the floor. All I can think about are the horrible things that could happen to E.J. "What did the sheriff say? How could they lose him?"

"Juliana, E.J.'s in a lot of trouble. Did you know about it? Does it have anything to do with that bruise?" He is trying his best to be patient with me, but his own exhaustion has him rattled.

I slink toward the piano that sits, isolated, across the room. Mom used to play it all the time when I was a little girl. She had a beautiful voice, though I doubt she remembers. I bang out "Chopsticks."

He plops himself on the couch with his arms crossed behind his neck. His stare means I will have to start explaining. I assure him that there's an explanation for all of it, but I am horrified that my Dad thinks E.J. would intentionally hurt me.

My fingers running across the keys drown out my father's worry. I make one last punch with my fist, and the piercing noise echoes against the walls. The silence that follows anchors me to my seat until I can't get out of the hole I've dropped into. The only way out is with words. He has been waiting so patiently.

I had last seen E.J. the day before the class trip. And we hadn't really spoken since then, either. I was mad. He was upset. We were a collection of stubborn. By the time I had gotten back, my mom was in the hospital, and E.J. was fleeing from the field. When I watched him being chased like an animal by that cop, his eyes found mine, and I could hear his heart pounding as his cleats hit the grass. He was asking me, with his stare, to stay quiet. And he was also asking for my forgiveness. I could keep only one of those promises.

"Daddy," I begin, "there's something you need to know." I am off the piano bench and sitting across from him, back in my "only child" chair.

"I'm listening."

"Before I left, E.J. was really upset. Something went down. He wouldn't tell me about it. I needed to get him to talk, so I skipped study hall, drove across town, and found him in the stairwell running late for class. There was no one around, and lately we haven't been able to see each other much. You run two-a-days; it barely gives us any time . . ."

"This isn't my fault. Go on."

"He told me not to worry, that there was some stuff he had to deal with. He hugged me and told me to go back to school before I got in trouble. Then this bag just fell out of his knapsack. Jewelry was all over the stairs. And it wasn't the fake stuff."

Daddy looks like someone who's had the carpet pulled out from beneath him. I go on, but I can tell he's furious. Mama throws her hands in the air when she's mad. Daddy gets that serious face that means trouble.

"E.J. freaked. He let go of me and started chasing the pieces. He was mumbling to himself about them getting scratched, and he had to hide them before anyone saw. I was shocked. Even though I knew E.J. wouldn't steal, I didn't know what to think!

"He said, 'Baby, it's not what it looks like.' And I panicked. I came after him with my fists *and* my words, telling him he was throwing his life away, throwing our life away. He tried grabbing my wrists to calm me down."

Daddy's enraged. "What does this even mean, Juliana? What are you saying? Do you know? Either he's a thief or not. He's done something he's not supposed to do—"

"E.J. knew about a burglary in town, and all fingers were pointing at Devon. He went to his father's house thinking he could talk some sense into his brother. He loves him. Ellis pits them against each other, but E.J. would do anything for Devon. They got into a fight, and E.J. took the jewelry. He was going to return it, that was his plan—he just needed time to think it through—so he left the stuff at Ruby's."

"Fool," Daddy says, shaking his head in disbelief. "The boy's a pig-headed fool. Haven't I taught him anything?"

"Daddy, he was trying to explain, but I was in a frenzy, and he was trying to duck my fists and fingernails when my foot slipped and I fell backward. He reached for me, he did, but it happened so fast. There was nothing he could've done . . ."

44

"He pushed you down the stairs?"

"I slipped!"

Dad pounds the table with his fist. "What is wrong with that boy? He knows better than to mess with Devon's mistakes. He knows how quickly everything he's worked for can be taken away. He should've never touched you like that. He's a boy. You don't touch girls like that. Ever." And then he pounds on the table again as though I didn't hear it the first time.

"He would never hurt me, Daddy!"

"I saw the bruise to your side, Jules. He did that to you."

"I came at him. I was the one hitting him!"

"Do you see how things can escalate?" he asks, not even trying to hide his anger. "E.J.'s like a son to me, but his life is dangerous."

"How can you say that?" I cry out. "You know E.J.'s good."

Daddy is too heated to respond. His nostrils start to flare.

"When will that boy ever learn? Did he think he was just going to drop off the bag at the precinct and walk out of there?"

"I don't know what he thought," I say, rather sadly.

"That's because he wasn't thinking. Reckless. Stupid."

"He was just trying to help his brother . . ."

"That's just it, Jules—not everyone wants help. We've talked about this. You'll be judged by the company you keep. Even sitting in a car with someone who is doing drugs puts you at fault. E.J. is enabling his brother by protecting him. There are repercussions to bad behavior. If they find him with that stuff, E.J. can lose everything. And for what?"

I am sick inside. E.J. has fought long and hard to overcome hardships. "It's his brother, Daddy."

"I understand that. I appreciate loyalty to family, but not when he risks everything. Devon's had a lot of chances. Someone's gotta pay for this."

I take a deep swallow, but I can't hold it in much longer. "I promised E.J. I wouldn't tell a soul."

Daddy looks me hard in the eye. "Are you prepared to see E.J. go to jail for this?"

"He's a kid!" I cry out. "They can't do anything."

"That's where you're wrong. E.J. ran from the police and is in possession of stolen goods. They can go after him as an adult if they want. The state holds grudges, and the Whittaker family is a prime target. Your boyfriend's going to be made into an example. He'll lose everything."

"No," I argue, shaking my head. "They can't do that."

"Oh, yes they can. And they will. We're going to find that boy and he'll come clean—or so help me God, there'll be hell to pay."

Infuriated, I get up and race to my room, slamming the door for extra effect. After dialing E.J. a dozen or more times, I finally give up. It's almost dawn and this middle-of-the-night foray has me wiped out.

When I hear Daddy's car pull up the driveway with Mama later the next day, I am reluctant to get out of bed. The blare of his horn nudges me from under the covers, and I throw the blanket off and greet them by the front door. Daddy comes in first, kissing me on the top of my head and whispering, "Don't bring up E.J. I don't want to upset her more than she already is." I wish everything weren't always about Mama.

We are finishing up dinner when she says she has an announcement to make. "Can we go in the living room and talk?" Her face is blank. I can't tell where this is going, but my legs direct me across the kitchen and through the living room, where we are surrounded by family pictures of better times.

The two of them sit on the couch, huddled together, closer than I ever remember them sitting. Dad's arm is around Mama's shoulder. She's leaning against him for support. I am in my special spot, the single chair to the left. I'm watching her carefully and thinking she looks better, but when I hear what comes out of her mouth, I know she's really gone crazy.

"An institution!" I cry out. "You're leaving?"

She stares down at her hands when she should be looking at me. "I think it's for the best."

"You think it's for the best?" I blurt out. Then I turn to Daddy with accusation in my eyes, "Did you know about this?"

"We talked about it on the drive home. Jules, it's temporary."

"Six weeks," she adds, perking up again.

"That's great," I fume. "You think narrowing it down like that makes *any* sense to me? I don't get it. None of my friends' mothers leave them. They don't do that. They stay."

"Your mama needs help," he says.

I begin playing with the threads dangling from a new hole in my jeans. "Fine," I mumble, "but why does she have to leave? Can't she get counseling from home?"

Mama looks as though she's about to change her mind. She clears her throat a little too long. "We've tried it that way before, Jules, and it didn't work." Then the defeat wears off. Or she's just reciting what the doctors forced her to swallow. "This is different. It's a place I can get extensive treatment without the pressures of home."

"You mean without me around," I say, furious. "What's so horrible about being here with us?"

This is when Daddy swoops in to protect her. "Watch your tone with your mother, young lady. You don't speak to her like that. There are things we can't expect you to understand at your age. You can be mad, but you won't disrespect your mother."

I have been bound up with bristling feelings for years. This news, along with E.J.'s undoing, has popped a hole in me, and my bitterness is bursting forth.

Throughout all my mother's episodes, I have always been attentive to her needs. I have been conditioned to put hers before mine. I have straightened my room and made my bed regularly so it's one less thing she needs to worry about. I have washed and dried dishes so the piles wouldn't topple her. I have encouraged her to take walks outside with me because I was told the vitamin D and sunlight would be good for her. I thought the changing leaves would open her eyes and fill her heart with beautiful things. I foolishly believed that the fresh air would wipe out the bad stuff. I have hugged her. Tightly. As though through the force of my arms, she would feel whole. I have willed that she would not be able to be sad in my presence because my love would be enough. When none of that worked, I tried laughing with her. We sat through marathon sessions of Will Ferrell and Adam Sandler movies.

I did everything I was supposed to do. And all she had to do was care about us enough to get better. If she really loved us, she would have gotten the help she needed.

"How can you be so selfish?" I cry out. "This is so unfair!"

He chimes in again. "What's unfair is that you're hurting. We all are. Your mama's making a commitment to get better because she loves you, loves us."

"I just don't get why she needs to leave. Can't she go back to Babs or Lois or one of the other mind mechanics?"

"I told you," she says, straightening up in her seat. "I need specialized treatment." Then she begins a monologue, her hands clasped together as if they are holding her upright. "Jules, I'm not well. This is not some passing virus that a round of antibiotics will heal. I've been too afraid for too long to get to the root of it. I couldn't leave you before, not when you were a baby, not when you were so young. But now it's time." She stops herself while what she's saying sinks in. It forces me to face her sad eyes and the hopefulness she's counting on to get her through this. "I know you're angry at me, and I can accept it. I haven't been the perfect mother. But I'm going to work through this, and I promise you—I promise you, Juliana—we'll be better and stronger for it."

Her speech is convincing, and I'm slowly backing down. It's futile to argue with her about this. It's not as though she's in my day-to-day life anyway. I have learned to get by without her. Sophie and Nicole, the twins, call it benign neglect, but I know her laissez-faire parenting style has more to do with her being damaged.

"I'm ready to make changes," she says, this time raising her voice, but my mind drifts to other things, like how I will explain her absence, where the hell E.J. is, and why this is happening to our family. "I'm ready to do what I have to do so I can be a better mother to you. I just can't do that until I fix the broken parts."

"Is this genetic?" I ask.

"Watch yourself, Juliana," says Daddy.

"I'm serious," I say, the concern seeping through my words. "Is this something that's going to happen to me?"

Her outstretched palm stops him from saying anything else. "It's a good question. I don't have the answer. I would think by now you'd know. I started having symptoms when I was a lot younger than you."

"Why didn't you get help back then?" I ask. "My God, our lives could've been so different."

"What are you saying?" she asks.

"Stop it, Juliana," he pounces again.

This is when my mother has had enough, and she collects herself and heads for the bedroom.

Daddy turns to me and his eyes are lit up pissed.

"I know you're upset about E.J., and the timing isn't great for your mama to leave, but you're being too hard on her," Daddy says.

I have to laugh—because if I don't, I will throw a lamp across the room. How long have I wished for a mother? Not one who lived in our house and snuck wine into her water bottle and thought I didn't notice. Not one who bought tons of clothes and shoes she'd never wear off the Internet so she wouldn't feel so empty all the time. And not one who stayed home 24/7 because she was too afraid to drive a car. Marlee's mom was the top litigator in the state and barely at home, but when she was, they spent all-out quality time together. Sure, I had a mother who was perpetually present—too much, if you ask me—but being around her was no different from being alone.

I finally say, "It's the other way around. Mama's being hard on me. She always has been. I know she's sick and we have to support her and accept her. But I just want my mom to be like my friends' moms. My boyfriend's in trouble. He could get shot and killed. Is it wrong to want my mother around? Is that too much to ask?"

"Come here," he says.

"No," I say, shaking my head.

"Jules."

My father can always get me to do things I fight hard against. I stand up, hugging E.J.'s jacket in my arms, which does not go unnoticed under his watchful eye. When I take the seat next to him, he wraps his arm around me and pulls me close. "How can I explain to you how much your mother loves you? Did you know that when she was pregnant with you, she didn't have these demons at all? She was a different person because you were inside of her."

"That sounds creepy."

"C'mon," he says, playfully giving me a little push. "Go easy on her. She's doing her best."

"I don't remember it ever being normal," I say, though I have been trained to keep these feelings at bay.

"No families are perfect. We're all just imperfect people who can't give up on one another."

I sigh and tell him, "I wish it were different. That we were different."

He hugs me hard, and I know what I'm asking is too much for him to give. He has already provided more than most fathers ever could. He has given me the love of two parents.

CHAPTER SEVEN

ABBY

It is late, and Juliana is locked in her room sulking while Ryan and I attempt to sort out my departure. "Are you mad that I'm leaving, too?" He's rummaging through a bedroom drawer and doesn't answer.

"Did you hear me?" I ask, draped across our white sheets.

He turns away from the dresser and whatever it is he's searching for, and apologizes: no, he hadn't heard what I said.

"You've been awfully quiet. Was that performance for Juliana's sake? Are you okay with my decision?"

Instead of leaning against the dresser, he perches himself atop of it. I'm not surprised that he passes up joining me back in bed. I am used to the way he flees the house at dawn to clear his head through physical exercise. Keeping his distance allows him time to process things.

"God, you look happy," I bark at him. "Or relieved. I can't tell. Why are you just sitting there?"

"Abby, what do you want me to say? I'm happy you're getting the help you need, but I'm not happy you have to leave us to do it."

"Right." I laugh, as we both realize the irony in what he's saying. I've been checked out for years.

"Baby, this doesn't have to be a bad thing. It's been hard, for you, for us, but you mostly, for a long time."

"You're being kind."

"Heck, I've suffered. We've all suffered."

"Are you giving up on me?" I cry out, feeling the separation wedge a space between us.

"I'm fighting for you, Abs. Even if it means we fight. If this gets you better, I'll do whatever it takes."

A montage of Ryan playing the hero reminds me of the reasons I must go. He is picking me up from the mall because I can't catch my breath, and I'm having what I believe is the third heart attack of the week. He is hugging me in our bed while waves of panic ripple through me. He thinks he can push the waves back to sea, though I know he can't. But he tries. He is looking me in the eyes when I'm in the throes of a depressive episode, and he is telling me how beautiful I am—not just outside but inside—and how he wishes I could see in myself a fraction of what he sees. And then there's the time we were flying to Dallas for the weekend and the turbulence got so bad—I was sure we were going down. The vodkas weren't the best decision. He had to carry me off the plane.

My mind is traveling along the Haywire Express while Ryan strides across the room and gathers me in his arms. I feel his misgivings against my chest. It's nice that he cares as much as he does, but sometimes the love and concern make me feel worse.

"Think about all you can do in my absence," I joke. "You can play poker with Wayne, watch ESPN uninterrupted, order in pizza every night."

"Babe," he says, smoothing my hair away from my face, "it's not nearly as fun without you."

But I know he is lying. I have held Ryan back for as long as I can remember. What started as a mistake has grown progressively worse. Sometimes the guilt consumes me. I wish I could be a better wife, a better mother. My handicaps prevent me from doing normal things that most women take for granted.

I reach across the bed and beyond the overstuffed pillows until I find the Cold Creek brochure stuffed in my bag, and toss it his way. Ryan fingers the pages and pretends to read the fine print. None of this could make sense to someone like him. Terms like *comprehensive treatment* and *continuity of care* are a foreign language, though I see his eyes remain on the cascade across the cover.

"You can go horseback riding and do arts and crafts . . ."

"Are you making light of my going to the cuckoo's nest?" I joke, sidling up to him, watching the pages written about my future temporary home flip through his fingers. I lean in closer, taking a breath of him through my nose and holding him in my lungs.

I never thought I would marry the love of my best friend's life. Sitting beside him, feeling his taut body against mine—it excites me and shames me as it has for the many years of our marriage. Ours was not a coupling that formed effortlessly, the way theirs did. Which is why when I feel these stirrings, the desires to touch his body, I retreat. Ryan used to complain that I would never initiate sex. "I can't," I would tell him. "I like when you take control. I like knowing you want me." That would arouse him even more, and we soon found some mutual gratification in his taking charge and my come-hither disguise. We circled around each other in this pretend dance, and most of the time it worked.

My memories of Lauren and Ryan were locked away in a vault, in the hiding places I avoided and fought to forget. It was years before I could stop comparing the way he would look at me to the way he had absorbed himself in her, or how he'd love me but not always like me.

Remembering can tantalize and torture. Ryan's lips graze my neck, and the stirrings I had tried to quiet are awake and alive. My body reacts to his. *It's okay*, I tell myself, giving him permission by way of spreading my legs wider. He's the initiator, the match to my flame.

"I'm going to miss you," he whispers in my ear.

"Lies. All lies," I say, smiling.

He is on top of me. He is peeling off his shirt that he had just minutes ago put on. I am always surprised to see his body and the meticulous way he has kept it firm and toned. I run my fingers along his forearms and back. His skin is warm to my touch.

When Ryan wants me, I become a woman under his influence. He laces his fingers in mine and leads me somewhere out of my body, where I am no longer myself. I could cup him in my hands and drink him in, feeling him pass through my veins until I explode.

An imminent good-bye makes me want him deeper and harder than I have in months. I fear my absence will harm us in more ways than the physical. I move against him to remind him of what he will be missing. My eyes close, and I am whisked away. He is making it impossible to think straight.

"Baby," he says. "Baby, it's okay. We're gonna get through this . . ."

I see their picture again, and I wish it away. And like the times before, it lingers. Close enough to remind me, close enough to punish me.

Ryan was Lauren's boyfriend in our first year at Davidson College. They met in Psychology 101—the irony of which was not lost on any of us. Professor Warsing was the most iconic teacher at Davidson. Though the class was required—a step up the requisite ladder for freshmen—students clamored to attend her moving lectures. That particular day she was discussing mood disorders: the biological and interpersonal factors, as well as environmental stressors that can lead to a devastating crash. Lauren burst into our dorm room, incensed about a debate she had had with one of the smug frat boys who sat behind her in the class.

"This guy stands up and says everyone has a choice. He said we can choose to wake up and see the world as a victim or wake up and—what did he call it?—be normal! Can you believe someone can be so small-minded? Really? As though someone wants to be depressed?"

Our friendship was too new for her to know of my secret suffering, so Lauren had no idea that she had just tapped into my psyche and given it a comforting hug. It was a sign that I had finally found my person, the one who would understand me as others before never could. A lightbulb went on inside of me. It connected me to Lauren at once. I loved her, and I loved watching her fall in love.

Their bickering continued all through the spring semester of freshman year. Having been banished to Professor Parco's class ("O Crap" spelled backward, and a fair assessment of his lectures), I was not privy to the banter, but every Tuesday and Thursday, Lauren shared detailed recaps of the boy who altered her philosophies and refuted her belief system.

I will always remember the perfect alignment of minutiae that led me to answer his knock at the door on a day when I was supposed to be in History of Educational Theory and Lauren should have been sleeping late before her literary analysis class. His knock was so mild it barely nudged me from sleep. Then it became stronger and louder.

"Dr. Horney, I know you're in there," he hollered at the door. I lay there thinking about Horney, the psychoanalyst known for challenging Sigmund Freud's theories about women.

I peeled the purple chenille blanket off my legs and jumped from the bed. Grabbing the gray Wildcats sweatshirt I had thrown over the chair the night before, I tugged it over my head and stretched it long enough to cover my bottom. In one or two hurried strides I was across the room and at the door.

"Who's there?" I asked, clearing my throat to rid it of the gurgle of sleep.

"Who wants to know?" he replied.

And so marked the beginning of my foray into the intrinsic force of Ryan Holden. Four words ridiculously innocuous and demanding, yet I obeyed him and answered: "Abby. Abby Coleman."

"Is Dr. Horney there?"

"You mean Lauren?" I asked, rolling my eyes and catching my disheveled reflection in the mirror against the wall.

"The girl who told the entire class that I have womb envy? My teammates are having a field day with this."

I was immediately impressed with Lauren's choice. Davidson was the thinking-man's college—*smart* football players attended.

I unlocked the door. What I saw on the other side stayed with me too long: confident smile, smooth jaw, deep stare. His long body draped across the doorframe, his hair a mess of indecision. The gleaming green of his eyes clasped on to mine, and I was certain there was a future for me full of babies and trips to the Outer Banks in their glare.

I became aware of my legs peeking out from underneath my sweat-shirt. His eyes were following my thoughts. I'd had sex with only one guy in high school, but my mind soon drifted from Hatteras Island to what it would feel like if this one grabbed me in his arms and flung me onto the bed. It didn't even matter that I hadn't brushed my teeth or hair. The way he was appraising me told me he liked what he saw. But Ryan Holden looked at all the girls like that. He couldn't help it. Sweet-ness spurted from his eyes, the need to elicit a reaction from anyone. He did it with small children, old ladies, and most every girl at Davidson. And they ate right out of his hands.

This cannot be the jerk Lauren complains about weekly, I considered.

"Is she here?" he asked.

"It's just me," I replied. And that's when my eyes fixed on the bou-quet of tulips he had tucked behind his back. They were orange, her favorite color. It plunged me back into the reality of what had always been my fate. Ryan Holden was not there for me. The kisses his eyes were sprinkling on my cheeks were meant for someone else. The flowers were a stab to the stomach, a dagger dissolving a fantasy into thin, shivery air.

I was angry, and I was horrified by my anger.

I fell in love with Ryan about the same time Lauren did, living through their courtship and "firsts" as if they were happening to me. And just because they hadn't happened to me, that didn't make me immune to the throes of first love or lessen the brilliance of the spark. I was happy for Lauren, and the closer she grew to Ryan, the closer he grew to me. Though I was the self-described third wheel, neither of them ever linked me to the gracelessness associated with that role. Ryan always made an extra effort to include me and make me feel welcome, whereas another guy would have resisted sharing that time with anyone but his girl.

Years later, on the day Ryan accepted the job to coach the Pine Ridge Giants, a community meet-and-greet was held, and I was asked to step up to the podium with my husband. One of the journalists who wrote for a local parenting magazine was gushing at the idea that Ryan was returning to his high school roots, and her questions were steeped in similar flattery. But when she asked, "How do you juggle the team and home life? Would you call these kids your own?" I was reminded that I was in another threesome, though this time it wasn't Lauren, but me and the game Ryan loved most.

We always knew that Lauren and Ryan would get married. Until they didn't.

Plenty of couples can say they shared a serious relationship in those formative years while *figuring it all out*, but none had the roots that locked together and sprouted like Lauren and Ryan had. Love came easily to them. It began with quiet reassurances and grew into bold gestures that flamed like fire. Their affection was as crisp as the sunrise;

their laughter, leaves falling wildly from a tree. It was more than their finishing one another's sentences and the gallant way that, throughout their relationship, he continued to compliment her and hold doors open for her. It was how, when we were all seated together in the taproom at Brickhouse Tavern, Ryan would drape his arm around Lauren's shoulder. His fingers would stroke her hair, reminding her he was close by, telling her in this gentle movement that she was his. She would press into him, their bodies fitting perfectly together, and she'd wipe the leftover food off his lips. It was how his eyes guided her through a crowded room. We girls would venture out of the bathroom, and his fixed stare would hone in on her, across a throng of drunken bodies, a knowingness that led her in his direction, because she usually couldn't see him with her nearsightedness. This bond ran deep and surpassed explanation.

Ask anyone in our close-knit group of friends about what defined Lauren and Ryan's relationship, and they'd say Profile. Grandfather Mountain's Profile trail was the toughest hike in the area. A group of about eight of us set forth on a long weekend en route to the 5,964-foot summit of Calloway Peak. It was nearing April, and Lauren and Ryan had just announced their love to the world, stepping out among their peers into their newfound couplehood. The drive from Charlotte to highway 105 in Boone was uneventful and spotted with conversations about declaring majors and the Final Four. The sky was a sharp blue, showing no sign of clouds. The temperature was unseasonably warm at fifty degrees, though anyone familiar with the Blue Ridge Mountains knows how quickly the weather can take a turn.

The seven-mile trail begins in a mid-elevation forest, growing steeper, with spectacular views and bluffs. Eventually you find yourself in front of Grandfather himself, the outline of an old man's face carved atop the peak. When parts of the climb were deemed a challenge to even the most seasoned hikers, the park installed large ladders to navigate the steep rocks. But those didn't help Lauren on that afternoon.

The most adventurous of our peers, Lauren was one of those girls who seemed to have emerged from the soil of the earth. Introspective and fearless, she was at her happiest and liveliest when she was in nature and away from the city lights, which burned her eyes. She unknowingly took risks because her poor vision and lack of depth perception made her miss what was right in front of her. Despite vision therapy, glasses, and contacts, she at times had difficulty sensing the distance of an object, especially when she was tired. But her handicap never slowed her down. She was the one who would run ahead on a hike, she was the one to hoist herself up a mountain effortlessly, and she was the one to take chances that none of the rest of us would dare.

Ryan begged her not to venture far ahead. He warned us all, but mostly her, of the chances of her eyes and feet failing her on the rough terrain. We all knew that if something happened to Lauren, Ryan would be lost. I remember Lauren talking about it at night when we were lying in bed, how tightly Ryan would hold her fingers in his. Sometimes they'd leave marks, as if he were branding her to his palm, permanently etching her into the folds of his skin so she would never escape. I used to marvel at the idea and blush inside, imagining someone feeling that way about me. Ryan's attachment never seemed to bother Lauren. She loved the way he loved.

By the time we hit the giant ladders toward the end of the hike, we had also hit the steepest climb, with the roughest, most ragged terrain. The rocks were covered in slippery moss, and the showers that abruptly fell from the sky coated the ground with slick varnish that most of our hiking shoes could easily tread. As soon as the wave of moist air passed through, a rainbow stretched itself over the peaks of nearby Sugar Mountain. It was a breathtaking sight, the colors loud and vivid across the cerulean blue. Lauren was the group photographer and saw nothing wrong with tramping off the marked terrain to capture the shot. She stepped down off the ladder and around some thick brush until we couldn't see her at all. We should have known she would miscalculate the depth of the drop. When Ryan found her, she was holding on to a narrow boulder jutting into the sky, and depending on whom you asked, it was an alarming number of yards from the ground. She told us later that she never doubted he would come. *He always did.*

Lauren barely made a sound; Ryan could feel her heart pulsing through the trees. The silent energy that connected them shouted louder than any of us could hear. And it continued while Ryan hoisted Lauren off the tightly gripped ledge. We only knew the details because we spent the two-hour drive back to Davidson listening to the two of them highlight the rescue. Lauren never feared for her life. The calming lilt of her recap was not that of a woman frazzled by fear.

I have returned to that afternoon in my mind many times. Lauren and I dissected it for days. She appeared unfazed by what I called supernatural destiny. To her it was the most natural thing to expect Ryan to always be there for her. That was when I knew they were connected more deeply than any one of us could fathom. And how I wished that kind of love could be mine.

The memory prevents me from responding to Ryan's touch. I am frozen in the chill of what I've done. "Stop," I tell him. "Please stop." He moves off of me, distancing himself from what he can't understand. "Just hold me," I say, and he cuddles me from behind without asking any questions. I feel his rapid breath on my cheeks and hair, and the feeling slows the pulsing of my chest. I have returned to our bed, to the place where coming together should be not only beautiful but also right. Instead, my guilt makes it impossible for me to move.

"I'm scared," I say.

"I'm here." He hugs me harder.

Certainty has crept under our sheets. There are things that have to be fixed if we're going to survive.

"When you're feeling bad," he says, "remember this. Remember us."

I tell him I'll try, though I wish I didn't have to leave him to take this giant step. And when I'm sure I can't hold it inside any longer, I ask, "Ry, what's going to happen to us?"

"What do you mean?" he says, lacing his fingers in mine, and I feel the worry spread to each finger.

"What if I'm different when I come back? What if I don't like what I find out about myself?"

"That doesn't make any sense. You're going to be healthier. Stronger."

I turn to face him, and the shadow around his eyes tells me he's afraid. I make it so he can't look away. His lips are waiting for me. I like the way the flush of our almost sex has warmed his cheeks. He has grown more handsome in his middle age while my fear has aged me.

"Abs," he says, pulling me close, reassuring the both of us with his arms around me. "You're so brave. You're going to kick some ass in there."

I snuggle deeper into him. It feels childlike, but I love the feeling of it. He says, "I have lost too many people in my life, Abs. I'm not going to lose you, too."

CHAPTER EIGHT

LAUREN

When you head northwest out of Charlotte, you reach the outskirts of the small mountain town of Beech Mountain. And whether crossing through the byways of Boone and Valle Crucis to the north or Morganton and Banner Elk to the south, there is one road that leads to the priceless property. The parkway is sharp and winding, with glimpses of Sugar Mountain and expansive views from any vantage point. The expectation of what lies ahead never gets old. It is as though the drive up the mountain is always for the first time.

The mountain covers a seven-mile terrain comprising steep switchbacks and dense forests. But if you pull back the veil on the robust trees, you find the real treasures. The vista provides a window into a land that is vastly open. Gushing creeks and waterfalls trickle from secret places, and breaths are deeper and roomier. The water that falls from the streams washes away troubles and calms the mind. Reaching the apex encompasses a journey, a storied history through time and memory. All the tales spin up, down, and through the mountain.

People seek the mountains for countless reasons. There are those on a quest for inspiration, while others are climbing to reach a vast oneness with nature. I've since stopped counting the reasons I come. Though when I last sought the mountains all those years ago, I came for one thing: refuge, to rid myself of pain.

This time I hadn't wanted to come back. The publishing house left me no choice.

"It's been a thousand years, Lauren. You promised us those final waterfall shots. It's time."

The call came through on a particularly dreary day in London, the kind that left me to question how I had lived without the mountains for so long. The mention of coming home transported me back in time. It was a jolt that inflamed my entire body, a loss I had fought years to escape.

"I know," I said into the phone, even though old wounds said I shouldn't go back. But I was also feeling homesick and lost around that time. The flat was empty; Jean-Pierre had given me an ultimatum. He had found the ring I kept in a drawer, a hidden promise that had painfully died, which led to a discussion about us. And I was never good at discussing us. Seeing the diamond in his hand set me off. I snatched it out of his fingers, and soon we were packing up boxes and saying our good-byes.

"I'm serious, Lauren. I can't stall any longer. You've already missed the six-month deadline. Eight months is very generous on our part. If your first three books weren't such damned moneymakers, I can assure you no one would care about this little hobby of yours."

Here is where determination hit memory, and I stalled.

The book was my life's work. A passion for writing and photography coupled with an ever-since-grade-school infatuation with waterfalls had led me on a quest to compile the most beautiful cascades in the world. Strewn across the thick pages were poetry and musings. The grand finale would bring me home to the North Carolina mountains, where I would shoot Linville, Toxaway, Looking Glass, and Elk River. Only what waited for me back there terrified me. And my procrastination was about to kill my publishing deal.

Once I made the decision to return, there was no going back. I assured myself it was to finish the book, that it had nothing to do with the ring that I carried around with me for days after I seized it from Jean-Pierre's hand. I didn't dare to put it on my finger, but I held it in my palm and stared at the shiny metal, knowing it wasn't the best way to block out his memory.

I packed my bags and the unfinished manuscript, and now, today—on a brisk autumn day, I am on a winding road feeling everything I've kept at bay, circling around. Abby, Ryan, me—all of it, chipping away at my defenses, reminding me that no matter how hard we try to move forward, there's always a past pulling us back.

I had spent most of my childhood studying the lushness of my favorite town. I was a nature girl, comfortable in sneakers and shorts with my hiking stick in hand. My father had taught me to start a fire with little more than a few twigs and an unpredictable wind. I had hiked Upper Pond and Lower Pond in all four seasons. I could tell the precise times the deer would roam the parkway, when the bears would hibernate for the winter. I knew the names of the birds and insects chirping outside our windows. By sniffing the air, I could predict when the ephemerals and lady slippers would bloom, followed by the daisies and the rhododendrons. And yet, later, when it came to Ryan and Abby, my instincts were all off.

Roaming the land was an enjoyable pastime. Even though the bear population had grown over the years, there was a stillness tucked inside my heart that made me at peace in the forest. My favorite place on the whole mountain, besides our vacation home, was the Falls Trail about a mile down the road. Had I only known, as a little girl, that the winding path I would take, the one by the roaring stream, would lead to my first experience with foreplay and that the tree-spotted lane leading to the open field and Buckeye Lake would be the climax. The flowers with their pointed stems would tease and tickle me, and the steps across the wooden bridge would brim with the mystery of what's below. The final wind-up would ascend along the steep climb to the clearing. It was there I first gave myself to Ryan. Ours was college-aged love, though our souls had been knotted long before we met.

As I climb deeper and higher into the hills, I roll down the windows so the fresh mountain air filters through the car. The breeze is a nostalgic whiff of my former self. I know the memories I've sealed off and cast aside will find their way back to me. That's what the mountains do. It makes it impossible to forget. I am not sure how to be here without him. This was our sacred place that nestled us in its beauty. As the mountain air cleansed our palates, we were able to see each other with that keen sense: our love deepened, our connection strengthened, our future looked as promising as the land in which we first fell in love.

My hands grip the wheel tighter. I had feared what the memories would do to me. Ryan holding me close, breathing me in by the river. I can feel him come up behind me, latching onto me and whispering something, anything, in my ear. It didn't matter at the time. I can feel in his hands the words his mouth wouldn't say. My climb up the mountain was fierce, and as he wrapped me in his arms, I thought I might not be able to take another step.

That a boy weakened me, and in the place where I most found strength and spirit, was alarming, all-pervading. He kissed my hair and forbade me to turn and face him. I gave in to his demanding hands, which meant succumbing to his fingers and the way they ignited something in me I could not contain.

My mind remembers that day, and I will it away. Only it's not so easy. Ryan is woven into my soul.

The house is as beautiful as I remember, a rustic mountain home set against a forest of trees, and when I step through the grand foyer, I think I might have made a mistake. The smell of fresh balsam startles me. That, together with the photographs lining the walls, makes me want to turn away and run. There I am a gawky teenager; a sensual woman; a frightened, wounded victim. Turning away, I drop my suitcases to the stone floor.

I knew it would be difficult to return, and I'm not prepared for the physical and emotional pull that unsteadies me. There is the balcony where we once touched each other beneath a blanket of stars. There he is coming through the door, guiding me to the Jacuzzi on the deck. There is the view that tonight will become purple and pink, and I'll see his eyes and the way they hold mine with their hazel flecks. The vision is beautiful and mystical, and in seconds it is gone.

Battling the revival of feelings had worn me thin; I am drained of tears. There were years of drops sliding down my face—each one a memory. They are hammering at me, closing in, and I am powerless to shoot them down.

Before I have even reached my room downstairs, my cell phone rings.

The sound of the buzzing startles me. I despise the cell phone. It was a safety measure my parents insisted on after college when I first left the country with my camera, though my fingers never quite fit comfortably around the wide body of the bulky device. Once abroad, shutting it off, or better, finding myself in international dead zones, was expected and freeing. It is my literary agent. She has no idea what I gave up to create this photo book. Fate had reared its head, and I had been forced to abandon not only one dream but two. Sweeping the misery aside, I did what I did best, and that was to write. Paragraphs became pages and feelings matured into fiction. Eventually the novels made their way to literary circles. My private success felt good, but the years away had gnawed at me.

"Yes, Quinci."

"That's how you greet me after you've dodged my last sixteen phone calls?" she scowls through the phone. "Welcome home."

I soften when she says the word *home*.

"How are we doing with the book? Are you ready to shoot the last of the falls?"

"Q, I just walked in the door. The plane from London was delayed three hours. I sat next to a screaming baby who stopped screaming only when her mom sang 'Itsy Bitsy Spider' to her. For seven straight hours. The traffic from the airport was gridlock, and a two-and-a-half-hour drive became five. Can we talk in the morning?"

"I see you haven't lost your cheery disposition."

"I know, I know," I say, stepping into my room and switching on the lights. "I'm here, aren't I?" The puffy red comforter beckons me, and I fall across the thick down. Quinci is talking to me, pleading actually, and I close my eyes, willing her away. I swear I can feel Ryan on the pillows. His arms are pinning me to the blanket, and he is teasing me with his eyes.

"Are you listening to me, Lauren?"

"Yes," I lie. "It shouldn't take me long here. I'll have everything to you soon." And then I hang up and fall back beside Ryan.

I love you, Lauren.

We lay in the bed after the Buckeye hike. Our coupling on that stretch of flowers and grass left a need in me that only he could satisfy. When I rolled over and faced him on the bed where I had had childhood dreams, his stare loosened a coil in me.

I had wanted to attend the postgrad photography program long before Ryan showed up at my dorm and let it be known that his teasing in class was far more than casual flirtation. Ryan was innocent enough to believe that our feelings would make it impossible for me to leave.

I stroked his face as he sulked about my leaving, and as the day got closer, I watched the shift in Ryan and the way his dark hair mimicked his moods. It was messy and thick when he was with me. He would run his fingers through it with an almost violent ferocity. I loved it that way, unkempt. I hated to abandon him too.

We were stretched across my bed again. "I'm going to miss you so much," he said.

"It's six months. I'll be back before you know it."

He was a little more forceful this time when he kissed me. I closed my eyes and let him in. Ryan mixed with the breezy air that leaked through the open window. The scent would forever remind me of all that we had lost, all the potentially beautiful things we could have created together: promises, a life. They all shot through a tiny splinter in the window screen, billowing in the sky. I often wondered if it was my fault for leaving Ryan alone. How foolish of me to think we could sustain the time apart.

That is why I haven't been back. Only something painful could keep me from the land I love. I roll over and face the wall. The pictures have changed. The night table with its cinnamon candle sits quietly. Like me, it has not been lit up for a long time.

Ryan's face has been replaced with a photo of my brother. I'm sure it pained my mom to remove him from our home, but at least she was replacing him with someone who would never harm her child. I know the years I spent apart from her were tough, but as a free-spirited woman, she understood the need to journey out into the world.

In my exhaustion, I don't even bother to undress for bed. It is better this way, or else I will remember his skin against mine, feel his hands touching me beneath the covers. Making love to him is buried in my skin. And that was Ryan's whole point. After, when he held me in his arms and smoothed my long hair with his fingers, he told me this: "No matter where you go, Lauren, you're mine. Always mine."

CHAPTER NINE

ABBY

Cold Creek is wedged into a picturesque mountaintop in Asheville. As you enter the compound, the narrow drive is bordered by maples and dogwoods, against an immaculate green lawn. The main house is an impressive white, with towering columns lining a stone patio. When you walk through the glass doors, high ceilings and windows frame the room with light and warmth.

I am greeted by a line of friendly faces with no judgments. Everybody's smiling, and it's a welcome and refreshing change. Though it feels wrong to have separated myself so completely from my family, I slowly embrace the idea of healing. Not only for me, but also for those who are counting on me.

My accommodations are on the west campus. My roommate is a pretty young woman named Rose. I am convinced early on her name isn't really Rose, even if she is prickly enough to be one. I find myself calling out to her throughout the day, "Rose! Rose!" and most of the time she ignores me.

Thorny Rose and I sit on our balcony and witness the most beautiful sunsets I have ever seen. When I told Ryan I had a balcony, I could sense his immediate worry and reassured him. "There are only two floors in the guest facilities. No jumpers." Our room is as simple and pleasant as an old hotel. It isn't fancy, though it gives the impression that people really live here.

The first day was tough. Ryan and I said our good-byes on the front porch, where he doled out one of his famous pep talks. "I'm proud of you," he said, and then he held me long and hard so my body would remember his touch. When he turned away and drove off, I broke down and cried, shielding him from the tears as he waved his hand out the window.

Jeannie Malone is my lead counselor. She's a nondescript woman in her forties with straight brown shoulder-length hair that she parts down the middle. Her eyes are a pale brown that complement her olive skin. Jeannie dresses as though she has escaped Woodstock, in long skirts with tan and orange flower prints. She even wears Birkenstocks. Her listening without judging makes it easy for anyone to talk. But in those first few days, I still resisted.

The trajectory of my stay was Jeannie's call. She devised my very own personal wellness team, which covered most every aspect of my life, from exercise to talk therapy, group therapy, specialized activities, and diet. I've never missed a basket of bread more in my entire life. It sounds dreadful, but it occurs to me that Cold Creek is exactly where I need to be. Here I am free of the responsibilities of home and the pressure to conform. Only that same freedom opens me up to scrutiny and self-improvement, and that kind of scrutiny scares me.

Seated in Jeannie's office that first day, listening to her trace my medical history from twenty-seven different doctors over the course of a few years, with the finale being a splatter on the bathroom floor with a bag of blades and pills, I knew the path of most resistance would inevitably be the one I couldn't resist. I was at my tipping point before I arrived.

Hunkered down, I studied the intimate space, which felt like a living room with its oversized brown sofas, beige chenille throws, and a sign that reads "The Loving Room."

Jeannie introduced me to a game called "emotions," in which I was supposed to write my dark feelings on index cards. I picked up the first card, and with the black Sharpie in my fingers, drew robust letters across the front: *scared*. After, it was followed by *nervous* and *sad*. I also felt angry. And though I didn't want to write that emotion on paper, I knew I must. So there. I wrote it on the card in big, bold caps: *ANGRY*.

Jeannie helped me sort out the words. She explained that for years, my body had taken over the natural expression of my emotions. As a small child, I might not have been allowed or able to articulate my feelings of sadness or rage, so they manifested themselves in physical symptoms. "We are going to say words aloud, own them, embrace them, and feel them," she said. For someone who had spent the better part of her life avoiding such emotions, I was terrified.

When we reached the card with the swirly strokes of *scared*, Jeannie and I began to decipher feelings that I had kept hidden inside irrational thoughts. She was right, the thoughts—however awful—protected me from the real pain.

Studying the next card, *ANGRY*, I focused on the emotion associated with the word. My first thought was of the picture of Lauren and Ryan I found in his drawer. *Asshole*, I thought.

"Which card is that?" she asked.

I turned the lined card with the big black letters in her direction and held it up for her to see.

"What are you angry at?" she asked. "Is it a person? A situation? Let's give it legs."

I saw Ryan looking through me. I saw the choices I had made. I asked myself, *Can you ever forget your first love? That person who gives you someone to dream about?* I wasn't about to tell this stranger all the doubts screaming to come out. "I'm mad at a lot of things," I said.

"Begin wherever you want. But I want you to start by saying 'I'm angry.'"

"Okay," I said, not really having to think it through, giving a string of thoughts a voice. "I'm angry because I know that I could have prevented this misery from dragging on as long as it has. I'm angry that my parents could have gotten me the help I needed but didn't. I'm angry because my illness and its wicked temper have caused me to do things I will always regret." This last one gripped me, and I had to pause. No matter how many years I attempted to cover up my mistakes, they snuck into my dreams and stabbed me in the gut when I was awake.

"I'm angry because my husband is closer to our daughter than I'll ever be. I'm angry because I can't be with her, and I'm angry at him for always being so darn chipper, for living his life in a most ordinary way. I'm angry my daughter's in a healthier relationship than mine with my husband." I let her digest this while the truths chipped away at me. I folded my forehead into my hand and searched the floor. I whispered, "I'm angry he loved someone else first."

Jeannie didn't say anything. I sat up again, fighting back the tears that were trying to escape. Anger felt so much better so I breathed the tears away. *ANGRY* stared back at me from the index card, and all the people and situations I was angry at, but Jeannie took the card from my hands and turned it in my direction.

"This practice helps you unleash a lot of pent-up feelings and emotions. That's what we do in here, clear a path for deeper introspection. There comes a point when you stop blaming others. Look at this card. It's your mirror. Do you think you might be angry at yourself?" she asked.

"No."

"Abby, are you sure?"

"Yes. I'm sure."

But *ANGRY* stayed with me the rest of the day.

Inhale. Exhale. There is a lovely woman leaning over me, and she is recit-ing a collection of words in my ears. Tamar is Cold Creek's Reiki special-ist, and according to my therapists, I am in need of her energy healing. I'm usually a skeptic when it comes to Eastern medicine, but when this petite woman with golden strands of hair told me she was going to free the negative energy from my body, who was I to refuse? If I could do what I did to the people I loved, perhaps there was hope for a stranger's hands to dislodge the pollutants clinging to my core.

I try to relish Tamar's fingers on my stomach and the bubbling sounds emanating from my belly beneath her palm, which lead me to believe I have a lot of messed-up stuff in my system, but instead, I am awash in those stupid cards Jeannie made me write down. Tamar wants me to close my eyes and imagine the word *thinking*. It floats in front of my closed eyes, though intrusive thoughts chase it away and dispel any meditation.

"Abby, I need you to take a few deep breaths. In through your nose, out through your mouth."

I am now facedown on Tamar's table with my head pressed against a circle that allows for half a nostril to inhale. She has come up from beneath me and is shoving a bottle of oil in my face. It smells quite nice, citrusy, and I breathe it in as though it will chase away demons.

"It's bergamot," she says. "It'll help with the anxiety."

My brain refutes this information. She is being kind. It is likely a potion for very bad people. Tamar's hands are resting across my shoul-der blades. I have been massaged a dozen or more times in my life, but I have never fallen asleep during the act. Something about her touch eases me toward the drowsy hush of sleep.

"I can help you," she whispers. Her hands shift down to the curve of my back. "These are your adrenals. Yours are probably depleted."

I am dreamily content with her hands on my body, and the drugs that are fusing with the citrus oil she has waved under my nose.

"Withholding your feelings is causing them to interfere with your body. You have to experience them. Rage, anger, guilt, sadness—they'll make you a very sick woman."

There is little fight left in me. I would chuckle, but my defenses are worn down and I am sleepy.

"Abby, you can learn a lot about yourself right now, if you take the time to work through this—really work through this. You don't have to feel like this for the rest of your life. You just have to want change badly enough."

I don't know what I want. I haven't known what I want for a long time. I thought I wanted Ryan and this life, though upon closer inspection, this life resembles an illusion. My body falls under the spell of the fraudulent fantasy. I am submerged in her words, and the peacefulness tells me that what she's saying might be true. I should be afraid, but the calm prevails. My eyes are closed and sleep is nearby, and the projector inside my head is spooling through memory. The images are checkered in black and white. They are moving so quickly I can barely pinpoint the faces of my childhood before I am in middle school and then high school and then Davidson. *Snap.* Everything slows down. The images halt. I feel Tamar's palms on my feet. It is the first time they don't jerk me into laughter. What's left is a vision. Only now it is brightly colored. I need to shield my eyes from the glow. It is Lauren. She is staring me in the face. Her fair skin is a deep red, shades darker than her hair. She is inflamed. Her eyes wide, her lips broken apart. It is a face I have learned to forget, to hide in the place where people are trained to hold their shame. I am repulsed by what I have done. *ANGRY.*

"Abby, are you all right? You just tensed up."

I slam my eyes shut tighter than before. I will Lauren away with each exhalation, and this time I am unable to block her all-encompassing presence. If what Tamar is saying is true, I fear for the feelings I have locked up, and if I let them out, how will I ever look Ryan in the eyes again?

I tell Tamar that I'm fine, but I'm lying. Her hands have to sense the physical discomfort I am unable to fix. There were times as a child and young adolescent—before I could give words to my fears and inner threats—that I actually wished for calamity. If only that rottweiler had taken a bite out of my leg, an area that healed quickly and didn't leave any long-term bruises. If only I had actually fainted, instead of always feeling faint. If only something truly terrible had happened to me, then my parents would have dragged me to a doctor and *experts* would have studied me to find out exactly what was wrong. Because I was sure there was something really broken in me.

On my next meeting with Jeannie, I creep closer to Pandora's box.

"Have you ever had suicidal thoughts? Have you ever wanted to hurt yourself?"

"No!" I shout, because it is vital that she believes me. "That's just it. That's the crux of it all. I've had anxiety, I've been depressed. But I have never wanted to die." And a thought popped inside my head. Lauren's face. And then me. A knife. My wrist.

"Abby?"

The picture is so strong it seems Jeannie should be able to see it for herself. I want to hand it off to her. I want to carve it out of me and plunk it at her feet.

"Abby? Tell me what's going on. I'm here to help you. You're safe in here."

Minutes tick by and Jeannie waits. I push the thought down as far as it will go and compose myself, sitting up a little taller. "I'm worried our marriage won't make it through this. I'm worried about Juliana."

Polluted thoughts are all over the room, covering the walls and landing near my feet. Ryan is standing by the window. I am running toward him, but Lauren stops me. She is tugging at my legs. "They scare me, these things I think about. I hate it." Then I begin to gnaw at my fingernails. The fear is overwhelming and I cry. I want to tell her, but I can't. The cauldron is on the fire and it is heating up inside.

She tells me rather calmly that I'll learn to accept this scary part of me.

I shake my head. "I'll never accept that ugliness. I want to get rid of it."

Jeannie straightens herself. "Then you'll be getting rid of a piece of you. Do you think there's a part of you that wants to destroy her?"

I let it wrap around me. I've already destroyed her, but I know Jeannie isn't talking about Lauren.

"I'm not sure what I've done is forgivable. And I'm tired of talking about the same stuff over and over. It doesn't change anything. Maybe I'm too messed up to fix."

Jeannie is writing and writing. I can hear the scratch of the pen against her pad. Then she places the pen behind her ear and begins: "I realize rehashing the past is tiring and repetitive for you, but it's necessary. You're stronger than you think."

I shuffle out of Jeannie's office and return to my room to find Rose on the balcony. She's wearing a sundress, despite the dipping temperatures. Goose bumps run up and down her arms, and it is the first time I notice they're papery white. As I get closer, I see how the bumps stop at the scars that stain both her wrists. We all suffer in our own ways. Some more noticeably than others.

People with psychological struggles know better than most the dangers of labeling, though it happens. There's a secret hierarchy of sufferers and distinct methods of coping, some worse than others. A small part of me—very small—feels lucky that my problem isn't more serious.

Rose knows what my eyes are honing in on, and she doesn't try to cover up her wrists. She has a closetful of jackets in our miniature closet, which could easily hide her scars. It's the first time she enlists me in conversation, and the first time I notice the welts. "I don't mean to scare you. When you spend your life avoiding bigger-than-you feelings, you get pretty good at hiding things, like slices across your wrists."

Rose looks twentysomething, but the sadness around her eyes has aged her. Her hair was probably once a vibrant, shiny blond. It is dull and combed forward to cover her face.

"You want to know why I do this to myself?" she asks. "Everyone thinks I'm crazy."

"No," I tell her, "believe me, I'm done throwing stones."

She says, "Physical pain feels so much better than emotional pain."

Her wisdom grips me in a powerful, unavoidable way. I get up, and she lets me wrap a thick shawl around her bare shoulders. She softens and takes my hand. Perhaps the time here has trimmed her thorns. I think about the two of us and the circumstances that brought us here.

"My mother told all her fancy friends that I've gone to some program in Europe. Like a Habitat for Humanity for rich people. I still get urges sometimes. But I know I can't succumb, so the most I do is scratch myself with my fingers. We've found a better release for my blood. When I'm able, I'm going to donate blood to the blood bank. I figure if I want to let it out, I might as well give it to someone who needs it."

I want to let things out too. Only what I need to give will hurt too many people.

I admire this young girl's bravery. If we weren't roommates in this facility, we probably never would have had the opportunity to meet. I am no different from Rose. Rose is no different from me.

CHAPTER TEN

RYAN

When Juliana was just a baby she fought us, and herself, for sleep. Neither pacifiers, a bottle, nor Baby Einstein lullabies could lull her to sleep. Abby took it as a personal affront to her mothering, which would send her into a fit of despair. I'd bundle Juliana up and drive her to my office at the high school with a stack of history papers that needed grading. Once Jules fell asleep, she was knocked out for the night. I could easily transfer her, and used the time to finish the papers in silence.

My office was a makeshift space by the locker room that overlooked the field. Listening to baby Juliana suckle in her sleep, her tiny breaths, was the lullaby I needed to get through some pretty awful essays. I cherished those nights as much as Abby detested them. The field I loved, together with my little girl—my heart was as full as it could be.

Sitting here at my desk, things have changed, while others have remained the same. Now my little girl's not so little. She's grown up, and she loves a boy from this field. And with him missing, my girl is feeling the loss and unanswered questions. I look beyond the window and beyond the sleeping grass. The lights are out and the grounds are still and quiet.

Thinking about E.J. and football keeps me from the other things that I've become good at hiding. Decisions and doubts are nothing compared to the magic of these lights. Ask any player, coach, or fan at a stadium football field, and they'll tell you this: the scene is electric, having much to do with the beaming flares that ignite the sky. Friday-night lights, they call them, and they sprinkle the stadium and its guests with stardust.

Friday-night football games symbolize different things to different people, though all can agree that the promises that fly above the field are what make dreams come true. Whether you're sitting in the stands or playing your heart out on a field to guarantee yourself a spot on a college team, or you're the girl being thrown in the sky on the shoulders of the other cheerleaders, or the guy toting the bassoon around during halftime, the atmosphere sizzles, and the sport touches you in some way.

I have always spoken of football as a way of life. For my players and me, it is not just a sport. The respect I command on the field is the same discipline I expect off the field. The young stud who shoots the finger after a supposed bad call from the ref is the same guy who won't be able to deal with mockery in the hallways. I teach my boys how to handle a football with dexterity and rhythm while facing a forbidding offensive line, all the while practicing self-control.

It may sound contradictory to expect these young loose cannons to exhibit fearlessness on the field, to run into a burning building, and then to know when it is time to walk away from an unsafe situation. It is a skill that some master; others don't.

I have coached a lot of boys over the years, though none like Evan James. His body is more machine than flesh, surpassing most every record for players his age across the country. He has already been offered over a dozen scholarships to some big-name schools. After careful consideration and hours spent in our kitchen, Evan James and I, together, signed with the University of Alabama.

Remembering a similar day when I committed to Davidson College was the highlight on a reel I visited often. My father was beside me with tears in his eyes. You never want to see a grown man cry, no matter the circumstance, but tears of pride are an exception. E.J. has all the mechanics, drive, and ambition to be a top athlete. The only thing he's missing—what I had on that afternoon when signing on the dotted line—is a dad.

There are pockets of Charlotte known for hardship and havoc. Often the two are interchangeable. E.J.'s one fault of birth was being born into an underprivileged family. E.J.'s oldest brother, Rodney, is serving a twenty-five-year sentence for narcotics distribution. The middle brother, the one born three years before E.J., Devon, is teetering on the brink of the same incarceration. Not even a short stint on my field could sway him from a life of trouble. E.J. was the baby, and although birth order assumed he should be taken care of by doting, mature siblings, it was he who was the caregiver.

Ruby Whittaker was a chunk of a woman who had withdrawn from her marriage after her husband resorted to the occasional left hook to show his appreciation for her. The first time she sat in my office, she was like a rusty faucet dripping with tales of their hardship. The years had not been kind to her, and she wore her stress on aged caramel skin. Ruby was terrified of her husband. Ellis Whittaker was a strong-willed man who had raised Rodney and Devon to use the bare minimum to achieve maximum results. Lying, cheating, and breaking the law were acceptable means of survival, viable means to reach an end. Those hurt in the process were bystanders, casualties of a socioeconomic war against their troubled neighborhood.

Why does anyone choose to marry a cruel-hearted partner? Ellis wasn't always that way. The way Ruby tells it, Ellis's parents were taken away when he was five. A car crash killed them instantly, leaving their only son in the shuffling hands of multiple foster homes. Ellis's pain ran deep; the foster parents mistook his silence for contempt. The lack of attention and love stripped the young boy of any good. This hardened version of Ellis got Ruby pregnant when they were high school juniors, and while there were signs of the loving boy who longed to be loved, there weren't enough of them. Marrying Ruby and having a child would provide accessories to his crimes. A team of thieves. By the time baby Rodney was eight, he had assisted in four drug deals; by ten, he had been the lookout for six burglaries.

Ruby was trapped and her children were pledges. Each time she tried to leave, Ellis would raise his hand and threaten. The years had tightened his hold on her, his temper finely tuned to blast through their house and seize her in its choking grip. When she considered the reasons to flee, E.J. was always at the top of the list. She could never leave him in Ellis's care. E.J. was special.

What set him apart from the other boys had nothing to do with the fact that he mirrored his mother the most. From an early age, Ruby knew he was more her blood than the others. Call it a mother's intuition, a connection that runs so deep it is immune to DNA, but E.J. distinguished himself early on as *her* son. When Ellis took the three boys to the mall and coached E.J. at the ripe age of ten how to scam the elderly or distract security so they could steal, E.J. protested in a way that set Ellis on fire. When he was thirteen, he unknowingly assisted his brothers in a scam while sitting in a car outside a bank. When E.J. found out what they had done, he gave Rodney and Devon the silent treatment for a week, which drove the boys crazy. At fourteen, his passion was discovered in a rather unusual way. When the cops chased E.J. and his brothers from an abandoned warehouse, E.J. found a measure to his limbs he had never noticed before. It was as though his body had arisen from a deep sleep, and it propelled him yards ahead of the others at lightning-fast speed.

The afternoon E.J. stepped into my office, I couldn't grasp the enormous weight on this young boy's shoulders. Nor could you ever watch him race across the field and know that he was carrying a burden that would slow most boys down. Instead, E.J. was graceful and fast.

He said, "My daddy wants to use my speed for bad things. My mama says I should put it toward good." Ruby Whittaker sat beside her son. Sad eyes peeked out of their sockets. The woman was terrified she might get caught defying her husband.

I have seen my share of these kids, deprived and discouraged. Their brains are hardwired into rough and tough bodies with the belief that sports will give them their lucky break and a ticket out of town. So many factors come into play for ultimate success. Six of my players have gone on to NFL careers. It isn't enough to have skill or talent, though. Dedication, discipline, and drive are vital to athletic success. When E.J. and his mom sat before me in my office overlooking the players' field, I saw a hunger in E.J.'s eyes and a wish in Ruby's. This was a mother who would scour the trenches of evil in order to protect him.

"Let's go outside and see what you've got."

Four years have passed since that afternoon. Four years of watching E.J. score touchdowns, break records, and lead our team to victory. Once his father intuited that his seemingly useless boy was going to be a pricey commodity, a potential NFL ball player, all hell broke loose. By then, Ruby had finally found the courage to leave Ellis, and she and E.J. had moved across town to a tiny, squalid apartment. Ruby had been working multiple jobs to save for her escape, and she squired E.J. away on his sixteenth birthday, a gift she said would last him for many years. Ellis chuckled when she slammed the door behind her, calling her good for nothing.

Battles ensued. Ruby tried her best to keep Ellis away from E.J., but Ellis Whittaker would show up at practices drunk and angry, belittling his son. When bullying him didn't work, he attempted humanity, which on someone like Ellis looked insincere and foolish. Then he would sic Devon on him. Devon was E.J.'s Achilles' heel, his soft spot in a hardened shell. E.J. was a young, impressionable teen, and though he chose a different path from his siblings and father, he felt a nagging sense of responsibility. "They're my family," he would tell me when I found him taking risks, getting into scuffles, committing petty crimes that fortunately didn't stick—all while trying to save his brothers from themselves. There was love, and there was hate. So deep, the two were indistinguishable from each other. Devon was a pesky reminder of their home where the three boys had once shared a bed and tossed a football. E.J. missed the raucous banter and practical jokes. Devon told him he needed him. Then he would promise to get a real job, and E.J. would think maybe this time it would be different. But it never was. Ellis controlled Devon in a way he couldn't unhitch.

Despite his family's shortcoming, E.J. was one supremely talented, resilient boy: Evan James Whittaker, the star of the Pine Ridge Giants football team.

I should have picked up on E.J.'s behavior in the days leading to his flight from Sheriff Buford. Usually steady and bright, his vigor had stalled. I had seen it before in his eyes. It wasn't the usual moodiness that accompanied a visit from his estranged family and shadowed him around the field. This was something else. Living with Abby and her moods all these years has made me immune to things I should be ashamed of. There were so many false alarms, cries for help, and bouts with hypochondria that I ultimately stopped recognizing when something serious was about to happen. So I should have seen that something was chipping away at E.J. I had thought about approaching him. He always responded to me like a sponge. Whatever instruction I threw in his direction, whether about life or football, he absorbed and put into practice. Hardships aside, he was a good study and eager to learn. And I gave him something that no other man would—unconditional love.

Things happened so fast with Abby's hospitalization, though, that I never got that chance to reach out to E.J., to stop the train from crashing. The day spiraled away from me.

And now, E.J.'s on the run.

Wayne has often asked me how I manage a team of teenage boys with more muscle than mind when I can't reason with my own wife. I cast him off as being witty, but the question has nagged at me more than once. If only I could get inside Abby's head and understand the inner workings. But I've never felt, from early on, that we really understand each other. Now she's gone, and I am here, the place she has referred to as "my mistress," my team, and I know her absence is the beginning, or the continuation, of the rift that has split our marriage.

I'm about to lock up when my cell phone rings. It's Buford. E.J.'s turned himself in.

Relief washes over me. "I'm on my way," I tell him. "You tell E.J. to hang tough."

CHAPTER ELEVEN

JULIANA

When E.J. was born, his mother loved him so much she gave him two first names, not one: Evan James.

And when the new school boundaries sliced through our lives, our house was one block away from what would have sent me to Pine Ridge with him. One block. But because Dad remained on the faculty, calling the exodus to a newer, shinier school cowardly and disloyal, our mismatched lives were due to cross. And they did.

I know I should be concentrating on Mama and missing her and being scared for her, but E.J. occupies every available space inside me. There's just no room for Mama right now. I think about this while my headphones are stuffed in my ears, and my iPhone is playing all the songs that bring E.J. close. My friends try to get me to come over, but I'm not in the mood for sitting around and Snapchatting when I have no stories of my own to share. I've been dialing E.J. for days and texting him all kinds of crazy messages. His silence has me in a frenzy. Being in my room only makes it worse, so I head for my parents' room down the hall and climb onto their bed, dissolving into the soft comforter.

E.J. and I met at a back-to-school bash. He was standing there in a corner with the football players, bulky juniors with attitudes as big as their egos. He was wearing my lucky number on his jersey, eighteen. The party, in the cozy neighborhood off Stettler View Drive, was jampacked. The line for the bathroom was twenty people deep when E.J. came up behind me, grabbed me by the shoulders, and whispered that he was ready to take me home. The look on his face when I turned around was at first shock, and then it transformed into something else.

"I'm sorry," he said. "I thought you were someone else."

Whether he knew I was Coach's daughter or not, he didn't let it show. "There's another bathroom upstairs," he whispered.

Every impulse in my body told me to walk away from this boy with the shaved head and cappuccino-colored skin, but instinct guided my legs to follow him upstairs to an abandoned bathroom.

"Shouldn't you find that someone you're supposed to take home?"

He shrugged it off, his quiet telling me not to pry. I had been warned as a teenager to never go anywhere alone with a boy who dwarfed me in size and stature, but there was something about E.J. that told me he wasn't nearly as secure as he sounded. The lock on the door was broken, and E.J. assured me he wouldn't leave without me.

After that first night, E.J. would show up everywhere I went.

"My daddy's not going to like you hanging around here," I would chastise him, with the early emergence of my soon to be "resting bitch face." I was working at Victoria's Secret in the Southpark Mall, and it was bad enough one of my father's controversial, gorgeous players was eyeballing me, but across the aisle from sexy underthings—words I couldn't bring myself to say out loud—was sure to irritate him. I would be there after school, folding and refolding those lacy numbers into these ridiculously tight cubbyholes, and he would hover as if I were folding something as everyday as T-shirts at Abercrombie.

"Juliana," he would say, over a pile of pink and black lace. I thought I might die of embarrassment, though when I stared up into E.J.'s prying eyes, a calm sheathed itself around my body. Perhaps that was the day he also wound his fingers around my heart and lightly tugged. I had no control over the madness that crept inside, the way he led me to believe that I was for the first time seeing the world.

I smiled at him instead of sending him away. I did it first out of curiosity, and then it became something bigger than even I could understand. I was terrified of the way E.J. made me feel, and it wasn't the kind of fear I could turn away from. Other girls acted silly and different when he was near. I didn't want to be like them, but something about his presence and his eyes and the way he curved his lips told me that I was. I felt goofy and girly around him. My laugh sounded decibels louder than I ever remembered it being. He occupied my thoughts in a way that other boys never could. Marlee would always tell me that love doesn't make sense: "It just grabs your heart and pulls you in directions you've never been." She'd say it plays tricks with your mind: "You'll see things brighter and clearer and feel them harder and deeper." When E.J. would circle around me in the store, I knew she was right. He was breaking me down, piece by piece. Whatever love was, it was something I knew I wanted.

"I'm not afraid of your daddy," he whispered at me. It felt like a tickle escaped this overgrown boy's body and slid down my back.

E.J. is five feet, eleven inches and two hundred twenty pounds. He runs forty yards in four point forty-eight seconds. I know this because I have studied every newspaper article about him and memorized his stats better than I will ever know calculus. He followed me out of the mall while the security guard eyed me, trying not to act as though he was concerned about a young girl being followed by an oversized boy. When he got closer and saw it was E.J. Whittaker pursuing me, he smiled and gave him a high five. After he got even closer and saw that I was Coach Holden's daughter, his surprise smoldered with a warning.

E.J.'s pace quickened with each step of mine. There was something provocative and sexy about leaving behind a pile of girlie lingerie and getting caught up in the tumult of the county's star football player.

Before I could reach into my purse, he was beside my car, opening the door for me.

"A gentleman," I said.

E.J. didn't say a word. He just stared at me as though he were afraid if he closed his eyes I would disappear.

"What are you doing here?" I asked, wanting to believe there was more to his presence than needing a ride back to his apartment. I wanted to hear the words leave his lips.

"You."

Me.

I would soon learn that E.J. was a man of few words. And the words he used would become the most meaningful ones I ever heard. I was sitting in the driver's seat when he sauntered over to the passenger side and opened the door. The parking structure was empty, the Charlotte sky sprouting a full moon. He had probably showered after practice in the locker room, something I would later learn he almost always did, far away from his crowded home and its dirty stall without a curtain.

The jeans he wore were a "gift" from a booster, the sweater from a girl who was best known for shoplifting at the local TJ Maxx. Yet E.J. reached across the seat and brought his mouth to mine with an irresistible ease. I kissed back. I kissed him with a desire that told him not to stop. His fingers cupped my face as if our lips together were not enough. My breath caught in my throat. I gasped and he pulled away, asking, "What's wrong?"

Everything was wrong. This was wrong. My dad was going to kill me. But I kissed him again. Harder. And through my lips he would feel the unwinding of my heart as it freed itself from a place I had kept well guarded. My hands fought to feel him on my fingers. I liked him. More than I had ever liked anyone before. It didn't matter that we'd barely spoken more than a few sentences, or that he was forbidden to me. Our different worlds had thrown us together, and I fell hard and fast for Evan James Whittaker.

I roll over onto Daddy's side of the bed when my cell phone rings, interrupting some of my favorite memories. Daddy's picture lights up the screen along with the football emoji I put next to his name.

"Did you find him?" I ask, jumping up and suddenly breathless.

"He turned himself in to the police. They're questioning him. This could have all been avoided if E.J. just went with Buford and listened to what he had to say."

I'm too happy to care about the politics of why and how he's at the station. He's alive and hopefully unharmed. The worries that had swelled my head stream out of me in an overdue sigh. Daddy's talking into my ear, but I'm busily texting words to E.J.'s phone: *I love u. Ur safe! I need 2 C U! Call me!*

"Do you hear me, Juliana? Get some sleep. You're coming with me to Cold Creek tomorrow."

I don't say yes or no because I'm hopeful he'll forget.

Daddy hangs up and I fall back into the pillows, this time using Mama's pillow to prop up my head. He said he's going to be at the station for a while since E.J.'s still not in the clear, but I know E.J., and he's going to do the right thing. He has to.

The sheet smells like Mama's perfume, and even her absence doesn't feel as bad now that I know my boyfriend isn't lying hurt on a street somewhere. E.J. and I will talk, we'll straighten things out, and he'll help me deal with the issues with my mama.

This is what had been missing from my life: someone like E.J. to help sort the jumble in my brain, to make me feel heard, to understand the constant state of alarm spreading through our house, 'cause let's face it, Mama's crazier than a wild turkey. E.J. and I connected through our imperfections. All of this made it easy for me to slip into his world, and I didn't think twice. I just jumped.

After E.J. stopped stalking me at the Victoria's Secret, and after hours of texting and late-night phone calls, he finally asked me out on a proper date. At first, I expected us to go to the mall, where all the kids from the neighboring high schools hang out, but there was nothing predictable about our first afternoon together.

"I don't like surprises," I said to him while hugging the phone to my ear. He said to dress comfortably and casual—sneakers. I worried that he was bothered he wasn't able to take me somewhere special, and that I was the one with the car. When he directed me to drive into the White-water Center, a recreational area for outdoor enthusiasts about twenty miles from downtown Charlotte, I saw this boy in a way I couldn't before. The E.J. who emerged from the car seemed taller and happier. Without the distractions of home and the gossipy stares, he took my hand in his and weaved me through the seven-hundred-acre park until we reached the canopy tour.

The excursion winds through the woodlands along the Catawba River and parts of the Tuckaseegee Ford and Trail. Only we were traveling beneath the canopy on a series of platforms, by way of zip lines, sky bridges, and rappels.

The afternoon sun poked through the trees, and our conversation became lighter. Though our worlds weren't meant to collide, everything about us fit together just right. I know this because I relied on him to keep me upright on the bridges and from falling through the net climbs. Even our guide found it sweet the way he hovered around me. She was an older blond woman with thick creases in her skin from the outdoors. "Let her go . . . You're holding her back . . ." I smiled, though I really liked the feeling of E.J.'s hands grazing my shoulders and the way his palms found my back. His hands were huge, so when they touched me they covered a lot of me, and I had nothing to fear.

As we trekked further into the trees, we reached heights in excess of sixty feet, and when it was my turn to zip across, E.J. was behind me, both arms encircling me in his famous grip. I leaned in to him, feeling close without saying a word. The wind was whipping past our faces, branches were snapping in the breeze, and the sky was a brilliant blue. Normally I would have been terrified. "This is crazy!" I shouted to the sky, as E.J. caught my words in his outstretched hands. "Hold on and take a breath," he said. "I'm right here." Then he pushed me forward so gently that I didn't realize I was dangling in the air from a single harness, my life secured to the line tethered around my waist and through my legs. The world hugged me in its hands, and I felt my body release in its grip.

E.J. waited on the platform behind me, and while my harness spun me in the breeze, I was facing him, watching his beautiful smile follow me through the trees. I could feel his blue eyes on me until I landed and then it was my turn to watch him fly in my direction.

"That was amazing!"

"I knew you'd like it here." He smiled. "My mom brought me with her church group. It's where I come to get away."

We walked the river trail, stopping a few times to take pictures. By then I couldn't take one step without E.J.'s hand. His fingers belonged around mine. We descended to the final tree platform, a rappel-style free fall that overlooked the river. I was blown away by what we had just done together. Anyone who said I couldn't trust E.J. was wrong.

The guide talked over us, describing the nighttime variation of the canopy tour—guests traveling through trees as the sun goes down. "It's a completely different perspective, a midnight sky," and I squeezed E.J.'s hand, imagining him guiding me through the dark under a shower of stars. E.J. saw the turn on my crimson face, and he walked me toward a secluded area surrounded by thick shrubs where we sat down on towels and unloaded our lunches.

And before I knew it, E.J. was telling me what I meant to him. "Don't be scared," he said. "I'm not. I've been waiting for you a long time, Juliana." My hand reached for his. "It's okay to let someone in." My brain was noisy with family-related clutter. The words coming from his lips wrapped around me and quieted the chatter.

"I'm not afraid," I said. "I won't even pretend not to feel what you make me feel."

Though we had kissed in the parking lot outside the mall, this time E.J.'s lips were different. They were more controlled, less frantic, as if he knew how I felt and trusted him. I wish I could say I closed my eyes and thought only of his lips, but I did not. I thought about my mom and how she pushed me away, right into E.J.'s arms. I thought about how my friends would react to my falling for someone so different from us, and about how I was going to survive E.J.'s leaving for college at the end of the school year. And my dad. It certainly didn't enhance the moment to have his warnings about boys creep into my ears while E.J. pulled me closer into his arms.

I think I was the first to pull away. It wasn't because I didn't love every second of his lips brushing against mine. I just needed to look at him, to study his face and his eyes. I needed to assess the reflection that was staring back at me. Would he have the same worries?

He started first: "Your mama's gonna hate me, no matter what I do. Coach, he'll hate me, too, at first, but he'll see how you smile."

"E.J.," I began, not really knowing how to say this to him. "It's your family he's worried about. And my mother hates herself more than she can ever hate you."

His long body stretched across the towel. I curled into him, and his arm wrapped around me, tickling my skin. The movement felt like a deep sigh, his disappointment rising to the surface and puncturing the air around us. "They suck, don't they?" he asked. I would have tried to sugarcoat it, but E.J. spoke aloud the thoughts that had crept into my head. He proceeded to tell me about a life I had heard about but could not fully imagine. It was rife with all the things one might expect from a family relying on crime to survive, though what I heard behind E.J.'s words—and there were quite a few of them—was sheer sadness. My heart, which minutes before had felt ripe and brimming with possibility, was suddenly achy.

"Do I scare you?" he asked. "You feel different," he added, caressing my arms and letting his fingers graze where my heart beat frantically in my chest.

I'm relatively thin, but my body is toned and strong from running. Except lying against E.J., I felt as flimsy and frail as paper. I was convinced my mind was a book that he was holding in his hands, and the pages and pictures were wide open for him to devour and explore. He was reading me rather fast.

"No," I said, nuzzling up against his chest. Dozens of girls had longed for this position beside E.J. I won't lie and say it didn't make me feel special to be with someone as famous as he was in our parts, but with fame came a slew of drama that I could easily have done without. I said, "I'm afraid of the girls at your school who think you belong to them."

He hugged me closer and our legs tangled together. Neither of us touched our lunch as we talked about his future in football, his mom Ruby, and his brothers. "I hate what they've done, but they're my brothers. And Devon, he's not lost to me. He goes back and forth, wanting to be better, tripping against my father's strong will. I've caught him watching me at games. He sits in a corner where he thinks I don't see."

"And your dad?" I asked, feeling his body tense up, reading him the way his fingers were reading me.

"There's not a lot to say."

Feeling that door slam shut was more powerful than any of the truths he had shared.

"I've said too much. You don't need to be near this."

"It's part of you. I want to be a part of you."

He laughed. I felt jilted and silly. Then he cupped my chin in his hands, and his ease around me altered short sentences into longer ones. "Beautiful Juliana. You're smart, yet naive. You're strong, but I feel your weaknesses. You're already a part of me. More than any girl has ever been. But I won't share you with the messed-up world of my family. You're too good. Too pure."

I might not have believed him had I not actually heard the words come from his lips. He kissed my cheek and then my nose and then my hair. "My family's pretty nuts, too," I finally breathed into him. "Drugs and weapons aren't the only things that destroy families. Trust me."

"C'mon, your dad's the man," he smiled. "Everyone calls him G.O.A.T, Greatest of All Time."

"He is," I whispered into his neck. "My mama's just not right."

"How do you mean?"

"There's always been something wrong with her, you know, in her brain," I tell him, not rushing my thoughts. I am uneasy sharing this part of my life, but I know it's okay to share it with E.J. It has to be. "When my parents sat me down to explain, it was as though all the question marks were answered with an *aha*. Everything sort of made sense."

"Like what?" he asks.

I tell him about the time I came home from school and she was holed up in her bedroom with the door closed. I had to be all of twelve years old, so I was more interested in what snacks were in the kitchen and who I could text about the upcoming math test. "Okay, that's kind of a lie." I smiled. "We would be texting about boys. Always." He laughs and I decide he has the most perfect white teeth I have ever seen.

"Really?" he said. "You were crushing on other boys before me?" So I swatted him on the cheek and he grabbed my hand, and I continued, feeling a well opening up inside of me. "I'd always pretend she was in there doing something productive, even though I knew she wasn't. There was a space underneath my parents' bedroom door so I knew when the lights were on or off. Those afternoons, the lights were off."

I felt guilty and disloyal elaborating and comparing, but it didn't stop me from switching to automatic pilot and letting it roll. Soon I was basically telling on my mom, and it felt, all things considered, good. "Do you ever go to your friends' houses and think how normal everyone is?"

He laughed. "Jules, come on, where I grew up, every house was crazy."

"I'm sorry. That was insensitive . . . It's just, when I'd visit the twins' house, I knew that something was really off in our home. We'd sit around the kitchens and the other moms would bombard us with questions about classes and boys. These Rachael Rays would literally throw food at us. I think they equated dessert with the depth of their love." I leaned my forehead against his and added: "I thought it was normal that my mom would nap every afternoon when I'd stroll in the door from school and be in most need of her mothering."

I continued: "Once, I walked into her room, and it was pitch black. I saw her there, wrapped under the blanket. I thought the sheets would swallow her up whole. I asked her where she went, I mean, she had literally disappeared." I sat up on my elbows and studied E.J.'s face. "Do you understand what I'm saying? This wasn't just a physical form of vanishing. She had no soul. Her eyes were hollow and empty."

His fingers gripped my face, and he brushed my cheeks with gentle strokes. "I'm so sorry, Jules. It had to be awful for you." My hand covered his palm until he pulled me down by his side.

"It's not easy having a mom who is *unwell*. That's the polite word my friends use to label her odd behavior. She never volunteered. PTA meetings were out of the question. Being surrounded by women who were staring her up and down with their beady little eyes was a definite trigger. Frankly, any social contact elicited fear." My mind passed through memories and I wasn't really choosing the ones to share. They were choosing themselves, slow moving, as I pretended to think out loud. I paused a lot between sentences. They were observations I couldn't rush. "E.J., I never felt entirely safe around her—you can't imagine . . . Well, maybe you could. And her behaviors and idiosyncrasies embarrassed me—she wouldn't drive a car! Would I inherit her claustrophobia or agoraphobia, or the whole host of ailments that plague her regularly?"

"There are all different kinds of crazy, Jules."

"I feel bad saying all this. I'm supposed to love and honor and respect my mama."

"No, baby, sometimes it's hard to love the people you're supposed to. I won't let anyone hurt you like that again."

I stare at the sky and think that all of my wishes have come true. "I'm not sure this is something even you can protect me from."

"I'll try," and he kisses me again, and I forget about my mama for a second while I taste his salty lips.

E.J. listened without prying. I'm sure my problems were nothing compared to his. For example, dinner wasn't always on the table at a set time. Sometimes Mama forgot to pay for my French tutor. She relied on June Harrow, Coach Harrow's wife, to drive us to appointments. Sometimes it was even worse for me when she actually showed up somewhere.

E.J. didn't judge, and he quickly caught on. "We're the same, Juliana Holden." And he was right. E.J. needed a father, and I needed a mother. Our collective needs strung us together in a beautiful, unpredictable way.

Drake and Rihanna were singing from the tiny iPhone speaker, and we lay on our backs staring up at a gorgeous Charlotte sky. E.J. whispered along with the words, and when it was over, he told me all the things Drake told her. He's going to take care of me. That's all I've ever wanted to hear from someone.

"It's not going to be easy for us, Jules. The world won't be kind. But you're my ever, and I'll do what I can to make you happy."

"Your ever?"

"It comes after forever. It's longer."

I could have stayed there looking into his eyes until the sun fell from the sky. He is the one person who makes me feel as though I don't need anybody else.

E.J. gave me a new and better life. He gave me an *ever*.

CHAPTER TWELVE

LAUREN

Imagine my surprise when I open the door to find Quinci's perfectly manicured, coiffed self bitching about Mohammed not coming to the mountain. She reminds me of the tumbling waters of Guyana's Kaieteur Falls, aggressive and loud. Like the falls, before you see her, you can hear her.

Quinci's luggage didn't make it to Charlotte, and she is about to sue someone at US Airways. She's screaming and swearing into her cell phone about the airline ruining her trip while holding up her finger and telling me, "One sec."

She hangs up and greets me with a kiss on both cheeks. "Isn't that how you greet people from Europe?" she asks through a mane of black hair and blue eyes. "Don't look so surprised, Lauren, I'll be gone the day after tomorrow."

I laugh at her. "Who checks luggage for two days in the mountains?"

"Who has a vacation home in the middle of Nowheresville?" she shoots back.

"What are you doing here?" I ask, guiding her through the house and to the sofa.

"You, my friend, need a pep talk. And I need to see what you've got for me." Then she reaches inside her ginormous pocketbook and applies a thick line of red across her lips. "Besides, the way you talk about this place, I thought I'd make a mini-vacation out of it. "It's pretty," she says, barely looking up from her compact and missing the view completely. "But where's the mall?"

Q can be funny when she's not so demanding. Her bag isn't supposed to arrive for twenty-four hours, and she is hard-pressed to be without her cosmetics and hair products for that long. Before she calls her attorney, who—she has reminded me three times—also represents Phillip Margolin, we are Google mapping directions for the fifty-minute journey to Johnson City, to the closest store, which happens to be Target.

The house is quiet without the clickety-clack of Quinci's heels. I hope she heeds my advice and picks up a pair of suitable shoes for the terrain.

Collapsing on the couch with the not-yet-named manuscript in my hand, I reach for the remote and switch through rows of channels. The soft voices on the local news remind me that I'm jet-lagged, and I fall back on the brown leather cushions and close my eyes.

The waves of emotion strike me hard. It is a lashing I have since forgotten, but being in this house brings it back all over again. It hurts more than I am willing to admit. So many years have passed, and it feels like only days. Maybe less. Could I have been foolish enough to think that hiding among the cracks and crevices of nature would heal me? And did any of it matter when starting anew had only led me back to where it all began?

The waterfall book rests against my chest. The story began immediately after college when I set off on a post-graduate photography program under renowned photographer Jean-Pierre Guichard. The focus of the six-month journey was to photograph the world's most majestic cascades: New Zealand, Croatia, Venezuela. I had plunged into the journey headfirst, leaving my present life behind. In some ways, it helped knowing Ryan wasn't right there, so accessible to me. I had to let go of him in order to fully experience the land without limits. Loving Ryan was never an issue;

he was in my heart. He knew I'd be unavailable for stretches of time while I hid behind my camera and the priceless views. And by sharing the pictures with him, I could see things through his eyes that my own could not.

Then everything fell apart. My trip was cut short.

Instead of traveling the world to places like Canada, Iceland, and Brazil, I was pushed in another direction, one that landed me in a flat owned by one of Jean-Pierre's friends in South Kensington, London. There I wrote novels under the pen name Virginia Sutherland, after the New Zealand and Zimbabwe falls that had been on my itinerary. Iceland's Seljalandsfoss falls were a good choice, but the pronunciation made Quinci's head spin, so we ruled it out.

If Ryan were a waterfall, he would be the Detian Falls on the border of China and Vietnam. Constant and contained, beautiful in their simplicity. That was before. After, he would become Canada's Virginia Falls. Brash and contradictory, tumbling out of control down an unruly abyss.

Because my eyes have failed me since I was a child, I grew to rely on the precision of the camera's lens to capture what I couldn't trust my eyes to see. At times I'd close my eyes and listen. The water spoke to me in a language only I could decipher. A trickling meant peace; a river, the seduction of impermanence. Whether thrashing falls or a docile surge, water has taught me that nothing remains unchanged. We can move beyond self-imposed limits. When sleep eludes me, the stream outside my bedroom window lulls me to sleep. My favorite trails have followed winding paths of weeping water. Water inspires me, and the falls are a pursuit I always need to follow. They were why I first left Ryan all those years ago, and the reason I stayed away for too long.

Having Quinci here is a welcome distraction. The publishing house has been breathing down her neck, so it makes sense she's breathing down mine.

Anyone who knows the workings of the publishing world knows that it is almost impossible for an unknown author to make it through the slush pile. Quinci was an ambitious warrior, which worked to my advantage. It began on a whim. After completing my first novel, I sent a query letter to her newly formed agency in Manhattan, and instead of outright rejecting me or requesting the first fifty pages, Quinci broke all the rules: she picked up the phone and called me in the London flat. She was impressed with my note and asked for the entire manuscript.

Within seventy-two hours, we were back on the phone. It was the most talking I had done in months.

"Who hurt you?" she came right out and asked.

"What makes you think I've been hurt?"

"I'm a trained reader," she said. "There's loss buried deep in your words."

"I have a keen imagination," I said, careful to bury the feelings that came along with it. "Besides, London has a lot of stories. There's a tale everywhere you look."

"It reads very personally."

"That happens when you write your characters in the first person," I said.

"It's got to be therapeutic to be able to release your demons that way. Your writing possesses such depth. You have the makings of a bestseller."

I laughed. The novel was a lark. My life course had shifted. Ryan and I were over. I couldn't go home, and I couldn't look at waterfalls. Visiting theaters and wandering the streets at dusk in London were my salvation. Writing was a cathartic pastime.

"I feel like I know you," she said, "the you who's played by Helene."

"Everyone thinks they know the author. We're not all protagonists."

"You're not the least bit romantic, wandering the globe in search of waterfalls? You refer to them like old lovers."

She wasn't wrong. The fingers of the falls had touched me deeply. Joy and pain trickled down those mountains. It was not easy to give them up.

"You must have really loved Patrick."

I let the memory wash through me.

"He sounds like one hell of a guy. I'd never let someone like him go."

I bit my lip. I hadn't let Patrick go. He had let go of me.

At Davidson when I fell for Ryan, I had just returned from a fourth date with Thomas Howard III. He was a likable enough guy who was exactly what you'd expect of a Thomas Howard III. But my thoughts would flit back to the arrogant boy in my psych class, even while Thomas's lips were pressed against mine. I couldn't admit it at the time, but I liked how Ryan teased me in front of a dozen pairs of eyes. The attention was thrilling, even though he was the antithesis of the guys I usually dated. I knew he was special when I returned to my dorm and found the bouquet of orange tulips. He later told me they matched my hair and how he would one day bury his face in there. I shivered when he made bold statements like that, and the quivering propelled me to do things I would otherwise never have done.

Thomas and I spent our fourth date studying at the library before heading over to the Soda Shop for some shakes. Returning to Belk Hall, he expected I would invite him inside, and I did, though what happened next to this day sends an ache down my body.

Abby was at a movie with some girls from the floor, and Thomas sprawled himself across my bed. An irony of college living is that these tiny spaces are created with two pieces of furniture: a desk and a twin bed. Though adults encourage kids not to have sex, once you pass over the threshold of your dorm room, you are essentially on a mattress. Thomas was handsome in a *Dead Poets Society* way—fair haired, blue eyed. His teeth were a little darker than I liked, but he was kind and opened doors and wanted to be a dentist. Go figure.

Our communal bathroom was down the hall, and while Thomas

stretched his long limbs across my deep blue comforter, I walked the few yards to its metal door. Ryan popped out of nowhere and pulled me down the hall. I saw the bathroom retreat behind me, though the heat that emanated from Ryan's hand doubled my pace.

Before my feet touched the ground, I was in the side stairwell used for emergencies, and Ryan had lightly pressed me up against the wall. Someone had opened the window in the dimly lit space, and a temperate breeze nipped at my bare shoulders, but I couldn't be sure it wasn't Ryan's looming presence wrapped around me.

I was wearing a sheer, coral sleeveless dress that fell right above the knees. Ryan was in jeans and a gray flannel button-down. Ryan moved his body closer to mine, so close I could feel his heart through his shirt. His hands found my cheeks. He wouldn't let me look away.

"Thomas is in my room."

"I know."

I looked to the floor, ashamed, and Ryan forced my eyes to find his again.

"What do you want, Lauren?"

None of it made sense, and everything fell into place—Ryan putting his lips on mine; Ryan holding me like he couldn't let me go; Ryan breathing me in like air, filling me up with sky. I whispered, silently, the answer to his lips, his neck, his hair: *you.*

I'll admit. I didn't think about Thomas Howard III at all.

"He's going to wonder where I am."

"Tell him you're with me."

"I am with you," I confessed.

"Do you know how long I've wanted this?" he asked.

I kissed him hard. His arms fell around me, and I melted into the grooves of his shoulders and chest. I had become one of those horrible girls who strings a boy along only to drop him for someone else. Not necessarily someone better, but someone who had drowned out the noises of the world and made it so I was spoiled for anyone else, a boy whose voice filled every part of my body, whose eyes I trusted to see things for me when mine could not.

When he backed away, I felt a mild panic inside. I didn't want to return to the other world. I didn't want to deal with Thomas on my bed, and have to explain what I didn't understand myself.

His fingers found my chin, and they lifted it up to meet his face. "Tell me you haven't thought about kissing me?"

"I think about you a lot," I said.

"Why are you dating Thomas?"

"He asked me."

Ryan took my hands in his, lacing his fingers through each one, and held them close to his heart. "I'm asking you."

My face burned from his words.

"You're so beautiful, Lauren Sheppard."

Ryan Holden.

His name is stuffed in a memory carriage I grew to avoid, and now it is resounding from somewhere else, somewhere real I cannot wake up from. I hear it again—*and Ryan Holden addressed the media today*—I open my eyes to Ryan staring at me on the screen. I jolt upright and reach for my glasses.

It is him. Ryan. And my entire body comes alive. Years strip away. My heart slips away from me.

Time can change a person, but it hasn't changed Ryan. Everything good about him is better, except the noticeable frustration that lines his face. I wrap the blanket around me even tighter to protect myself from the feelings that are piling up. He is talking about his team and the struggles his players are facing this season. Under the footage, the ticker reads "Pine Ridge Poised to Win Championship Again?"

Mom and Dad don't have a DVR, so when I try to rewind and listen to what he was saying, the message is gone. I hear his voice, the deep inflection of how he cares about this team. The same whisper that would wake me in the morning and kiss my cheeks at night. His eyes are honest and pained, but a beautiful swirl of deep green and brown, and the scar above his eyebrow has hardly faded. It is hard to look and not feel cheated of the years I missed. He was mine, and I was his. Forever. We had agreed on that. Now I am looking at a stranger, though I swear he feels me staring back at him. And he is telling me how he misses me, and I am blushing because it feels so good.

As I sit here, on the couch where Ryan and I wrapped ourselves around each other too many times to count, I wonder if my choosing the land first, before Ryan, sealed our fate. His mouth tosses words into the air, and his eyes tell me he is the same gracious man I fell in love with when we were young. It strikes me with little warning, like a gushing fall slapping the pool of water below—the seal of the cracks has been only temporary. I may have forgotten how his lips taste against my tongue, but I have not forgotten what being around him does to my heart. A stirring within is erasing what I had seen and what caused me to run. Ryan betrayed me, but hadn't I betrayed him first? Somewhere in the blurred perspective there is truth.

This longing begins in my belly and moves through my chest and lungs. It is physical, like sex, and nostalgia laces with unforgotten memory. I can feel him pressing deep into my skin. My protective layer crumbles just at the sound of his voice.

Seventeen years is a long time. I had thought I left those long-ago feelings and sensations behind, though being here thrusts Ryan into my head, like the thrashing of the falls.

CHAPTER THIRTEEN

ABBY

I awake refreshed and eager to begin the day's dig. Rose is gone, quietly slipping out to her morning yoga on the deck. Tamar has left her imprint in my body. Last night, she explained how the energy of any electronic devices interferes with the work she does, so she asked me to refrain from turning them on. Though I thought she was nutty, I couldn't refute the state of calm my body had seemed to casually enter. It was hardly a sacrifice. I had relinquished my cell phone and Internet access when I arrived. Being cut off from the device has been good for me.

I have much to consider. The doctors and my personal peace corps have laid out the groundwork, and it is up to me to decide my fate. Struggling with mental illness is a lifelong, full-time job. It invades every crevice of the mind and body, and when it is dormant, it will later resurface when you are most vulnerable. I remember watching an infomercial that promised to cure anxiety. I was suffering from agoraphobia at the time, and it seemed logical to order the $399 manual, complete with ten CDs for relaxation, meditation, and self-talk that would be delivered to our front door. The thing that really hooked me—besides not having to leave the house—was when the pretty lady on the screen bellowed, "How far down do you have to go before deciding to make a change? How long are you willing to suffer?"

When I found that picture in Ryan's drawer, lava poured through my veins. Jeannie had said, "It's not the emotion, but rather the level of intensity." My eruption had been volcanic.

A knock at the door resounds, and I rise to let Ryan in. Before kissing me hello, he walks over to the TV, the only electronic device allowed, and with the flick of a switch, I learn of the ongoing allegations facing one of his players. Because the player in question is a minor, they don't use his name, though I can tell by Ryan's eyes that the drama is centered on my daughter's boyfriend.

My on-screen husband looks tired and beaten. He is trying to keep in step with the reporters' questions, but I can see through his steely reserve. They are provoking him with bristling theories. His eyes are glossy red. He clasps his hands together and waits for the frenzy to pass, in an attempt to regain some composure, though it doesn't work. They poke and badger, and Ryan is irate.

"Just awful," he says, gesturing at the television.

"What happened?" I ask, taking a seat at the edge of the bed. "How come nobody told me?"

"There's nothing you could've done. E.J.'s being stupid, and now they're charging him with a crime he didn't commit."

I ask about our daughter.

"Not good," he says, coming closer to the bed. "She's in with Jeannie now." Part of treatment means family members have to meet with a counselor. "It was a fight, but I got her through the door. More important, how you doin'?" he asks, changing the subject completely. This is one of my husband's many gifts. He can turn the table so that everything has to do with me, and for years I lapped it up, taking a seat at the head. When you're stuck in your mind the majority of the day, it is easy to forget that other people have problems. But today feels oddly different. Which is why I begin to cry. At first quiet whimpers escape, which turn into loud heaving noises. Snot drips down my face, and Ryan cleans it with his finger before finding a tissue beside by the bed. That's what he does. That's how deeply he loves me.

"Baby, what's going on?"

"I don't know. I think those pills are unlocking my sadness. I cry a lot in here." Or maybe Tamar's palms are unleashing something else.

He takes one of my hands in his and when the tears slow down, I tell him two words: "I'm sorry."

It's not the first time I've uttered those words. For years I have apologized for my weaknesses, my sickness, things beyond my control, though today's apology is for what Ryan is blind to, things he could never know. Things I never told him and the carefully constructed story I will have to unwind. Not today. Today I must be sure that he's okay.

"Tell me about E.J.," I say.

"The police got a tip that the Whittaker boys had something to do with a burglary. Buford showed up at the field like a bull and called E.J. out in front of the team. He didn't steal the jewelry, but he may as well have, the guilty way he ran away from Buford's questions. He took it from his brother and hid it at Ruby's. Knucklehead thought he could fix it." His voice trails off because he had known the likelihood of something like this happening.

Ryan sits on my bed, and I move over to make room. His face is worn, and his body slumps forward. I want to console him, reach my arms across his shoulders and ease his distress, though I don't know how. Something stops me. It has always been me in need of care; I have forgotten how to soothe someone else. The hesitation that swamps me is rooted far back in our relationship. It was how we began, how my comforting him destroyed everything he once loved and trusted.

This is not E.J., the gentle giant who ate dinners at our house, whom Ryan is describing. Panic churns around me, the real, tangible kind. Panic derived from the unknown is far more perilous than real, concrete threats. When the waves pass through me, I am drenched with thoughts of Juliana. "She can't see him anymore, Ryan."

"She loves him."

"He'll hurt her," I say, pressing into him, feeling his heart tickle my cheek. "She can't be a part of that world."

"He is her world. This isn't going to change it," he says, his voice trailing off somewhere.

I think of how Ryan once had another world with someone else. Things change. People move on. I shudder at the memory.

"What are you thinking?" I ask.

"The police are taking the charges seriously, despite the fact that he turned himself in. Those minor infractions over the years have added up. And running away from Buford will only add to their case."

"Didn't he tell them how the stuff got there?"

"He's not talking."

"Not even to you?"

"Not even to me."

Ryan curls around me atop the miniature bed, and before long he is dozing. I am weirdly calm from my Reiki-induced rest, though deeply concerned about Juliana. His warm body against mine spreads the flow of energy. If she loves E.J. the way I love her father, she will heed no warnings, and she'll do things she can't undo. She will accept circumstances that may alter her path and those of the people closest to her.

Scanning the small room, I see the reflection of the two of us in the mirror on the wall. There have been memories over the years that I have observed from a distance. Sometimes it is easier to block out the images, as though they really didn't happen. Because when you hold up the mirror, you don't want to see the disgraceful person staring back. Tamar dug into my memory bank to ones that are too painful to remember. I had tricked my brain into believing that what I did wasn't so bad, but it was. It was awful.

Lauren had left for wherever it was in the world she claimed she had to go. I had my own feelings about this, but whatever they were, Ryan's despair trumped them. He was losing his girlfriend, his *future bride*, he called her. I was losing my best friend, the only person I knew who didn't see me as a weirdo. I was crushed. And even though I had lingering feelings for Ryan, I had kept them in check out of loyalty to my friend.

But when she left, I was angry.

Watching them say good-bye to each other was tough. How do you divide two who together had always been one?

Then Ryan's father died. It was twisted and cruel that God would take these two people from Ryan's life so quickly, one right after the other.

Ryan was enduring a brutal form of grief. Lauren was unreachable. Most of us who had tried to summon her on her cell phone weren't even sure she got the messages. When you're twenty-one and traveling the world, you don't consider that it might fall off its axis if you don't go home to set it right. A week turned into two, and friends and family returned to their respective lives just when Ryan most needed the sounds of voices in his empty kitchen.

It was easy for me to think at the time—and I would never have said it aloud—that *I* wouldn't have left him in the first place. And that isn't because I had always secretly worshiped him. With all my phobias, I would have to have been knocked unconscious to board an airplane.

So there was a fair amount of resentment both in me and in Ryan when I showed up in Myers Park, in what was once his dad's house and then his own, with the intention of consoling him. He was still mourning, though his grief seemed more hollow and less fluid than before. His hair was long and tangled, falling almost to his shoulders. He was pale, and his jeans hung loosely on his hips. I think being with me reminded him of her, and I stuffed myself with the attention.

I came with a bag of noshes from our favorite gourmet deli, and it was Ryan who brought out the bottle of wine. Drinking often made unbearable situations easier. It also caused dangerous side effects. More than a few glasses and I'm deluded into thinking I can karaoke, though that afternoon a bottle of wine meant possibility to me. I should have known by the rough way he handled the bottle and tossed down two glasses that something terribly wrong was going to happen. When he switched to scotch, I saw the subtle way in which his anger became defiance and then dissolved into sadness. Traces of the Ryan I knew well had been erased by a drunkenness that slapped his face. When he looked at me, I swear he was looking for someone else. There was a desire in the flecks of his eyes that touched a place deep inside of me. Even if it wasn't for me, I felt his passion wash through me and I, too, became drunk.

We were seated at his family's breakfast table. The furnishings were tired and outdated, though it reflected the essence of Ryan's family: unassuming and close knit. Ryan had two older sisters who had moved down the street to be near their aging father, and from the pictures that lined the walls of the home, one could see how the family had gathered happily between these sturdy walls. A large window surrounded us, the afternoon sunshine streaming in and casting a glow on the backyard with its wilting flower garden. People are not the only ones who need human touch.

Ryan didn't ask me to drink. He didn't even offer me scotch. When he got up to clear the plates from the table, which he insisted on, I took his empty glass, refilled it, and swallowed the gold liquid down in one hungry gulp. When he returned to take a seat next to me at the table, he had no idea of what I'd done. Then I asked him for a glass of scotch.

During our years together at school, Ryan had always treated me like Lauren's baby sister. Whether it was because I was not nearly as sophisticated or self-assured, or because he saw me as the shadow of the girl he loved, the result was the same—he worried about me. He never came right out and said it, but I could tell by the way he'd ask about me, fix problems for me, realign my thinking when I went off on some wild tangent. It was obvious the guys on the team were rolling their eyes or ignoring me. Ryan listened, and sometimes I felt he cared.

"You don't drink scotch, Abs. And you shouldn't mix it with the wine."

"I want to try it."

Ryan was buzzed when he poured another dose of the smooth liquid into a glass. When he held it up in the air, I couldn't think of anything to say. It seemed like an awful idea at the time, but we continued. "Today," he whispered, "let's toast to today. Right now." It was an empty promise, though it shot missiles through my body. Or perhaps it was the liquor. Our glasses clinked and I couldn't wait to feel more of the same.

Except Ryan started to get more upset. He was slurring words, and I was casually filling and refilling my glass with a liquid I had quickly learned could squelch my inhibitions. It really liked me. When I checked my anxiety levels—a self-monitoring system I had in place for situations like these—I didn't feel the swells of impending doom. Panic was not lurking under the table, waiting to gnaw at me limb by limb. Quite the contrary, I felt better than I had in years. I was channeling the spirit of the goddess Athena, only she wasn't prepared to hear Ryan's "I miss her." When he said it, it was as though his heart left his body. The pain was raw and primal. He hung his head on the table and crossed his arms.

"I miss her too."

Then he asked if I had heard from her, which I had not. We were all finding it hard to believe that she hadn't retrieved our messages, but the sketchy cell service made it possible. I said, "I'm worried about her."

This was when Ryan stood up from the table and staggered across the room and down a few steps into the family room. He plopped himself on a nearby couch with a fresh bottle of scotch in his hands. "She's fine," he struggled to say.

I followed him into the other room. The books spanned an entire wall, floor-to-ceiling. Each shelf was sorted by color, forming a rainbow wall. "How can you be sure?"

"I'd know if something were wrong."

"Then why isn't she here?" It came out as a whisper, a legitimate question that hit Ryan like an accusation. He stood up again, agitated, and reached for the poker beside the fireplace. He stabbed at the logs until one fell to the floor and crackled by his feet. The fire was blazing, and I am certain he was too. He didn't bother to clean up the mess; instead, he kicked it to the side and headed back toward the couch, where I had taken cover under one of the rumpled blankets. It made no sense to have a fire going that time of year, though I suspected nothing made sense to Ryan without the people he loved around him. He guzzled another half glass of the scotch.

Ryan was close enough that I could smell his alcohol-laced breath, feel his skin against my arms and legs, burning holes through the blanket that divided us. His face was so immensely sad that I prayed for the power to extinguish the pain. His head drooped to the side and rested on my shoulder. I was light and dreamy there beside him. I was Athena. And I took my hand out from beneath the blanket and touched his shoulder. And then his hair.

Shattered, Ryan did not move away when I slid my fingertips through his messy brown hair. He was drunk, and while I knew it was wrong and spiteful and selfish to take advantage of him in that vulnerable state, it didn't stop me from doing what my body wanted most. We didn't fall in rhythm against each other; instead, we sank into flesh and leather. Ryan was, for the first time, clumsy and incoherent. His words, which usually inspired his teammates, were disjointed and slurred. His head was bobbing up and down. I imagined the mess of thoughts running through his head: *Why did my dad have to die? Where is Lauren?*

My hands drifted out from under the plaid blanket and touched him. They made subtle motions at first, as my fingers sized up his response. I purposely leaned against him, let him feel me beneath the slight fabric around my chest and shoulders. He didn't move away. He let me rub my hands along his arms until I felt him release himself into me completely. He sank deeper and deeper into the couch, and I grew ravenous for him in a way that logic and loyalty could not overturn. He was openly crying, and when my mouth settled on his, I knew I would taste Ryan for a long time. He turned his head away to hide the buried pain, and my hand reached for his chin and cheeks to bring him back. The eyes staring back at me were hollow and lost. "I can make you feel better," I said. "I can take the pain away." He shook his head no, and I took that to mean the pain was too deep. So I pressed harder.

In all my fantasies of seducing Ryan and having him for my own, in no way did I imagine how it could have happened like that. His eyes were pursed shut, heavy with grief. He was not the agile player I had watched on the field; he was not the animated man I studied while he snuggled around Lauren in bed. He was lifeless, strewn across the couch. I knew I had to breathe life into him. When I lay down on top of him, one of my legs cramped and I fell to the floor. When I picked myself up, he was resting peacefully against the stack of pillows. I should have known by those first awkward movements that we did not fit together like he and Lauren did. I should have left him there. I should have given him that moment of tranquility when hurt dissolves into sleep. I owed him that much. And her.

But I didn't. I was on my knees in a pair of jeans that hugged me in all the right places. I unzipped them and let them fall down my legs. Then I unbuttoned the front of my blouse until the only thing separating me from Ryan's body were his clothes and my doubts.

Though my fingers fumbled with the top button of his shirt, by the time they reached the third and fourth, they were alert and nimble. Ryan was lovely in the most wholesome, unspoiled way. His head slumped to the side and his breathing was deep and purposeful, like mine. He was too large for me to move, so I tucked the ends of his shirt away from his chest and traced his stomach and chest with my finger.

I was twenty-one years old. No longer a child, though hardly an adult. Everything I was thinking and doing had the power to screw up my life and those of the people I loved most. I searched the room for a sign. I could get up, put my clothes back on, and leave Ryan to miss his father and pine for Lauren. No sign came. My palm was drawn to Ryan's skin and common sense had vanished along with my clothes.

I unzipped his pants.

By now, Ryan was awake, and when I had finished pulling the jeans down his legs, our eyes met.

"Abby, what are you doing?"

I slid my body on top of his and let my hair fall down the sides of his face. I touched him in forbidden places and made it impossible for him to refuse. When I kissed his mouth, at first he didn't let me in. He grabbed my shoulders and tried to push me away, though I kissed him deeper until he could feel all of me lying across his body.

He smelled of alcohol and dying wishes. I was going to revive him. I was going to make him whole.

"I want you," I said, pulling his hair back so he could see my eyes. "I'm here. I can make it better."

And that's when I felt him come alive. His eyes brightened, and the renewed emotion washed away the lingering sadness. He grabbed me hard and started to kiss me back. Then he touched me in all the places I had dreamed about. He wasn't gentle, and he wasn't kind.

And then he stopped.

"Please don't," I begged. "Please."

"I can't do this, Abby."

And my heartless comeback: "She's not here."

Then I slid his boxers off and did the worst possible thing I could have done.

And when it was over, and I lay spent in his arms, I whispered, "I wish we could stay like this forever."

CHAPTER FOURTEEN

RYAN

Abby is curled in my arms on her bed at Cold Creek. She's talking in her sleep, and I hear her say she wishes we could stay like this forever. It knocks me for a loop. I hadn't thought about those words in a long time. I'm pretty sure I've blocked them out, like most of my memories of that day. I educate my boys to strengthen their body muscles, but I have come to learn the mind is the toughest muscle of all. There are places I have trained it to never revisit.

She stayed over. I remember that much. I wanted her to leave, though the gentleman in me didn't have the heart to kick her out. The truth: I was sick about what we did. Abby was our friend and confidante. The three of us had grown up together during our four years of college, and parts of us were fused together, but I didn't expect it to be those parts.

I always knew Abby had a crush on me. That's why she let me tease her about her obsessions and weird habits. She never got mad at me. She covered her face with pounds of makeup to hide her acne scars, but when I made her laugh, I could see the true color on her cheeks. And I knew.

When we went boating on Lake Watauga, Abby would wear these skimpy bikinis and flaunt her outrageously large breasts. As a college guy, it was tough to look away. She could be sexy at times, when she wasn't falling apart or having some crisis. Especially when she drank. When she drank, her confidence soared, and we saw a side of her that wasn't meek or anxious. She would spring to life with the alcohol boost, and she was actually fun to be around. She'd pull her long dark hair off her face, and her brown eyes would widen. When she let her guard down, she loved to play games and practical jokes. She could be quite a little schemer. She would say her mind is like a superhighway, a maze of overlapping roads. We always knew there was a lot going on in there, but to hear her describe it like that made us feel sorry for her.

Abby was never comfortable in her skin. Either she tried too hard or she didn't try hard enough. There was no in between. I knew of the onslaught of highs and lows, the edginess that lasted for days, though at the time we didn't know the clinical name for it.

I'm not saying it's her fault for what happened with us. I stopped her at one point, and I could have stopped her again. I missed Lauren with such ferocity that when I felt Abby's willing body against mine, my flesh descended into a needy state that only another human body could satisfy. I was horny and drunk and pissed as all hell. Her body was smooth and ripe and begging to be touched. Nothing at that point could have prevented me from falling off that cliff.

We talked about that night just once.

She gathered her clothes and her shoes and her purse and skipped out of the house early the next morning. I didn't try to stop her. When she returned a month later to talk, the first thing she asked was, "Why'd you let me leave?" I thought the reasons were obvious. "It was a mistake," I told her, though her recollection was completely different from mine.

"You didn't even call." Her whiny desperation made my heart palpitate. I was irritated. "It was beautiful. The things you said, the way you held me after," she said.

I was drunk, half passed out, and thinking about Lauren the whole time. I didn't hold her after, like she claimed I had. I didn't lovingly stroke her hair. And I didn't tell her that this would be the start of anything.

"Your eyes. You never looked at me like that before. I saw how much you cared, Ryan. I saw it! It meant something!"

How could I tell her that maybe what she was seeing in my eyes was my need for someone else, that maybe what she felt in her heart was someone else's love story?

It didn't really matter that our recollections were so at odds, not when she told me she had missed her period and was pregnant. I couldn't insult her with the question of paternity when I saw how her eyes locked onto mine, sealing our fate. The news hit me swift and hard.

I do remember her saying to me she wished we could stay like that forever. I was twenty-one. Forever meant, like, five minutes.

There was no use trying to make sense of Lauren's absence—no understanding why she hadn't written or called. I forbade myself the pain that thinking about her would induce. Instead, my guilt convinced me that it was my fault she was gone and my fault she stayed away. Maybe the town chatter reached the peaks abroad, and Lauren knew what I had done and what was to come. My contrition kept me from reaching out to her. My losses prevented me from reason. I knew there was no way I could fix things.

Slowly—and I mean slowly—I did come to love Abby. The pregnancy looked good on her, and we drifted into a pattern of spending time together that turned into dating. She was glowing in that way people say someone filled with budding life should. She was all belly and boobs, and something about her smile had changed. Her pregnancy was the healthiest time of her life. The doctors and her family had their theories about it, though I was spending enough time with Abby and her belly to know that this baby filled her with expectation. However it came to be, this child gave Abby something to latch on to. Life was no longer about her and her moods. Or maybe it was because she was properly nourished, eating all the right foods, not worrying about staying skinnier than the other girls. Or maybe it was because she had complete control over me.

I was fully devoted to the baby, which made me entirely devoted to Abby. She moved through each trimester seamlessly and with glimmers of complete calm. Lauren had always loved Abby, and I found myself loving the aspects of her that Lauren used to praise. She could be flirtatious: "I'd tell you to kiss my ass, but you might like it too much." Or sarcastic: "That's funny, but I don't like you so I'm not going to laugh." She had great taste and style. When she mellowed out on the makeup, she was less dramatic looking and cuddlier. She was affectionate. She spoiled me with gifts and playful notes and cards. And I loved the way she made the holes in my heart feel full again.

We never discussed marriage. Like two young kids starting our futures, hers in motherhood and mine in coaching, we coasted through the days, waiting for things to happen around us. When Juliana arrived, that changed.

"I think we should talk about moving in together," I said.

"I thought you'd never ask," she replied.

And though I was starting to feel again, and even love again, I think I was mixed up about whom I had fallen in love with. Juliana was intoxicating. I couldn't get enough of her. Going home to my parents' house with its painful memories depressed me, and soon Abby, Juliana, and I were closing on Reacroft Drive in South Charlotte. It was a sturdy brick ranch house with three bedrooms and a sprawling deck for my grill. The street was lined with birch trees and young families. I loved waking up in the morning and seeing Juliana's face, training with my other kids during the day, and coming home to Juliana at night.

At first, it worked. Abby's postpartum depression was mild. Statistically she should have been a magnet for the affliction, with all her crossed wires. "Maybe I'm cured," she said to me one night after we put Juliana to bed. "Maybe having a baby was all my body needed to heal itself. Maybe loving her is enough. Loving you."

Indeed, two people who shared a home and a child together have to discuss the subject of love. Things like waking up in bed together and bathing your baby together elicit strong emotions that should translate into sentences like "I love you." Not so with us.

It took me a while to say those words again.

It was the first game of the season, and she was swaddled in a thick scarf when I found her in what would become her spot in the bleachers. She was staring back at me with a smile. Juliana was in her arms, about six months old. From that distance, my wife was striking. The dark hair and eyes, the beautiful baby in her arms. Momentum scattered across the sky. My players were pumped. I was pumped. Friday-night fever poured off the sidelines and filled up the field. My heart beat to the sounds of the drums in the marching band. My whole body was awake and alive and ready. Everything I needed was right there under the silvery lights. I smiled back at her and mouthed the words, "I love you." And she mouthed back, "I love you too."

CHAPTER FIFTEEN

JULIANA

When I open the door to Mama's room, the first thing I see is my father lying in bed very close to my mother. I should probably close the door, as I was trained as a young girl to do. Yet when I step in for a closer look, the two of them look serenely at peace and connected. Mama's cheeks are brushed with color, and she appears to be dreaming of something that has her looking peaceful and happy. Daddy looks like a young boy, as though wherever his mind has gone has erased recent events. I take a picture of them with my phone.

The click of the flash startles my mom awake, and the calm turns into fear, as if I caught her doing something wrong. Dad comes alive next and makes room for me to sit beside the two of them.

Mama reaches for my hair and attempts to untangle the golden brown knots that fall down my shoulders. I know by the way my mama is lovingly touching me that my daddy has told her everything except the part about the bruise. Still, E.J. was arrested and neither of them can be happy.

The shrill of the phone interrupts the silence, and before I can get another lecture on the perils of dating someone with dangerous ties, Daddy is talking into his iPhone, careful to hold it a few inches away from his head, which is funny to me since everyone knows football causes more brain injuries than the phone. He steps out of the room, and we both know the call is about E.J.

I didn't want to come to Cold Creek and meet with Jeannie, and I certainly didn't want to be left alone with my mother. Neither of us knows who should start first, so the ticks of the clock allow us to study one another. She looks better, less creepy, though her moods have always been temporary and fleeting. I finally ask her how she's doing, and she shocks me with a "better." "That's good," I say. She seems as nervous as I am, and the feelings collide in a stream of quiet we can't come out of.

"Do you really think he had nothing to do with it?" she asks me cautiously.

My body tenses. There's a part of me that wants to share E.J. with her. It would feel like I was having the conversation with Sophie and Nicole's mom, or Marlee's, and the words would slip from my tongue with a friendly ease. Talking would help us find a way back to each other, but I don't trust what we've never had. I am exhausted and guarded.

"You don't know him like I do."

"You can tell me," she says. "We don't always have to be pitted against each other. I love you, Jules. I want to know you and your life . . ."

I close my eyes and hear E.J. telling me I'm his *ever*, how he's going to take care of me, like Drake sang to Rihanna. Someone who says things like this to you doesn't have the ability to steal or intentionally lie or push you down stairs. He's innocent.

"He didn't do it, Mama. You'll see."

Dad returns, and the crack of the door pushes away the unrest. His concerned voice says, "That was Ruby. They're coming after E.J. aggressively. Seems he's the scapegoat for the rest of the family."

My earlier assurances weaken. "I don't understand."

My mama tries to comfort me, though I have moved away from her. Her hands can't quite reach me.

"The charges are serious. E.J. told them where to find the jewelry. And now the state doesn't want to release him into Ruby's custody. She provides him with more stability than Ellis, but with two jobs there's little supervision."

"Is he in jail? Like in an actual cell?" I ask, clearly not understanding the criminal justice system. "E.J. hates closed spaces, Daddy. He's gotta be out of his mind."

"Then your boyfriend should start talking."

Daddy mentions bail being set and I become frantic. "Daddy! They have no money! You can't leave him there!"

"He's okay, Jules. I saw him. He's hangin' in there."

I am jamming myself in his face, thinking the tears in my eyes and the insistence in my voice will jerk him into action. "You said he wouldn't have to spend the night there!"

My dad is being evasive and quiet. The next thing he says must cause him a great deal of apprehension. "If he makes bail, there's the issue of where he'll stay. I'm petitioning the court to release him to my custody."

"What does that mean?" I ask, my voice trembling, and Mama says, "Ryan, do you really think that's necessary? Now?"

"The evidence is strong. Real strong. At least he can be with us at the house with proper supervision. It's the only answer."

"E.J.'s going to live with us?!" I blurt out. I don't know what more to add. I'm shocked, and grateful. Daddy looks my way and says, "Juliana, I'm not happy about this decision, but E.J. is running out of options."

I am shivering all over. Once I had admired E.J.'s loyalty and ability to detach from his family without cutting them off completely, but now I am incensed at the faithfulness that is going to ruin him. My daddy wraps his arms around me, and my mama tries to do the same. I am terrified. The bruise on my side no longer aches, but it may as well. I have to talk to him. We have to fix this.

The first night E.J. sleeps in our house, it takes me less than five minutes to get up the nerve to sneak into his room. My daddy is snoring madly. I can hear it through the floorboards, and I am desperate to talk some sense into E.J. He's not asleep when I tiptoe through the doorway. "Jules?" he whispers into the darkness. "Oh, man, Coach is gonna fillet me."

He is in our guest room, though we never have any guests. The room is dressed in gray and black with hints of yellow. The touch of color gives me a sense of hope, as if there is light at the end of this long, dark tunnel. He is holding the covers up for me to slide next to him. I can't make out his face or his hands, though his body against mine feels a lot like home.

E.J. starts talking at once. It's as though he has saved his words for me. When people say he is quiet and shy, I smile, knowing that I spark the valve in him that makes him want to share. But tonight he needs to stop yapping and listen to what I'm saying.

"You're making a mistake, E.J. If you'd just tell the truth, we can help. Daddy will help you."

He stiffens and says he can't.

"This whole thing is ass backward. You shouldn't be taking the blame. It's just plain stupid. Why are you doing this?"

He is tickling my shoulder, trying to distract me. Even in our disagreement, we fit together just right. "You do things for people you love, Jules. No matter how pitiful they are."

The words swing at me like a pendulum, back and forth, and I'm not fast enough to catch them. Or my resistance won't let me.

"I don't know if I can ever be that forgiving," I say, and he mistakes that to mean how he hurt me.

"I'm sorry about the stairs," he whispers into my hair.

"I know you didn't mean it," I say. And after he's had a chance to think about it, I ask, "How come you didn't call me?"

His arms come tighter around my waist when he says he was ashamed about what he'd done. "I thought I'd hurt you. I never want to hurt you, Jules. I was scared you'd hate me. I didn't want you involved. The less you know about this stuff the better."

"The only thing that hurt was not hearing from you. It was an accident. You know that, don't you? I missed you so much."

"I missed you, too, but I thought if I got out of here you'd be safe."

"You're always trying to protect me, but the person who needs protecting is you. Why would you run from the cops like that? Buford could have shot you. Then what would I do?"

"I was in a safe place. You don't need to think about it."

I tell him he's crazy, fitting my head against his chest and running my fingers along his warm skin. "I can't stop thinking about you."

He lets this idea sit between us and then I pry. "What was it like in there?"

"Terrible." He nuzzles me closer so as to show me how much.

"At least you turned yourself in. That's gotta mean something. Please think about telling the truth. The only person you're hurting is yourself." I stop myself because I sound a lot like Mama's therapist. E.J. asks about our session and it rolls over in my brain.

Sharing with her and hearing about Mama's progress made me aware of newer, more uncomfortable feelings. I didn't even know that was possible. Mama hasn't always been the easiest person to live with, but she is my mother. By fault of birth, I am required to hate her and treat her cruelly, while excuses like moodiness and being a brooding teenager prevent me from permanent punishment. But now I miss her. Seeing her at Cold Creek gave me a deeper appreciation of the hell she's lived in. I say it out loud, rolling it off my tongue. I miss that crazy woman who makes me love her with her many-sidedness.

"It's like whiplash, E.J. Every time I think we have a chance to be close, something happens and it stretches us further apart." Once I slip through this door, I'm off. "I miss her. I hate her. I love her. I want what I didn't get for all those years. It's so unfair."

E.J. doesn't have to say anything. His hands and his fingers give me all the comfort I need.

"She's my mother! How can she be so selfish?"

"I don't think she does it on purpose, Jules. I don't think she can help herself."

I abruptly sit up and stare down at him on the pillows. "That should make it all right? My mama's limited, so I should fend for myself? You know how long I've bought into that crap? And now this Jeannie lady tells me I need to accept Mama's limitations, too? What if I don't want to accept them? What if I want my mama back? The one who was pregnant with me and loved me so much she wasn't sick! Maybe it's me. Maybe I made her sicker."

"That's impossible," he says, trying to calm me down, reaching for my arms to bring me back down in his. "Your mama loves you and that's why she checked herself into Cold Creek. My daddy has no chance. But your mama does. She's not a bad lady, Jules. She just needs help. You got Coach, and I got Ruby. I'd say we're pretty darn lucky."

"Why is it that what we don't have can overshadow what we do?"

He gathers me in his arms and soon he is curled around me. Talking to Jeannie lessened some of my anger toward Mama, but the coils were still warm, and they brought forth a real sadness, which E.J.'s body wrapped around me could temporarily block. I think about all the people in the world who could have found each other, and I know it is no coincidence I found E.J., and that he found me. I see how Daddy has changed both of us.

Before my daddy came into his life, E.J. had a difficult time with trust. Soon he was worshipping him just like I had always done. E.J. was always telling stories about Coach and the team, things I'd always known about my father but that seemed brand new when I heard them come out of someone else's mouth. My daddy gave the players chances. He treated them with a respect that helped them respect themselves. It was Daddy who went to the office to speak with the principal when one of his boys got in trouble. It was Daddy who visited the family when there was a problem with a teacher or an unsatisfactory grade. He wasn't just a coach on the field. He was a life coach, guiding and steering and laying down rules.

Knowing this should have stopped me from letting E.J. spoon me in the dark. We were inching closer and closer to breaking one of Daddy's biggest rules: no sex.

E.J. and I have talked a lot about sex. It's hard not to, considering how excited we make each other when we're together. It's maddening to be handed these overpowering feelings without a way to release them. Sure, we listen to our parents' advice about abstaining or using condoms, but when you're trapped in a heated moment, it's hard to get out without being scorched. E.J. hasn't pushed me at all. We sometimes talk about sex as though we're swimming toward an island. Neither of us knows how far out we are, but we see it in the distance.

Until tonight. When it's right in front of me.

I'm ready.

When I touch E.J., I can tell he's ready too.

He is kissing my neck and running his fingers through my hair. I arch my back into him and let him kiss me, while I close my eyes and imagine where those kisses will take us. His hands are inside my pajama bottoms, and his breath is coming out in deep, long gasps.

I wouldn't be his first, but I would be *the* first. The first one he loved. I'm surprised he has withstood the wait. The knuckleheads on the team are always teasing him, and he doesn't care. His self-control always impresses me. Especially now.

Maybe because we aren't looking at each other, it makes it easier for me to tell him I want to do it. "Please," I say.

His body stiffens. Warm breath slithers down my neck. I think our hearts are pounding in the same measure.

"We can't," he says.

"Why not?"

"You're crazy, Jules. No. We're not having sex in your house with your dad down the hall."

I turn to face him. *E.J.* He is fire and light. My ever.

He kisses my cheeks, and I close my eyes while he dots my face with his lips. He always says my timing is terrible. I figure I am a girl and can get him to do what I want, so I touch him again.

He takes my hand and moves it away. "That's not going to work."

"You love *him* more than you love me."

"Not possible," he says, holding my hands in his so they can't move, while he traces the line of my collarbone with his mouth.

I think I may scream. I'm on the cusp of womanhood. I'm ready, willing, and able, and the boy who's supposed to make it all come true rejects me. The wave passes through me and numbs my body. It collides with the earlier upset, and I am at first kissing E.J., and then I am pulling away, fighting back frustration. He feels me go tense and hugs me close. I fight harder. He pulls me tighter. "Why's everything so messed up?" I ask. I don't want to fight E.J. I want to be swallowed up in his arms. I want to peel back his chest and take his heart in my hands because mine feels frail and tired.

"I'm broken just like you," he says. "It's going to work out."

"You don't know that!"

"I know that you're not going to fill those holes you have inside by having sex with me."

And just like that, he sums up everything in a sentence. I bury my face in his arms, and they hold me close enough to ease away some of the emptiness.

He whispers into my hair, "I want to have sex with you. More than I can tell you. Damn, Jules, I think about it all the time. All the time.

The only thing better than crossing that goal line is thinking what it'll be like. But we can't. Not tonight. Not like this. Not the first time."

His refusal stings, and after a while it changes into something else.

"I love you," I whisper into his ear.

"I love you more," he says. "Forever and ever."

CHAPTER SIXTEEN

LAUREN

Quinci has returned to the city with my partial manuscript in her hands. So far she's enjoying the read, even though she doesn't understand my fascination with what she calls the "wild." Coming from her mouth, it sounds like a dirty word. Quinci is Park Avenue and cappuccinos.

I have sunk into the crisp golden hues of fall with a fervor that quenched my earlier misgivings. It is as though I have never left, and a tiny part of me is sorry I did. I missed the views. I missed the smell of pine. I missed the cool air.

I'm finishing a morning stroll, a steep, uphill climb from the rec center below. The walk energizes my legs, and I feel the strain in my butt. The weather is a chilly forty degrees, and the trees that line the road and its switchbacks are in full October splendor. I haven't forgotten how the breeze invigorates, how the quiet fills me with deep thought and centeredness. A few miles away, the crowds have descended on downtown Banner Elk for leaf changing and the Woolly Worm festival that marks the peak season. After a quick shower, I will drive down the mountain to join the throngs of people craft shopping and racing worms.

Every third week in October, thousands of visitors flock to the town's center, where they purchase a "fuzzy worm" for a dollar, give it a name, and race it against other worms, up a three-foot length of string. The winner and its unique markings are interpreted to predict the fate of winter.

As I climb into my truck and move down the mountain, the temperature rises about ten degrees, though the fickle sun and its intermittent glimpses behind the clouds make it seem colder. The streets are crowded with visitors from all over, and I find a parking space next to the Banner Elk Cafe. Crossing the street, I quickly join the masses en route to the park entrance. I am strolling along the line of booths stuffed with art, crafts, and specialty items. The dog park is corralled and filled with yappy pooches. The smells of festival food fill the air— elephant ears, roasted corn, barbecued ribs—and I stop to chat with a local artist whose work I'd always admired. I notice at once that both she and her talent have matured. She paints oils of scenic vistas of the region, and captures detail in her emotional colors, blended and brushed onto the page.

A painting in the corner behind her tabletop catches my eye. It's a fairly large canvas, and I can make out the delicate strokes of the murky lake and the trees in the background that form a canopy over the hidden path. I am pulled into the frame against my will. Free floating, I feel his lips on my forehead, the trail of drops against my skin. It is a good-bye and a future shooting off the canvas and knocking into me until I have to reach for the table to stabilize me.

In the foreground there is a couple seated on a bench. Their backs are to the artist and to me. His arm is around her. She is leaning into him protectively. There is no way to decipher their ages, only the sadness that swarms around them, reflected in the somber-toned clouds. Indeed, on first sight, the picture appears gloomy and dark, though on closer inspection the lake is shimmering with light, and I know the fate of two. A bright orange sweater covers the girl's shoulders. The man is kissing her hair.

The artist studies my face before she speaks. "You're Claire and Arthur's daughter?"

I nod. "Yes, I'm Lauren."

She stretches out her hand to meet mine. "Meline Stapleton."

"I know who you are," I say, pulling myself together. "I've always admired your work."

"How are your parents? I haven't seen them here in a while. Almost as long as you've been gone."

My eyes are fixed on the picture, though I make pleasantries with this kind woman. "When they're here, they prefer to stay at the house. They're not much into crowds."

"Where's that young boy of yours? He could never get enough of you. The ladies and I used to admire the two of you every year."

"That's some memory," I whisper with a half smile. All the years we were together. Three festivals. His worm lost to mine each time. Lance Wormstrong and J. K. Crawling. We were quite a team.

"Such a handsome couple."

"Tell me about that piece over there," I say, pointing to the masterpiece on the floor.

Her tired, round body moves toward the corner and lifts the canvas for me to see. It is almost bigger than she is. "*Lake Coffey*. She's not for sale."

I gaze at the painting with a mixture of pain and regret. The couple is contained in the frame, but I feel them reaching off the canvas, reaching for me. "It's beautiful," I say.

"I think so. My husband had gone to the lake to do some fishin', and he kept me waitin'—a good forty-five minutes—when I was ready to pick him up. I had just driven to Walmart for supplies, so I started to sketch as I was waitin'."

I'm staring too long, and my eyes feel full. The sadness coats my words when I ask, "You never knew the couple on the bench?"

"Don't very much like to paint people I know. My fingers find a way of marking their ugly parts. She had that bright orange sweater on, and the sky just right there opened up and cried on them. Poured. Darn good thing, 'cause it finally got Al to get his butt in the truck. I got a photographic memory. Those two didn't move a muscle. He just kept right on saving her from everything. Even that sky."

"It's really something," I say, because I don't want to hurt her feelings. I have no other words for the pain the picture induces. "Would you consider selling it?"

She hesitates. "*Lake Coffey*'s always been mine."

"I'd like to have it."

"Nobody's ever wanted her. She's either too big or too expensive. Some folks say she makes them sad."

At once, I am desperate. I don't want to let the painting go: "Name your price."

"Well, now, she's one of my older paintings. Before I became attached to her, she was priced at $750."

"I'll pay double."

Meline turns deep red right before my eyes. She rests her index finger on her wrinkled cheek and says, "Al won't be too pleased if I say no to that. It'll be tough to lose her."

"I understand. I'll take good care of her."

"Darn tootin', you got yourself a painting."

I reach for my checkbook, though not before noticing the wet filling her eyes. Her hair is gray, falling down her shoulders. The sadness makes her seem smaller and older than she is.

"Can I leave her here while I do some shopping?"

"Take your time. I want to spend as much time with her as I can."

I thank her, watching how she gently places the painting beside her. She handles the things she loves with delicate care. I would have done the same. It makes me think about what I've given up, and the sadness that picture evokes in me.

Meandering over to the stage where the worm races are held, I am reminded of our gang of friends piling into the car to enjoy the absurdity of it. There was no training your worm. There were no frontrunners. Yet the thrill of cheering on a caterpillar as it climbed up a string had been ridiculously fun. Besides, the $1,000 prize for the winning caterpillar was a bonus.

The stage is packed, and the surrounding audience is jammed against one another. It is a tidal wave of colorful jackets and furry hats. I love the anonymity of it all. To be among thousands of people who don't know my name. Though the novels I'd shared with the world were personal, my pen name gave me a veil to hide behind, a shield to protect myself from scrutiny. I reveled in the secluded life I had created for myself in London, complete with a phony author bio that included five cats: Sam, Driver, Simon, Ally, and Bailey. The author photo, we randomly pulled off the web.

Virginia Sutherland, the English recluse, did not have a website or a Facebook or Twitter account. Her fans accepted her agoraphobia by creating their own fan page, which had more than half a million followers. I knew this because Quinci was a social media wizard who tracked stats with words like *tweets*, *likes*, and *shares*. This would change with the new book. I had decided when I stepped through the doors of our house and confirmed it when I saw Ryan's face staring down at me from the TV: I can no longer hide behind the moniker of Ms. Virginia Sutherland. Lauren Sheppard will be in ink across the new cover.

I want my life back.

A little boy with a worm named Vincent van Go is jumping up and down on the stage. His woolly friend has just taken a slither closer to becoming a finalist in the race. If only life followed the predictions we make. How much is predicated on fate? How much is opportunistic planning? I cheer for the little boy in the bright yellow parka and resume my walk around the festival. The wind picks up, and I hug my jacket tighter around me, stuffing my hands into the lined pockets. I am at ease perusing the booths, and soon I have bags of knickknacks I will probably never touch.

The skies are changing rapidly. The sun has given up in its fight with the clouds and abandons the sky. This is how the weather works in mountain country. The brash forces of nature blow through the valleys and temperatures drop, skies quickly darken, and erratic conditions descend across the land. The festival guests are collectively layering their bodies with extra warmth. I didn't think to bring gloves, as the day started out so gloriously, but I am freezing now, the chill biting at my bones. Shuffling through the swarm of people, I reach Meline's booth, and there is a small crowd gathered around her space. I wait patiently until she finds me standing there.

"Lauren!"

I wave, telling her to finish with the last of the customers, but she ignores me and heads my way.

"There's a young lady over there admiring *Lake Coffey!* I told her it was sold, but she's pushy."

My eyes land on the four teenagers surrounding the painting. One of them is rolling her eyes, as though art is the most boring thing on the planet. The others are prodding the girl in the middle—the skinny one with the highlighted hair—to hurry up. They're impatient and clearly uninterested.

"My daddy talks about this lake and these mountains all the time."

Meline whispers to me, "It's sweet. Kids today hardly think about their parents." Then she says to the girls with the never-ending hair and legs, "Here's the lucky lady who's taking *Lake Coffey* home." They all turn in unison, and I wave as the older woman positions herself behind her table to talk to other customers.

The leader, the one they call Marlee, is texting away on her phone and doesn't look up. The other two, who look like twins, are slowly slinking away from the booth, and from me. And the one whose father loves the lake, the one with the transparent green eyes, is studying me.

No matter where you are on Beech or Banner Elk, folks ask where you live: "Do you have a house on the mountain? Are you visiting? It follows "hello" and "nice to meet you" because it sheds light on who you are.

I didn't expect the question, though, from the fresh-faced teenager. She smiles and says, "Do you live here?"

I smile back. "That's a good question."

"Not really," she says. "It's either yes or no." One of the twins elbows her in the arm.

"We have a vacation home on Beech."

"My dad loves that little lake and being on Beech; my mama, not so much . . ."

"Your dad has good taste."

Marlee stands between us with her hands on her hips and her long blond hair peeking out from beneath a fur-lined hat. She is chic and fabulous and very pretty. "Her daddy's *hot*," she says, swaying her body dramatically.

"Marlee, that's so gross," says one of the twins, while the other chants, "Eww."

The green-eyed girl begins talking again. "I wish he'd pick up the phone. I think he'd like it for Christmas. Do you take installments?" she adds.

"He's visiting the wacky ward. They don't allow cell phones," says Marlee, who doesn't take her eyes off her phone. "C'mon," she adds, "what's the fascination with art? You didn't even want to come today.

Do I have to remind you of how we had to drag you away from your boyfriend this morning?"

One of the twins berates her with a stabbing look.

All three look at their phones and try their best to move away from Meline and her work, and I am transfixed by the young girl who wants my painting. She creates distance with her eyes, but there's a kindness in her face when she smiles.

She asks, "Please wait until I reach him. This place has so much meaning for him. Let me just see if he's even interested. I can take a picture and send it to him."

I clear my throat. "I'm sorry. I've already purchased the painting."

She looks away while one of the twins moves toward her and shields her from my stare.

"Is she okay?" I ask, recognizing something in her plea, though not wanting to pry.

"PMS," a twin says, but I know there is much more behind this girl's disappointment.

Marlee flits back into the conversation. "Her daddy's famous around these parts. Best football coach in the state. Her mama, on the other hand, let's just say she's got some loose screws."

"Marlee!" they all shout in unison.

The girl pretends not to hear, but the comment colors her cheeks. She says to me, "Don't listen to her. She's partially crazy herself. My dad is kind and sentimental. He used to take me here when I was kid and we'd hike and fish. He changes when we reach this altitude."

The shape of her eyes and the curve of her nose say one thing, while the man they describe sneaks into memory. A subtle ache extends throughout my body. The pull toward this young girl feels inescapable. My heart beats a little stronger, and I have to stop my hands from reaching out. "Do you have a home up here?"

"Nope. Daddy wishes we did. Sometimes we rent in Fox Pointe or Klonteska."

I know I have never met this girl before, but something in her reaches deep inside of me. The similarities are too striking not to say anything. I see her dad hiking, I can picture the boy she's talking about, the one who came alive when we reached the mountaintop. The words force their way out of my throat. There is fear and curiosity laced in their tumble: "Is Ryan Holden your father?"

She brightens. "Do you know him? Oh, my God, this is totally random!"

The air I've been holding in my belly releases into the sky. Along with it are the shattered dreams and promises we made to each other long ago, on a bench by a beautiful lake. Everything I thought I saw moments ago is screaming at me. The way she stands, the thickness of her hair. She has his eyes and her nose. His warmth and her grit. She's a unique combination of the two of them. I'd say she got the very best parts. She is an astonishingly pretty girl. Her beauty makes me want to run away and never come back.

I say with a forced smile, "I haven't seen your dad in years. We went to college together at Davidson."

"Then you must know my mama . . . Abby . . ."

I pause. "Yes, I knew her very well. We were roommates for a while. Best friends. We lost touch after college."

The other girls walk off, bored by our revelation. "I'll meet up with you guys in a sec," she tells them.

"I'm Lauren," I say, reaching my hand out to hers, tentatively, because I know that I'm about to touch the two of them. The friend who betrayed me, the lover who did worse. It's painful to look at her.

Her fingers wrap around mine, and I fight the surge that Ryan and Abby's daughter is sending up my arm. I should loathe her and walk away, though her innocence shields her from any blame. I'm also curious.

"I'm Juliana. Juliana Holden. But you know that already."

I try to breathe, and the cold air mixes with nervous energy. The girl has me shivering, and it has nothing to do with the frigid temperatures.

"Daddy's coaching at Pine Ridge. They're state champs, and if you know anything at all about my daddy, you know he's just obsessed with football." She beams proudly when she speaks of him. "He's good," she says, nodding.

"And Mama's okay too . . ." She seems less sure of this and turns away from me, fixes on her Uggs. "She's not feeling so good these days."

Remembering the roommate I once cherished, the nights we talked ourselves to sleep, I thought Abby's fragility might have gone away when she got what she wanted.

"She's not sick, like cancer sick. She's been having a hard time with stuff lately . . ."

I nod because I feel almost nothing when she says this. I don't mean to be cruel, but the wound feels raw again. Juliana's face has sparked a notch in me that I had blocked out. Her face brings it all back. Feelings are knocking me around, and I'm unable to protect myself.

"Anyway, I'll tell my daddy I saw you and you asked about him." And then she is gone. And I feel my heart unravel inside my chest.

I am sure she will forget my name, that we met, and all will go along as it has since that painful day many, many years ago.

Meline says to me, "You look as though you've seen a ghost!"

How can I tell her that I have? That I saw the apparition of what might have been.

My hands are shaking as I drive the old Suburban up the windy mountain roads. *Lake Coffey* moves in harmony with each turn; the brown paper Meline used as wrapping crinkles in the air. The skies are dark, and the leaves are falling briskly from the trees. Soon they will mix with rain, a fusion of color and cold.

I can't get Ryan's daughter out of my head.

I can't get Ryan out of my head.

"My mama's not well."

The young girl's words are whipping around in my head.

Abby had had an episode one afternoon when we were driving this same route. I had to pull into Fred's parking lot and get in the backseat with her to cradle her in my arms. She was hyperventilating and crying. Abby never sat in the front seat. She didn't say why, and we accepted it as one of her quirks. I learned rather quickly that what threatened Abby was in her head, much worse than any logical, external dangers. It came on without warning and immobilized her. I could usually talk her through her bouts of hysteria, though this one was worse than the others.

She had clutched my shoulders. You would think she was possessed, as though someone were coming after her and she was racing away. I told her to breathe, and I rubbed her back and assured her she would be fine. I had no clue what I was up against. I was a baby myself at the time.

When she calmed down, she said to me, "Lauren, I don't know what I'd do without you. You're the only one who understands."

Clearly she had no idea that I didn't understand at all, that I was doing what any friend would do. Then I pried: "What's going on with you?"

Abby's disoriented eyes pooled with water. Behind the brown, I saw a melancholy gloom. She shook her head and cleared the tears that painted her cheeks. "It's okay. I'm okay. These moods . . . they come and go. It's passed," she said, pulling herself together, tucking away the angst, back inside her secret places. I knew it would only be a matter of time before Abby cracked and crumbled.

I just never thought she would take Ryan and me down with her.

CHAPTER SEVENTEEN

RYAN

We are quiet at dinner. Me, E.J., and Juliana. I'm worried about her mama and her boyfriend, and I expect her to show some concern too, but she plays with her food instead, shuffling it around the plate with a fork, as if I won't notice.

The one good thing about having E.J. living in the house is that he is a necessary buffer between me and Juliana. Though her mother has been absent for a long time in ways that made Juliana independent, her complete withdrawal from our lives has proved more difficult than either of us had expected. Like waves, we crash into each other. Right now Juliana needs someone to blame, and that someone is me. I can live with that.

"How was Woolly Worm?" I ask.

She doesn't look up.

E.J. interjects. "Jules, your daddy's talking to you."

She rolls her eyes and says it was fine. Then she tells me how she ran into a friend of mine from Davidson. "Lauren . . ." she mumbles.

The name crashes in to me, and not even E.J. can cushion the shock.

"Do they really race worms?" he asks, oblivious to the fact that I have put down my fork and reached for a beer to help digest the words my daughter just threw at me. "That's one of the dumbest things I've ever heard."

Juliana rolls her eyes again. She's in a mood. So am I, but I can't show it. "Don't get me started on dumb things," she says. When she sees how she has slapped him with her sauciness, she shifts in her seat. Strands of her hair fall against her porcelain skin, and I watch as their eyes meet. "It's not all about the worms. There's people watching and awesome food and some cool stuff to buy. The weather's almost always perfect this time of year." I see how this boy softens my daughter.

"That woman bought a painting of Lake Coffey. I tried calling you. I wanted to send you a picture of it to see if you might want it, but she bought it first. She said she knew you and Mama."

"She was Mama's roommate." I use short, hollow words to describe someone who once breathed life into me.

"I've never heard her name before."

I start to say something, pausing because I know I will have to say her name. I begin again, but I can't get the word out. Two sets of eyes are asking me for answers. My unbreakable dam may fail to keep my feelings inside.

"Daddy?" she asks.

"She left the country after college. She followed waterfalls around the world for some elite photography program. No one ever heard from her again."

"How cool is that?" they say, impressed by her willingness to leave us, to leave me.

"I wonder why Mama never mentioned her," Juliana asks, while I quietly pretend that I'm not dying inside.

"E.J.," I say, clearing my throat for words that won't come out. I am bristling with forbidden thoughts. I need to change the subject and move away from Lauren and all the pain associated with her. I need to fix something I before wasn't able to fix. "E.J., are you sure there's nothing more you want to tell me about the jewelry?"

They exchange guilt-ridden expressions, and I wonder how long I'm expected to support this boy without full disclosure. Only there is a part of me that admires his willingness to protect his family. There are no limits to how far any of us will go to safeguard those we love.

E.J. met with the court-appointed attorney and was going to plead guilty. In one swift poof of air, his dreams of college seemed to evaporate. The story spread like wildfire around town. E.J. was lumped together with his criminal brothers, and a dreadful picture emerged of a boy raised in a cradle of crime. The court of public opinion tested his character, his football ability, and his love for Juliana. Girls came out of the woodwork, claiming they had had sex with E.J. in the locker room and on the field. Coaches criticized past transgressions, a single missed catch, the few yards he came up short at the goal line. These were indicative of greater infractions that would soon be exposed for all the world to see.

Yesterday's football star is fodder, overnight, and I am furious.

I cannot let E.J. spend another day caught in this disaster. I can't let him throw his young life away. Not when there is so much potential at stake.

"E.J., let me make this easy for you. I know you didn't take the jewelry."

He drops his fork and stares hard at my daughter.

"Don't go looking at her. She's not the problem here. You are. When you love someone, you protect them. Even from themselves. You can't expect her to let this go on. Not when it'll destroy you. And her."

E.J. doesn't agree or disagree. He simply nods his head and looks down at his plate. "Yes, Coach."

Juliana squirms in her seat, and I do her a favor by asking her to go to her room and to give E.J. and me a moment alone.

E.J. is playing with his string beans. He's mixing them with mashed potatoes, and I know he doesn't see the mess he's making on the plate and in his life.

"You want to tell me what happened or should I tell you what I know?"

"No, sir."

"No to which part?"

He repeats the story I heard from Juliana, only this one is laced in regret.

"Did you think you were going to knock on the front door of the house your brother burglarized and hand back the stolen property without consequences? C'mon, E.J., you know the system doesn't work like that."

"I thought I was helping out my brother. I thought I could make it go away."

"E.J., Devon is up to his neck in trouble. Why would you sacrifice so much for him?"

"He's my brother."

I push my chair away from the table and stand up, raising a finger in E.J.'s face. "He's your brother in blood. The boys on the field, they're your brothers. They'd take a hit for you. They protect you. Devon and Ellis, they've only hurt you. They've put you in harm's way. That's not what brothers do."

E.J. listens to me spout. He winces when the tone of my voice scratches at his face. "Do you know how blessed you are? Do you know the God-given talent you've been born with? You have a ticket out of here. An honest, righteous way to make a name for yourself in the world. You continue protecting you brother, and the authorities are going to make an example outta you. You'll never play ball again. Are you ready to lose something you love, because," and then I feel it all at once, that sick, sad feeling I spent years pushing away, "I'll tell you,

you're never down until you lose something you love. You never recover from it." My eyes are holding his and I pause to let the feeling pass. "No pads. No offensive line can protect you. I can't protect you."

Emotion racks E.J.'s face. His fork is splayed across the plate, and he looks pensive and scared, unlike the E.J. I have seen flash across a field with dynamite in his legs. "Devon didn't want to take the jewelry. Daddy gave him no choice. When someone points a gun to your head, you do stupid things."

"A gun?" I am shaking my head in disbelief. "Why would he do that to his own son?" The idea sickens me, though it sheds light on the kind of life these boys have been exposed to.

"Daddy has rules. Devon has to earn his keep."

"Your father has no right to treat you kids like this." The idea of doing that to one of my boys makes me physically sick, but I need to focus on taking care of E.J. right now. "Son, you're going to come clean, and we're going to deal with this mess straight on. I'll be there every step of the way, just like on the field. I'll do whatever I can to keep you safe and protect you from the opponent. Anyone who messes with my boys messes with me."

"I'm sorry I let you down, Coach."

"That's just it, son, you've let yourself down. There's nothing any-one can do to you that hurts you more than what you do to yourself."

"It won't happen again."

"I know. Now clear that plate, and my lazy daughter's, too. Both of you in your own rooms by ten."

E.J. doesn't say much else except, "Yes, sir." He doesn't need to. I can tell in his eyes that he is thankful for my loyalty.

It is not until later that night when I am tucked in bed, the one I share with my wife, that I allow myself to think of Lauren. I am adrift under the covers and don't dare to venture on to Abby's side. Her pillows remain fluffed, the sheets pulled and flat.

I always thought I would know when Lauren returned, that I would feel her presence. Seeing the picture of us by Abby's hospital bed brought her back, but it was different from the intrinsic signal I thought would tell me she was close. We were lovers so long ago. Had time managed to break the last threads that tied us together? I had loved few women in my life. A young football star can easily collect a bevy of beauties, but losing your mama so young teaches you to protect yourself. Lauren stormed in like thunder, and my heart didn't stand a chance. From the day I met her, I knew she was different. Her blistery disposition and relentless need to be right had me tongue tied and wanting to be wrong just to watch her gloat in victory. We fell in love quickly and without pretense.

Lauren was laughter and light. She was kindness and friendship, the one you'd always want on your side. I loved the way she defended Abby, even though it took up a lot of our time. I admired the way she didn't give up on her when so many others had run. She was her best friend first before she became mine. And she was the love of my life. The one that got away.

I feel tricked. I was supposed to know when she was near.

When my boys get sloppy on the field, I remind them to stay centered. Staring up at the ceiling of our bedroom that evening, I push the thought of Lauren away. Thinking about her cannot do me any good.

Immersing myself in busyness is what I do best. Confidential meetings with attorneys who have read E.J.'s recent statement leave little time for unnecessary reasoning. I juggle the potential fallout and manage Juliana, all while supervising practices. My little pep talk has steered E.J. in the right direction, and he changes his plea from guilty to innocent, something not done very often in criminal court. The state doesn't buy E.J.'s turnaround and needs proof that he wasn't the one who stole the jewelry. Having the property in his possession is enough to find him guilty. We are treading lightly, trying not to point fingers, since the only way E.J. agreed to move forward with the plan was if Devon wasn't implicated.

We had a tough game on Friday against a formidable team, the Patriots, and my players were uncharacteristically preoccupied. Dropped passes, missed blocks, and miscommunication on the field had me concerned that the boys were being as careless as E.J. was off the field. That one of their own was facing the possibility of jail time stifled their instincts. Instead of sobering them, the entire team was asleep.

We were down three touchdowns at the half. The Patriots' defense was crawling all over our offense, and the boys were panting, their heads held down in premature defeat. We sat in the locker room, and I did what I do best. I reminded them that they had faced far worse challenges: "We are not giving up. We don't ever give up. This fight is not about skill or talent. You've got all that. This is about which team wants it more. When you want something bad enough, you go after it. You don't let anything get in the way. Now go out there and win me some football."

As we stepped back on the field, the energy had shifted. My motivational speech revived them, and my words were a boost. Immediately I was reminded of how football is not only physical. Our boys had the talent. Like any of us, they needed a mental adjustment to steer them on course.

Instantly, our boys scored on an interception of the Patriots' seasoned quarterback. Braylon Jones ran thirty-two yards down the field, and the momentum changed, like it often does in competitive games. The shift's nothing tangible—though suddenly the fans are on their feet and energized, feeding off the players on the field. One touchdown is a confidence boost, two is a shot of steroids to the system. At once, the boys were united, confident, and charging the field. The clock read five minutes left in the third quarter, and we were back in the game. Whatever misalignment we saw earlier fueled the boys forward.

On most nights, I hear the crowd without seeing them. I feel the energy ebb and flow in tune with the mishaps or triumphs on the field. Tonight is a packed house. The air is alive, and even the band sounds more cohesive than usual. The clock winds down on the third quarter, and soon we are deep in the fourth. Our team is closing the gap. We are down one touchdown with minutes left in the game, and I have my eyes on a win. Edging closer to the end zone, we are poised for an eleventh-hour victory. With three seconds left on the board, our quarterback throws a bullet to Jerry Goihman in the end zone for six. We have a tough decision: whether to go for two. A kick will tie the game; a run or pass will give us the W.

"Go for it," I tell my team, barking out the play that concludes in our extra points.

And before my players can rejoice in their effort, officials blow their whistles and huddle up. Our two-point win is suddenly under review. In question is whether our running back broke the plane.

In decisive moments such as this one, there's nothing a coach or a player can do but wait. I cross my arms and search the sky. My gaze passes over Abby's empty seat in the stands. It's a fleeting glance, something I don't even know that I'm doing until I feel the pull of something else. The force is guiding me in a direction my body could never fight.

I see her sitting at the top of the bleachers. Far right, resting her shoulders against the fence that borders the field. She is wearing green, and the color pops from beneath her flaming hair. Unlike hers, my vision is perfect. She is as clear to me as the stars.

The ref signals for the coaches to meet them in the center of the field, and I steal my eyes from her, try to wade through my emotions before approaching the other men. Her presence makes me stumble. I have waited years to feel her again.

After hearing arguments from both sides, the refs decide that my running back, Tre Foster, did indeed break the plane to win the game. My boys surround me and hoist me onto their shoulders. We are in the playoffs. We are one step closer to state. The victory is hard earned, and I am proud of them. I tip my hat to the screaming crowd and watch as the kids charge the field in ribbons of red and blue.

Before I can look up in her direction, I know that she is gone, her absence as heavy as the first time she left.

CHAPTER EIGHTEEN

LAUREN

Ryan and I always had an awareness of each other's physical presence. I hoped that by showing up at his game that he would feel me there, even if he didn't see me. I also knew by watching the blurred bodies on the field that I was due for another eye exam. The faces and features faded into one another, though I could make out the shape of Ryan's shoulders and the tumult that had become his thick, wavy hair.

The game was a good one, and I was impressed at how he coached his team out of a deep tunnel and into a fourth-quarter victory. Football had been good to him.

When I decided to attend the game, I was only a spectator with unanswered questions. The stands, packed with attendees, were the safest place to study him from without risk of getting caught. And though I didn't know what I would do if we found ourselves face-to-face, I knew what I would do if I saw Abby.

"How could you?" I would ask her.

She would turn it around and blame me: "You're the one who left. You destroyed him. I was the one who had to pick up the pieces."

Then I might laugh because she and I both know exactly what she did. And the nervous squeal would sneak out of me, embarrassed for her, embarrassed for me.

The blaming game would stop right there and nothing would change. I would back away, holding everything inside.

I made off as the boys hoisted Ryan onto their shoulders. I felt the energy between us, and it circled around me in the form of a soft breeze. The leaves from the nearby trees scattered on the ground. I had planned to make the two-hour drive back to Beech that evening, but it was too late and too dark. I wanted to pull away. From him. From that life. And all the reasons I came. Instead, I spent the night in Charlotte in a restless sleep before waking at dawn to head home.

Now I am driving out of the city, taking the deserted stretch of road through Morganton that curves around the fingers of the Blue Ridge. It is a gorgeous fall morning. Around me, the foliage is budding and alive, and I believe, foolishly, that it can make sense of the troublesome thoughts circling my head.

The sign up ahead reads "Silver Fork Winery, turn left." A new winery in town. I should have chosen the other route home, the one that wasn't checkered with memories and deceit. We'd snuck into Grandfather Winery once with our fake ID's. Ryan and I were seated by the stream in our Adirondack chairs. The water was high that time of year and the sounds were loud, but calming. It was a week before I was set to leave. The three of us had been together daily, though I needed some alone time with Ryan, and he with me.

"Am I supposed to babysit her while you're gone?" he'd asked, his anger in my leaving starting to surface.

"Don't say it like that. You know she's a good friend to us."

He poured me another glass of wine and I fell back into the chair, the warm sun making it a perfect afternoon. "You're what connects us, Laur. Without you, there is no us."

I'd laughed it off at the time. The wine. The way it made me feel silly and happy inside.

I shudder at the memory and seeing how we were all pinned against one another. How long it took me to get over the hurt, the devastation. How cruel fate could be. I stare at my bare fingers gripping the wheel.

When the Pisgah National Forest sign comes into view on my right, announcing the entrance to the Upper Creek Falls, I slow down for a glimpse, the windy drive filling me with visions of long ago.

I feel his heart beating while I lay my head across his chest, and how we tanned our bodies against the cool, gray rocks. I see Ryan carrying me across the creek, his lips cold and wet after the last slide of the afternoon. And then I see her face: Abby's.

On our last weekend together, Abby had taken a video of us tubing down. We were all smiles, laughing and letting out playful shrieks, the three of us piled on the tube together. Later, I would watch the video in slow motion, searching for the angle, the close-up. I needed to pinpoint our descent, when we became less together. Was it possible that the cold water had battered our bond?

I have tried not to hate Abby, though it's been impossible. That she captured our last moments in her video steeps me in accusation. No matter that we had a collage of moments, which painted our montage, the final evidence of Ryan and me was held in Abby's hands, and she destroyed it.

It's easy to blame her for everything, though I can't leave Ryan out of the equation. It didn't take him long to forget me. We spent so much of our relationship with Abby, and discussing Abby, that I wondered how much time they spent discussing me. What could they have possibly said?

Christa's sandwich shop comes next. We'd stop there to pick up lunch on our way to the falls. Christa was blue eyed and blonde, with a kind personality to match her face. We loved filling out our checklist lunch orders with names like LaDainian Tomlinson and Gisele Bündchen. The more original the name, the more freshly baked yeast rolls she would throw in.

Being away for so long has kept the memories at bay. Being back, they are closing in on me. *The book*, I keep telling myself, that is why I made the journey back, though all the reasons I fled in the first place are confusing me. I feel him tugging at me. I smell him all around. *Just a few more photos. Just a few more musings about a place that has captured my heart and spirit.* I keep telling myself that, but the minute I stepped off that plane, I felt my resolve weakening. He was the air, and if I breathed, he would be inside of me again.

CHAPTER NINETEEN

ABBY

Rose has become my friend and confidante. Though she is much younger than I am, we share a pain, a deficit that binds us, joined together by our third roommate, Sybil. No joke.

Sybil arrived this week with an alarming level of anxiety. Fast-talking and jittery, she's an over sharer without a filter, so whatever thought pops up in her head she spouts out. "We're all here because we're not all there," is how she greets us the first day. Shocking platinum hair outlines a face hidden under mounds of war paint. It is hard to tell if her raccoon eyes are blue or black. Her breasts are so large and perky that they peek out from the top of her blouse and call attention away from her face. Because of our weeks of wisdom, we know that as soon as Sybil strips herself of the mask and finds a better-fitting bra, she will find her real self and some acceptance.

The contrasts between my two roommates are startling. Cold Creek has brought out Rose's true beauty, the kind that emerges from self-awareness. Jeannie says that the prettiest people are those who are happy within. Their energy makes them smile deeper; their glow comes from confidence, not cosmetics. Which is ironic since Sybil has made it her job to experiment with makeup and hairstyles—on me. In between therapy, yoga, and long walks around the property, I am being painted and primped like the girls in *Toddlers & Tiaras*.

"Close your eyes," she tells me, while powdering my nose and lining my lips. "You have to shape and contour your eyes. It'll make them pop."

Whether it's the palettes of gold and purple she uses to shade my eyes, or the mental dirt and grime that Jeannie and I extracted in our sessions and continued withdrawing later in group, the reflection staring back at me does look exquisite.

Rose refuses to allow Sybil near her face with the brushes and pencils she forced on me. Instead, Rose's blonde hair is combed back neatly in a ponytail, and her cheeks, once vacant of color, are now glowing with wellness.

"You don't need makeup," I tell her, as Sybil tries out a new shade of plum on my lips. "At my age, I need all the help I can get."

Sybil chimes in. "You're not the prettiest girl in the Carolinas, Abby, but you've got a lot of strong features to work with. I'm barely using any makeup. It's a very natural look." Then she takes scissors to my long hair and cuts and shapes it better than any stylist in Charlotte.

Sybil, outside the confines of the Cold Creek grounds, is a high-powered executive who runs a multimillion-dollar cosmetic company. She won't tell us the name, even though Rose got it out of one of the staff members the very first night she arrived. Rose is easily one of the most popular twentysomethings I have ever met. She receives no fewer than ten postcards a day from friends who are traversing the world, and she has a waiting list for visitors to come and see her.

"Nothing is ever what it seems," Sybil says to me. "It's a lot easier for people to imagine that your life is perfect than to take the time to see the cracks underneath."

It is liberating to be among intelligent women with varying degrees of craziness. One of the great lessons of the weeklong therapy and group sessions is learning you are not alone. I had no idea that the general populace suffers as much as I do. The insight makes the thoughts less scary, less pervasive, and allows many of us the ability to accept ourselves in ways we never could before. One thing we all agree on is everyone has weak spots; no one is without some form of neurosis.

Take, for example, the mothers at Juliana's school who can't sleep without popping more than the recommended dose of sleeping pills. Or the ones who can't make it through the day without a bottle of Chardonnay. They're not quite alcoholics, but they're dependent nonetheless on numbing all feeling. There are others who are addicted to activities that give them momentary highs. Workouts, Botox, and shopping are great substitutes for masking and avoiding what we don't want to see or feel. All the pleasures of life we abuse to hide what's bothering us. The residents of Cold Creek are no different, and it raises our hopes that we too can have a better life. Jeannie says, "It's the strongest ones who seek out help."

"I've never felt strong."

"You showed up. And you show up each day. You're opening up and learning about yourself. You're working hard in here. Even when you've seen something about yourself you don't like, you're willing to fix it instead of blaming those around you. This new way of thinking will be very valuable to you when you leave here."

The time spent in Jeannie's office has ripened me. She illustrates the process with the metaphor of a maturing fruit. I was a peach, at once hardened in my obstinacy, my colors dull and unlively. Her poking and prodding me has softened my skin. My coat is wearing down now, allowing light to come through. When you squeeze me, I am beginning to feel soft. "You're ripe."

Why had my mind played this nasty trick on me my whole life? Filling my brain with scary thoughts and voices had depleted me. How could it hold so much power? These are questions Jeannie and I devour in our sessions. And it doesn't stop there. The psychiatrist is managing my obsessions and compulsions with the newest of drugs. The dual therapy feels like peace, and I soak my toes in its warm water.

Although it's helpful to examine my earlier self, I have learned that my psychological blueprint relies on a combination of triggers. How neat and tidy it would be to be able to sum up what caused my problem in one word or one person: *Aha! That's the reason I'm so messed up!* It's rarely that exact. One day I was blaming my domineering mother and her lack of attention. The next, I had to put myself in her shoes to look at the broader picture. The cause and effect spans through generations of genes and behaviors. Our minds are too complex for its dispatches to come down to one variable.

Blaming your defects on an abusive father or alcoholic mother can lessen the magnitude, but that shortsightedness blocks you from resolving the deeper problem tucked under layers of protective armor. One of the most significant aspects of my work with Jeannie is putting an end to my search for those answers. I am not being punished. The thoughts aren't a nasty trick. Instead, she tells me, I am being *tested.*

Of course, I have to revisit my childhood from time to time—everyone in here wants to blame their problems on their childhood. And just as quickly, we move toward the present day and the basket of emotions we need to sort out. When a scary thought nips the surface, she asks, "Do you remember the thought you had before the scary one? I know you want to focus on the unthinkable threat, but what preceded it is what we need to analyze. What were you feeling at the time?"

My eyes close while the string of words work their way out of my lips: "Lonely. Sad. Unloved."

"Tell me, Abby, have you ever heard of a term used in therapy called *mindfulness?*"

I shake my head to tell her I have not.

"Mindfulness is about living in the moment. Mindfulness backs up the overused phrase 'live your life to the fullest' with useful studies and tools to put in to practice. By committing yourself to mindfulness, you are an active participant in your life, observing your thoughts and feelings without judging them."

I long for that ability immediately.

"I want you to try mindfulness while you're here. If you find yourself having seemingly irrational thoughts, instead of labeling with negative self-talk, like 'I'm crazy! I'm a horrible person! What's wrong with me?' be aware that the thought is *just* a thought. Imagine a crowded bus. There's noise, chatter, and movement. It is best to imagine that you're a passenger on that busy bus. You're not driving. You always have voices in your head telling you things. They're just like people beside you on the bus, distractions, and you have to stay on course, continue to move forward, riding the bus, without letting the noise in the background get in your way."

I hear everything Jeannie says. Her knowledge and insights always move me in some way. I take her lessons seriously. But this is a big one. Sure, I'll just tell the thoughts that have tortured me for thirty years to quiet down so I can get to Costco without distraction. No problem.

Sybil is gushing about the masterpiece she has created.

Rose watches us, not judging. She's smiling the wry smile that I have learned to appreciate and envy.

Tonight we are having dessert outside by the campfire. I've come a long way since the sleep-away camp of my childhood, the summer getaway that plagued me with separation anxiety and crippling homesickness. I look forward to experiencing the grown-up version of something I could never enjoy as a kid.

"Is Ryan coming this weekend?" Rose asks.

Rose worships Ryan. He always had a way with kids, and, despite her age, Rose is childlike and enthralled with Ryan's energy.

When Ryan first visited, the two of us would walk along the perimeter of the property and talk about everything, except for us: Juliana, the team, E.J. The more comfortable I became at Cold Creek, the less comfortable I felt about my old life. Soon his visits were filtered through Rose and eventually Sybil, who would challenge him to a game of basketball or chess. He always let the girls win. He is that kind of guy. Sybil's assistant would arrive for a visit, joined by Rose's friends and siblings. The lively group would descend upon Cold Creek and enlist her in a game of touch football, and soon Ryan was calling out plays and commanding the field with his athletic prowess. He could quickly make chaos into calm and orderly formations. And just as the players on the field turned to him for approval and leadership, so, too, did the women at Cold Creek.

This was an area that I was working on with Jeannie.

I loved Ryan's playfulness. I loved his enthusiasm for life. But I didn't like the way I felt around him. Unknowingly, he made me feel weak and small.

"No one can make you feel anything you're not already feeling," she would tell me, and each time she said that, it was met with a dull throbbing between my temples.

Many of my dreaded symptoms had been alleviated. I had a system of checks and balances in place so that when I was feeling particularly at ease with myself, I imagined one of the horrific thoughts, to elicit a response, to test how far I had come. Lately, I was convinced I was getting well. Only there was an area surrounding Ryan that I couldn't quite come to terms with. I knew I loved him, that the fear of losing him was so great it would knot my insides, though there was something distracting me when we were together that left me with questions. Instead of joining the group on the fields, I watched from the sidelines.

"Earth to Abby. Come in, Abby." It is Rose's voice, and Sybil is laughing at her. "Not only is he too old for you, Rose, but he's married, and

I'm sure he doesn't like blondes." To which Rose responds, "No offense, Abby, I'm not into your husband, and Sybil," she says, swatting her with the hairbrush, "I thought you were working on your filter."

I have a sister, though we never laughed and accepted each other like the three of us do. Admitting faults and imperfections has a way of knocking down pretenses and defenses. So does honest, full disclosure.

"Yes, Rosie," I tease. "Your boyfriend is coming this weekend."

She smiles. "I may let him win this time. Poor guy."

Our chuckles fill the bedroom.

We return from the campfire hours later. Sybil is the first to admit she is ready for bed. "This schedule is more rigorous than my business dealings."

"Working on yourself is tough stuff," I tell her, sounding like one of those life coaches in a self-help seminar.

I spend an extra few minutes in the bathroom scouring my face with a washcloth and removing Sybil's artistry from my lips and cheeks. Studying my face in the mirror, I consider the changes I've made over the past few weeks. But something else is clawing at me, and it has distracted me much of the night.

These are the feelings I most feared when I thought of coming to this place. There were things inside of me I didn't want to know, realizations I didn't want to accept.

What if truths brim to the surface and have the power to drown all of us?

CHAPTER TWENTY

RYAN

In football, I take risks. I have been known to take a chance on fourth and inches or go for two when we need the extra points. That's because I have faith in my players, faith in my team. As a coach, you see the whole field—the weak spots, the holes, the challenges that can be converted to victories. It is up to me to make history. These young men turn to me for guidance, and it takes years of preparation and developing my skills to make the right call.

In my personal life, I am far more cautious and predictable.

When Lauren told me she was leaving, I could have fought harder for her to stay. Letting her go was what she wanted. I couldn't hold her back. When my father died and Lauren was overseas, I turned to Abby because she was willing and available. Abby had a range of personalities that drew me in. Instead of me being the leader of the team and making the tough calls, she guided me through the trauma of being orphaned at twenty-one. She tried so hard those early years. Despite her ups and downs, she was an attentive wife who listened and strived to create a peaceful home. There was a vagueness to her I would never understand, silences I couldn't break through. There was a time they intrigued me and made Abby a sensual, mysterious woman. Until I learned that the mystery was depression, and instead of tempting me, it turned me away.

Like most marriages, our disjointedness linked us together. We each had our role, and for years it worked. Raising Juliana was paramount, and when Abby disappeared into her cave, I compensated by giving Juliana more love. There was a cadence to our marriage and Abby's struggles. When she came out of one her thick fogs, she'd be better than ever—loving, wickedly funny, flirtatious. Those days I couldn't get enough of her.

I love her. I love my wife. So why am I in my car on a Saturday morning following the lengthy road to Beech?

Wayne saw me after last night's game and said I looked as though I'd seen the devil.

"I have." But I wasn't sure she saw me. Lauren was practically blind.

"Why else would she have shown up if she wasn't here to see you?" he asked.

I knew she was there to see me. "Why now?" I asked my friend.

"I'm not sure."

Then he asked, "Do you think this is the best time for this?"

I had to see her. I had to know why. It didn't matter whether Abby was beside me in our bed or sound asleep in Cold Creek—I needed to know the answer. That was my excuse, so I wouldn't feel deceitful when choosing the clothes I would wear, making the climb up the mountain, practicing what I would say when she opened the door.

My hand grips the wheel, and I am afraid and ready. Though I have studied her every nuance and know the feel of her body in the dark, I have no idea what I am up against.

The rain falls hard against the windshield and there are spots along the windy road that force me to ride the brakes. I know these roads. I know each landmark. The Farm at Banner Elk. The curve that splits highways 194 and 184. The cell phone graveyard where all calls are dropped. The computer repair shop. The old wooden sign that reads "Snow Chains." There's Cynthia Keller of Emerald Mountain Realty racing to her truck with her drenched dog on the seat beside her. Fox Pointe. Jackalope's. Fred's. I am getting closer and my heart emits a warning. There is a buildup of tension in me that makes every turn of the wheel an exercise. I can manage a team of overgrown, wily teenagers, but when it comes to Lauren, I have no big play up my sleeve.

Anger ignited me this morning when I drove off in the dense Charlotte fog. I know that if I have carried my anger at Lauren all this time it means that I have loved her just as long. I am torn. Conflicted. I hate what she did to us. To me. And with a baby on the way all those years ago, I could look only forward and not back.

The rain is coming down harder at the top of the mountain. The clouds are stormy and full, galloping across a gray sky. I stop at the scenic view just below the Alpen Inn. The bench and map of the mountain are coated in the harsh slap of rain. The view is shielded by fog, but the marker tells me that I have arrived on Beech.

It is about eight minutes to her house. We had done the drive so often, we knew exactly how long from her road to the market, to the ski lifts, to our favorite hikes. I also knew exactly how much time it took for Lauren to collapse into my arms and fall asleep at night, or how hard she needed to be held when we said good-bye, how many freckles lined the inside of her right thigh.

The thought forces me to close my eyes, and the sounds of the heavy rain drown out a forgotten stirring deep inside my gut. *What are you doing?* I have always been a man of logic and facts, stats, numbers. On the field they make sense. Up here, I am trying to calculate the time we have missed, the lost hours, the broken promises. As I continue the descent toward her house, I don't know what I'm doing. I am on automatic pilot, being pulled by a force that I've never been able to control.

I see her before she sees me. I know this because she is wearing her glasses, and they are fogged up from the condensation. She is sitting in the old wooden rocking chair on the front porch with a blanket wrapped around her shoulders. The house is large and daunting, and at once I am thrown back into another time. I pull into the gravel driveway, and she stands up. Lauren. She is a shock to my system. If it were not pouring down on us, I know she would hear my heart asking her questions, the ones I'd held in for so long, the ones that can no longer remain quiet.

I run toward the covered veranda, through the thick glaze of wet, and we stand across from one another. She is my Lauren. Only more beautiful.

"I knew you'd come," she says. They are the first words I've heard from her lips in seventeen years. I feel them circle around me. "Come inside," she says, waving me in, not touching me with her open hand. She's dressed just the way I'd imagine she'd be: faded Levi's, white T-shirt. Her rain jacket is bright green.

I realize I haven't replied to her. I have not said her name aloud, though I had imagined this moment repeatedly in my head. My sweater is soaked, and she offers to throw it in the dryer. I decline by shaking my head, because words escape me. I don't want to undress in front of Lauren, even with Under Armour protecting me. We step through the foyer, she hangs her jacket on a hook, and we sit down in the open living room.

"Can I get you something?" she asks. "Coffee? Scotch?"

I shake my head no.

"How've you been, Ryan?" she asks.

There is a singular thread of normal that makes being in her living room the most natural thing on earth. I blink. She is still here, and nothing is the same between us. I am staring at her, tracing the changes in her face, studying the sapphire eyes. All at once I hate her. I hate what we have lost. I hate all the things we missed. I hate that I hate, because I know it can mean only one thing. I have a wife. I have a life. But I am looking at Lauren, and I love her. I still love her.

"Ryan?"

She is seated on the brown leather couch. I am across the room from her, on the bench that is carved out of tree bark, in front of the fire. We had sex on this bench.

I grip my knees with my fists and look toward the floor.

She sits proud, seemingly unaffected by my presence. It is hard to determine which one of us has the right to be more pissed.

"Lauren," I finally say, finding her eyes and releasing her name into the air.

The rain tickles down the exterior of the house and thunder rattles the windows and floors. The winds have picked up again, and the howling noises crawl along the rooftop.

She has gotten up from the couch and takes a seat beside me on the floor. I can't avert my eyes from her. Her pale face is gently lined, fuller and prettier. Everything good about her at twenty-one is even better today. Her hair is long and falling around her face, past her shoulders. And it makes her sexy as all hell.

"Ryan," she says again, looking up at me. And it is then I notice a difference in her. It is her eyes. They are the same deep blue, the same depth that once pulled me in, though what's in them I'm not really sure. Her hands are clasped in her lap. She is waiting. I am waiting too.

"Why didn't you come?" I ask.

Maybe she doesn't hear me because she doesn't say anything. So I say it again: "I need to know why. What happened to us?"

The indifference in her face moments ago is replaced with something resembling shock. "You really don't know?" she asks.

And this puzzles me. "Know what?"

She seems mad. And sad. Her eyes are many shades of confusion, heavy with something she can't say out loud. She turns away and says, "Oh, my God." She repeats it over and over and I want to touch her lips to make her stop. When she finishes, she turns to me with a distant look in her eyes. "I'm not sure it matters anymore."

"Yes, it matters. I fucking loved you." This wasn't the Lauren I once knew. The Lauren I knew would understand that it mattered, the way we once mattered.

"I guess everything happened the way it was supposed to happen," she lies, locking her defeated eyes onto mine.

"I don't understand you. This isn't how we talk to each other, this philosophical bullshit," I say.

"You're with Abby, Ryan. What do you want me to say?"

The way she says it pummels me. I was trained on offense and defense. I am failing at both. A silence comes over us and she breaks it by asking me if Abby's all right. Quarterbacks have to be careful about letting their opponents read their plays through their eyes. It's a skill I have drilled into my boys. I turn my head away from her so she can't see how much she is killing me. Those eyes could talk me into anything. I stare out through the glass doors and study the rain that by then has slowed to a drizzle. It makes the things we aren't saying louder, and I sigh. "Is this how we're going to do this, talk bullshit pleasantries? She's fine, Lauren. Fucking great."

"I don't believe you. You were never much of a liar."

I bring my eyes back to hers. "I never had reason to lie to you before." She is hooking me, stringing me along.

"We were happy, weren't we?" she asks.

The question makes me want to get up and run. It hurts. I have never been able to protect myself from Lauren.

"Abby's sick," I admit. "She's been having a hard time the past few years."

"I can't imagine why. She got everything she wanted."

We absorb the harshness of her words, until she takes it back. "I'm sorry. That was uncalled for."

I want to touch her face. I want to touch the hair that falls against her cheeks. I want to smack her, scream at her.

"You left me no choice," I finally say.

"How wrong you are," she says, though it is barely a whisper. "We all have choices. At least now I know what Abby did with hers . . ." And before I can get more out of her, she stops. "I'm sorry, maybe it's not good for us to rehash the past, Ryan. That's not why I showed up last night. I don't want to play the blame game. I can't. It took me too long to move beyond it. It shouldn't matter anymore. I needed to see you. I needed to see what it felt like."

"Yeah," I whisper to her eyes, "What does it feel like?"

Her face is inches from my own and our stare is painful and deep. If I close my eyes I can inhale the old, familiar smell of lavender. She uses the same shampoo. This is what she does to me. My head falls into my hands. The blackness brings images of us across its screen. She is spreading her legs for me to come closer, she is grabbing my face in her hands while she kisses me, she is pulling at my hair. She comes to me in fits and feelings. My whole body responds to her being near.

"It hurts, doesn't it?" she finally says. "Everything we lost."

I know Lauren, and her defenses are wearing thin. Long-forgotten feelings are finding their way back, making it impossible to pretend we don't matter anymore.

"You left," I say. "I would never have stopped you, but you could've stayed."

"That's not fair," she says, shaking her head back and forth. She would push me away, but that would involve touching me. Instead, she straightens and says, "You know I loved you. That's not how we got here. And showing up last night, I had to know you were happy."

"That's it? That's all you wanted?"

She crosses her legs like Juliana and watches me, to see if she can see through me. If there is something else, she isn't budging. Then she abruptly gets to her feet, her long legs following her like flower stems. She grabs her laptop off the table and sits beside me on the bench. "My literary agent has my only copy, so I have to show it to you digitally—this is what I've been working on."

I pretend not to feel her leg against mine. The screen comes alive and before me are the reasons Lauren left: Jog Falls in India, Murchison in Uganda, Plitvice Lakes in Croatia. She is describing each one to me, and I am immediately struck by the beauty in her photos. She always had a knack for capturing the best in her camera lens. I hate myself for being jealous of the places that took her from me.

"There are excerpts about how I photographed each fall, stuff Jean-Pierre taught me, and passages about what each fall evoked in me. You have to adjust the light and camera speed when you're shooting falls so it doesn't look like a blob of white. You have to be precise. One millisecond off and the image isn't caught. Timing is everything."

I really don't give a shit about Lauren's waterfall pictures.

"These are one of my favorites," she says, pointing at a stack of falls that she explains are nestled against the Brazil-Argentina border. "Iguazu Falls. We spent two weeks there. It took us that long to get the right amount of light to shoot. They're much larger than Niagara Falls. You would like them. There's Devil's Throat." She points again, and I am half-listening, pledging to myself that I will not inch closer to her on the bench. "It's one of the widest cascades of the falls. Just breathtaking. You don't realize how big the world is. That's the lower falls," she says. We took a boat ride right through it. It was incredible. And this is a shot I took from the river, looking up."

I wonder if she can tell what she's doing to me. The world is by no means that large, not when you love somebody you can no longer have. When you love somebody like that, it's small and cramped.

"It's nice," I finally say, not bothering to ask about Jean-Pierre or any other men in her life. I hadn't expected her to be alone all these years.

"That's all you have to say?"

"What do you want me to say, Lauren? They're beautiful? Part of me hates these damn falls."

She doesn't disguise the accusation when she says, "You did this, Ryan."

She recedes from my side, getting up from the chair and pacing the floor. Her ass looks small and tight in her jeans. I pretend not to notice when she catches me staring. She's thinking about something. I can tell by the way her forehead scrunches into lines, lines deeper than they used to be. She wants to say something more, but she shrinks away from me instead.

I turn back to the computer and follow Lauren through the China-Vietnam border, all the way through New Zealand. Each fall is unique and spectacular in its own right, though I have always preferred the hidden falls we found on our many hikes through these mountains. Less traveled and close to home, they were ours alone to discover. When I reach the end of the project, Lauren has scribed her acknowledgments onto the page. They read: "All my life I have been hampered by issues of sight. Without lenses, I am legally blind with limited depth perception. For someone who enjoys excavating the beauty in ordinary things, I am thankful for the devices that allow me to witness, capture, and preserve the pure beauty of our world. Not very often do we find a beacon in another living being whose light guides you toward your dreams, when futures and landscapes are blurry and indistinct. This journey would not have been possible without the encouragement and support of one very special person. His vivid memory inspires me daily. It is because of him I am able to see things clearer today than I have ever seen them before."

I have no doubt those words are meant for me. "I'm glad I could give you clarity."

She is standing beside me, running her fingers along the mantel of the fireplace. There are photos in frames that used to hold pictures of us.

"You inspired me," she says. "Would I have preferred it to have happened in other ways? Yes, but I wasn't given a choice, either. I never forgot what we had. I never forgot what we meant to each other."

I place the computer on the table in front of me. I am stormy mad. Whatever's left of the surge outside is now inside of me and clamoring to come out. "My father died, Lauren. If anyone knew what that would do to me, it was *you*." My voice begins to crack. "You didn't call. You didn't come back. You didn't do anything!"

My questions circle around her, and I can see her struggling with the answers. Agitation spreads across her cheeks as she holds back, something she's never had to do with me before.

"Say something!" I say. "Give me a reason. Tell me you didn't get the messages . . . Anything!"

"I got the messages!" she shouts.

"Then what?" I say, "What was it? What was it that kept you away from me?"

She turns her head, but I can see she's rattled. Her cheeks turn pink and she forces her eyes closed, hiding what she doesn't want me to see. Maybe my accusations and demands are too much for her. Her silence is too much for me. It pokes the air around us, making it difficult to breathe. I can't sit here much longer. But then she faces me again and starts talking. Her voice is tangibly sad, her words full of regret. And something else.

"There were reasons—there are reasons—I can't expect you to understand. But I swear to you. I *swear* to you, Ryan, if I could have been there for you, I would have been. Nothing would've stopped me." The tears are spilling down her cheeks, and I am at once off the bench and standing in front of her. She is staring into my eyes with a fierce, forgotten longing, and though the crystal blue remains fixed on mine, drops fall from each eye. The fine lines down her face want me to touch them, but I can't.

"It doesn't make any sense," I say. "I loved you. I know you loved me."

"I did," she says. "And it's complicated."

"You loving me, or something else?"

"I loved you completely," she cries out. "I loved you with everything I had. I gave you pieces of me I will never get back. No one else has ever been able to fill those places."

"Why come back? Why now? Lauren, it's so much easier knowing you're far away. I don't know how to be here without you. I don't know how to be this close without touching you."

"It was time to finish the photographs for the book," she says, her cries becoming softer while she takes a tissue to her nose. "Believe me, I knew how hard it would be to return. And you have Abby," she says, straightening herself. "I didn't do this to us."

"You did, Lauren. You disappeared. We were supposed to have a life together. I gave you a ring." Here is where I have to stop myself because I'm saying things I can't. I'm talking to her as though I'm free to love her again. And I'm not.

She dries her eyes with the back of her hands and rubs them on her jeans. We take our seats at opposite ends of the couch. I was prepared to feel this way about her, but I hadn't expected it to happen so fast. I thought we would catch up and get to know each other again, and the old feelings would crawl back into their respective places. Instead, it has been instantaneous. So dangerous we have to rewind the conversation, make it so it never happened.

"Tell me how you've been," she says, the traces of what we'd once meant erased from her cheeks.

I let out a painful laugh. "I can't do this with you."

"It's all we have, Ryan."

"It's crazy," I say. "It doesn't feel right."

Lauren's tender gaze gives a small token of comfort. "I didn't want it to be this way. I really didn't."

I knew this better than anyone. At the end of the day, I was the one married to her best friend. Our grudges were linked together so that neither of us could forgive. When she starts asking questions about the team and football and Juliana, I think I've had about enough. The small talk eats away at me, and I want to stand up and leave. Only I want her to follow me and try to stop me, to try to fight for me, to make sense of all of this. We were supposed to survive everything. She was supposed to feel me in every breath she took. How could this have happened to us?

The crackling fire is the only sound I hear. She doesn't have answers, so she tells me again, "I'm really sorry."

I give up and tell her what she wants to know. "The team is undefeated. I'm teaching ninth-grade world history. My daughter's sixteen. She's a handful, like most teenagers. Touchy and cross one minute, a real charmer the next. She said you bought a painting of the lake."

This prompts her to head through the kitchen toward the mud room. The house is wide open with high ceilings, so I continue talking to her, even though she has turned a corner. I ask her about her parents, and she replies with one word. She emerges with a large package sealed in brown paper. I know it's the painting by the size and shape, and I move across the room to help her with it. We lean it against the large armoire and begin to rip at the paper.

Before the entire picture is uncovered, I know it's us.

She says, "We had no way of knowing. Meline, the painter, was sitting in her car behind us. That's why you can't see our faces. It should've been a happy day for us, but it turned into the saddest day of my life. I had no idea six months would turn into forever. Saying good-bye to you."

The admission pulls us apart, and she stands up. "I'm going to put up some coffee. Do you still take yours black?"

The day Lauren left the mountain, it had been raining on and off all morning. We had finished brunch with her parents when the skies cleared up and we decided to get some air. The house was stifling us with the mixture of emotions. We would regularly take walks around the circular path of the lake and on the wooden footbridge. Lauren always slid on the green moss where the trees canopied the planks underfoot and moisture collected. Sometimes we'd sit on the benches overlooking the water without anything to say. She once told me how she could say nothing at all when she was with me, and I'd always understand. Then there were those who hear you speak a thousand words and can't understand you at all. "That will never be us," she said, leaning her body in to mine.

Lauren was in the bright orange sweater. I was wearing blue, an extension of my emotions. I was a wreck that afternoon. We had only a few hours before her flight to New York and then her connecting flight overseas. The minutes ticked loudly on the clock, and the steady prompt preoccupied me. Savoring her and those last few moments was impossible. Instead, we clung to each other and let the quiet define us. When the miles separated us, we would have to draw on that silence to bind us.

At no time was I ever more certain about anything than that day at the lake. Lauren would photograph waterfalls, she would return, and we would start a life together. The permanent kind. I know those thoughts were going through her head. I could tell by the way she clung to me and how every part of her fit so neatly into me. When you're young and in love, it doesn't occur to you that things happen. People change, curves are thrown at you. You think you're invincible. We were invincible.

I loved her so much I wanted her to be happy. I loved her so much I believed we would weather any storm. And when the skies opened up again, drenching us in rain, we held on to each other, and I made a promise to Lauren that I wasn't able to keep: "I'll be waiting for you when you get back." Then I reached into my pocket. "With this," I said, holding up the silver ring with the tiny diamond. She cried out, "Oh, my God," and covered her face in her hands. Then she sank deeper and deeper into me, while I held her in my arms and we played with the ring on her finger. We were so happy that we were oblivious to the wet cold. We didn't need a ring to unite us. We were already tightly stitched.

She takes a seat next to me on the bench, and we study *Lake Coffey*. Her mug rests on the table in front of us, along with some fresh bread and jam. My eyes fix on her hand. I think of the ring that meant she was mine. Its absence goads me. To think it would be there is foolish. I turn away and it occurs to me how hungry I am. It is not the hunger that follows a lengthy practice. It is a mounting hunger that hinges upon desperation. The sensation inhabits my whole body—my fingers, my toes, my stomach, my chest. I want to feel again. I see the two of us in the strokes of the brush, and I know I want to feel *that* again.

"We were so young," she says.

My words are a whisper. "That's not what I wanted to be."

"We had our whole lives ahead of us."

I hear the crack in her voice and mine splinters too. "It never felt like enough."

"I'm really sorry about your dad," she says, her hand coming close, but not enough to touch me. "He was a good man. It's got to give you some comfort knowing he's with your mom."

"I miss him," I say. "Every single day. Driving home from practices, we'd always talk on the phone. We had some of our best conversations. The quiet on the way home kills me."

"I'm sorry. For you. And your pain."

I turn to her. Those eyes drain me of any fight. I let my fingers dig into my pants, though they want to touch something else. "It never goes away."

"Does she know you're here, that I'm back?"

The question brings Abby to the forefront, and I forget the illicit thoughts that send me somewhere forbidden. "Abby had to go away. The anxiety thing got out of control. She checked into a facility."

I let that admission grab her before saying anything more. She takes a sip of the coffee, and I feel as though I'm watching junior-year Lauren studying for an econ exam.

"I'd like to go see her," she says.

I want to touch her hair and her cheek. I want to give her all the answers. "I'm not sure that's a good idea. She's already having a hard time."

"Maybe it'll be good for her," Lauren says, pausing, searching the room, meeting my eyes again. "Abby and I have a lot to talk about."

CHAPTER TWENTY-ONE

JULIANA

Daddy says I have to go back to Cold Creek for another session with Jeannie, but I don't want to. "And you need to spend some time with your mama," he says, but I want to do that even less. We've had the discussion no fewer than ten times since Jeannie called about my next scheduled visit. Daddy kept putting her off with excuses about the drive and school, though the truth was that I refused to go. Daddy doesn't realize that I try to block out that part of my life. It's like Alice's Wonderland. I take careful steps not to fall through the rabbit hole and land on the other side. Instead, I call Mama every Sunday. It fills in the gaps, and I save my neediness and impatience for our awkward conversations.

I vacillate. One day I miss her to infinity, and the next I feel nothing at all. I told her this on our last phone call, and she told me not to be hard on myself. "I've been swinging from the same pendulum, Jules. Do yourself a favor: accept that you're unsure about your feelings."

Her wisdom should have appeased me, but it had the opposite effect. "Don't compare me to you," I hissed through the phone.

"I won't be spoken to like that. When you're ready to treat me with respect, then I'll be happy to finish this conversation." And she hung up.

I went out for a jog after that. It was freezing outside, but I had to get away from the invasion of feelings. I don't know how to respond to this woman who claims to be my mother. Her absence marked so much of my childhood that I got used to it, and missing her was impossible because it was something I never had. This strange, assertive woman wants me to be her daughter, but we are too far apart. How can I trust her when our seams have always come undone? I know she means well. I know she is working on getting better. But I am angry at the time we lost.

My mind pushes my limbs to a speed that is unnatural. The peaking sensation floods my bloodstream and I gasp for air. Mama said this is what her attacks feel like. A small part of me feels sorry for her, sorry for my anger. Which makes me feel angry all over again.

This is why I am lying in my bed under a thick blanket of blue, positive I won't be visiting Cold Creek with Daddy today. The house is quiet, and I know E.J. is breathing just a few doors away. He's been broken up about Ruby and what his arrest has done to her. She calls daily and comes by the house when she can, but it's not the same as having him in the apartment. Their separation is taking a toll on both of them. Football was always his stress-relieving outlet, and while he's banned from playing, it's left to me to distract him from a sadness he didn't want me to see. I haven't slept very well since he moved in, though my head is crowded with dreams.

It's also been left to me to take chances in the pathways connecting our rooms. E.J., with the charges piling up against him, and respecting my dad in a way only a player can, is less interested in being risky. That's why I jump when I hear a faint knock on my door, and E.J.'s head pokes through.

"Have you gone crazy, too?" I ask.

"He already left," he says, nudging me over and sliding under the covers. "Guess he knew you weren't going."

E.J. is wearing a pair of white gym shorts and a black tank top. He smells of morning and the organic soaps my mom buys from Whole Foods because she's convinced that manufacturers are trying to kill us with their ingredients.

"I feel bad," I say.

"You should go see your mama. We only get one of them."

I watch E.J. get comfortable under my sheets. And I feel his every limb against my shorts and top. I nuzzle into him and let the covers fasten us together. Soon his lips are on mine. "Morning breath," I say, getting up from the bed and filing over to the bathroom to brush my teeth.

I return to find him staring at the picture next to my bed of the three of us: Mama, Daddy, and me. It's their wedding day, but most people don't know that. She's not wearing a white dress, and he's in khakis and a pale green shirt that makes his eyes shine. He's holding me in one arm with the other wrapped around Mama. It was just the three of us, since Mama barely speaks to her side of the family, and Daddy's sisters, my aunts, moved to another state. An unconventional ceremony for an unconventional family.

"What's it like to live with parents who like each other?" he asks.

I shrug my shoulders. E.J. knows our house is certifiably nutso. He has his serious face on, and I'm more in the mood to touch him than talk. I sneak under the covers beside him, and I force him to look away from our picture and instead to look at me. His eyes are the clearest blue. I can see deep inside.

"I shouldn't be here," he says, as I run my hands up and down his back. I love his body. I love the smooth brown of it. I love the feel of it against my fingers and feet. I love the way his legs get tangled in mine and how he thinks I don't feel his hands prying my knees apart.

"Then why are you?"

He says it's because he can't be so close without touching me.

My fingers and hands are stroking E.J. until he abruptly sits up and swats me away. "I'm serious, Jules. I can't do this." The covers have shifted off my body, revealing a small, stubborn remnant of my fall. I like that it hasn't faded. He touches it with his fingers. "I did this to you."

"It was an accident."

"I didn't want my family's troubles to interfere with you."

"Then Ruby shouldn't have made you so darn cute."

"It's not funny. Ellis is mad. Real mad. Devon was supposed to bring him that bag. He expects that money. It's not just the police after me; he's going to come, too."

I am used to living in fear and things not being stable at home, but the fear E.J. lives in is of another kind. People in his world shoot and kill each other. Anger turns to violence. Sometimes I am able to forget where E.J. came from. He isn't like his brothers, and he is nothing like his father. The few times I've met Ruby, I could tell at once she is the reason E.J. is who he is, maybe why he's even alive today. And yet, I wonder, how can he risk everything to protect them?

"I'm not scared of him, E.J."

"Jules, he's dangerous. He doesn't care who he hurts."

"You'll tell him the truth. You did it to protect them."

"He doesn't think like that, babe. He's different from you and me. We're not people. We're things that can be replaced."

"What are you saying?"

"I don't know. Maybe we should stop seeing each other."

E.J. is my heartbeat. Those words bring it to a halt. "Why would you say something like that? You have to stay here. The courts said it was the only way they'd release you. How can we *not* see each other?"

"That's not what I mean."

"Then what?"

"Maybe we should take a break."

"I love you, E.J. You love me. We don't take breaks. You told me to open the door and let you in and I did. You told me I was your ever!"

He's touching the tender spot along my back. "Look how I hurt you. I should've been able to save you."

"You're hurting me now," I shout at him. "You think this doesn't hurt? You think you don't have the ability to crush me?" I get up from the bed and begin to pace the room.

"Ruby's coming today. We're going to petition the court to let me stay with her. She quit one of her jobs and she'll be home after school. Things will be tight, but she needs me."

"I need you! I thought you loved me. I thought you couldn't live without me."

"I can't," he says, hiding his face in his hands. "That's why we need to end this. I don't want you getting hurt. I don't want my problems touching you or your family."

"Please don't do this," I beg him. I am on my knees on the floor while he is under my protective covers. "You can't just come in here and lie down next to me like that, and then, two seconds later, tell me we're breaking up."

"Jules, I love you. I don't know what I'd do if something happened to you."

"I was ready to have sex with you!"

"You'll have to save it for somebody else."

"I don't want anyone else."

He is resting on his side, and his face is staring up at me. The whole scene is crooked and wrong. I should be under the covers with him, and we should be out of breath from a thousand kisses. I shouldn't be on the floor, begging this boy in *my* bed not to leave me.

"Come here," he says, pulling me up alongside him and covering me with the sheets and blanket. I collapse into his body, bare and needy. He curls around me, and I know I will never be whole again.

"Please don't do this," I say again. He is kissing my hair and my damp cheeks, and it's making it worse. "It doesn't make sense." He pulls me tighter to him as if force will make my pain go away. It won't. E.J. is decisive. He's made up his mind, and I hate the falseness of his body against mine.

Deep, heavy sobs fill the air between us. His arms contain me, and I hate him and love him all at once. The wound fills my lungs. My arms fight to break away, but he is stronger than I will ever be.

His cell phone is next to the wedding picture, and it is vibrating in tune with my sobs. The glass screen lights up, and it distracts E.J. from protecting me.

"I have to get that," he says.

I am too numb to speak. Lifeless, I let him reach across me and take the phone into his hands. He doesn't say hello to the voice on the other end of the line. He just listens. After a few seconds, he hangs up. He lies back on the pillows while I remain turned to the side, studying my closet of clothes like I've never studied it before. My back is to him so I don't see the message that comes up on the screen, but I can make out the reflection of something in the mirror. The text is a warning. The picture on his phone is of me, and the call was from Ellis Whittaker.

CHAPTER TWENTY-TWO

ABBY

Nonfamily visitors are allowed at Cold Creek, but they first have to obtain proper clearance from the patient and his or her lead counselor.

Jeannie and I are about to begin today's session when she informs me that a Ms. Lauren Sheppard has put in a request for admission. "This is Lauren, the best friend Lauren, right? Ryan's ex?"

The way she says it simplifies it rather nicely, though the way my heart pounds inside my chest means there is nothing simple about traveling down this road.

"Have you been in touch with her?" she asks. "Did you know she wanted to see you?"

"I'm the last person Lauren has wanted to hear from."

"The decision is yours, Abby. I can reject her request rather easily. You're my patient and your well-being is paramount. Say the word and I'll do it, but this is an important discussion for us to have."

I'm sitting in my favorite chair in her office. Jeannie and I have talked about this, how patients assume the same spots over time. It's so proprietary I am convinced that this is truly my chair and no other person has ever sat in it. Which is kind of what happens in the patient-therapist relationship. The sessions are so personal you can't believe they happen with anyone else.

"It would be so easy for me to have you do that. The thought of her coming here petrifies me."

"Talk to me about it."

Jeannie has mastered getting me to divulge the most painful parts of myself. Lauren breezes in between us, and I see her right before my eyes. "It's always her face," I say. "It's staring at me. Lauren's a pretty girl with these damaged but persistent eyes. I can't free myself from the glare."

Sophomore year, Lauren and I moved from Belk Hall to a two-bedroom walk-up on Larimer Street. By then, Ryan was our third roommate with his own drawer, and our toothbrushes would commingle in the bathroom the three of us shared. I pretended not to notice when he'd walk past me freshly showered. Images had a way of piling up inside me and making it difficult for me to concentrate.

Senior year, we were studying for winter finals when my peculiar moods progressed from bad to worse. I was twenty-one years old and on the verge of something awful. Ryan was draped across our couch, his long legs resting in Lauren's lap. That's how intertwined they were. Lauren's flaming red hair fell all around her, and her pale vanilla hands were tickling his arm. Black-rimmed glasses framed her blue eyes.

Snow had fallen the night before, and the windows revealed a coat of white covering the street. Most everyone we knew was hunkered down for the day. Brian, Ryan's teammate, came bolting through the doorway without knocking. The beefy linebacker was out of breath and at the mercy of his tears.

Oliver James is dead.

How could this be? Oliver and I had gone on a few dates! Finally, someone who had made me laugh! The disbelief made it impossible for me to react. Ryan jumped up from the sofa, leaving Lauren and her fiery hair to sink into the dull, lifeless beige. I thought he was coming for me. He went to Brian instead.

"He's dead," Brian repeated, reaching for the refrigerator, the dining room table, anything to stabilize him as he told us this shocking news. Oliver was a gifted tight end. He was young, healthy, and in his prime. "He killed himself," said Brian. "He fucking hanged himself. The guys found him."

My heart began to race at an unusual pace that signified bad stuff to come. The news alone was alarming and disturbing. The thought of Ollie gone sent me into a panic.

Lauren folded into Ryan, who had returned to the couch and scooped her in his lap, and it's not as though Lauren was petite or small. She was medium build—not skinny but not fat. And when she curled herself in Ryan's grasp, he rested his head on hers, and the two of them just bawled. No one could believe it. No one had seen it coming.

I watched them, aching for the comfort that was rightfully mine, that I thought I deserved.

Already I knew my insides were beginning to seep out. I was broken over the loss of someone so young, someone I had grown to like, but my sense had shifted from grieving to danger mode. Though this was likely the most terrifying threat, it had not been the first time I had fought off frightening thoughts. I was having an acute reaction that sabotaged me wholly. Fear had injected itself into my veins.

Ideas raced through my brain at an uncontrollable pace. One in particular crept up on me and hovered in my mental desk drawer for the days and weeks that followed Ollie's death. Lauren, Ryan, and the others thought I had stopped eating and almost flunked my finals because I was distraught over what Oliver had done. They attributed my melancholy and disinterest in the usual parties and happy hours to stress. My parents thought that, coupled with being on the cusp of graduating and entering the real world, I was poised for the perfect storm. I knew better. Something infinitely worse had taken over and locked me in a personal prison. A sinister question almost wrecked me: *What if I were to do what Ollie did?*

Lauren was not about to abandon her roommate. She was the one who passed up sleeping beside Ryan, instead, choosing to curl around me until the shaking stopped and I fell asleep. It was her voice that coaxed me out of bed, convinced me to get dressed, and made it so I got to my exams. She gave up a lot for me.

And I thanked her by stealing the one thing, the one person, it would destroy her to lose.

So yes, it is her face that comes to me, and it comes to me often. Eyes that once sympathized with my struggles and made it so that taking a step each day was possible, a smile that told me she cared.

But that face changed over time, replaced with madness.

"Do you think I'm ready to see her?" I ask Jeannie, before changing my mind. "No, don't tell me. I already know the answer." She asks me what that answer is. "I don't think anyone is fully prepared for a confrontation this big. Seventeen years is a long time, and what I did, well, facing Lauren could be a big part of my healing."

Jeannie nods her head in agreement: "The interaction might assuage some of your guilt. And guilt is anger turned inward. You've held on to it for a long, long time. This could be a painful and rewarding lesson for you."

I think about things and it feels doable, though Lauren's face reappears again, as if she's taken residency over Jeannie's head, just past the desk and by the window. In her stare she is asking me all kinds of questions. Accusations that may sound confusing to someone else but that make complete sense to me. I feel defenseless and exposed. My nerves begin to sense the real danger ahead. I am traversing the darts she is throwing, shielding my face with my hands.

Jeannie interrupts Lauren's attack: "What do you think was going on at the time that made it possible for you to go after Ryan? Understanding those actions will help you . . ."

"Jeannie, there's no way that telling Lauren I had lower than low self-esteem, and took whatever I could get from anyone who would pay attention, will lessen her anger or help her forgive me." I exhale, and loudly. "Maybe I'm not ready for this."

"What stops you?"

My eyes rest on hers before I speak. My fingernails find my mouth. "I know I've been heading on the right track. This just makes me think there are too many things to uncover, and they all revolve around Ryan and Lauren. They always do. I know he loves me. I do. He's the most loyal, honest man in the state . . . But what I did, to the two of them . . . It's much worse than what you think. It's much worse than bedding my best friend's boyfriend."

Most people would ask, "What could be worse than that?" Not Jeannie. She asks, "Abby, what's going on here?"

I stand up from my favorite spot because my body is hot with fire. I need to stretch my legs and arms. I've seen ugly parts of me, but this one is the ugliest. Telling Jeannie can only help me defend myself from Lauren's wrath. The words don't come out of me as much as they slowly seep from a hidden reserve. And when I'm done, Jeannie nods her head and doesn't judge.

My voice comes out in a quaver: "I was selfish and cruel. I played God, thinking I knew what was best for my two friends. I kept secrets. You're right, though. This is something I need to face. As scary as it feels, this showdown, the aftermath, it has to free me. Maybe it will fix my marriage, maybe it won't, but it's something I have to do. I don't see any other way."

"Well, then, it's settled. I'll clear Lauren Sheppard's visit."

CHAPTER TWENTY-THREE

LAUREN

All I can think about on my way to Cold Creek is that Abby hadn't told Ryan. It is racing through my brain in spiraling repetition, and I can't shut it down. I can't press stop. I am helpless in a loop that drowns out the sounds of NPR and a woman talking about problems with Obamacare.

She didn't tell him.

I have called ahead of time to secure a spot on Abby's visitor list. Yesterday's storm brought in a front of colder weather, and the trees are noticeably bare. The bowed stems are bare and crooked, their jagged fingers branch into the bright sky.

Seeing Ryan was not how I'd pictured it. When he said my name, I was dragged back in time, feeling the whisper of his breath running up my neck. It was his fingers touching me again, leaving no part of me unexplored. At first I thought our college love would become worn and tired like that of all the other couples. It never happened to us. Even after years of his chapped lips on mine, I could never get enough of Ryan touching me. I had it. I had it all. It's hard to shush the voice in my head that echoes his words: *So why'd you have to leave? Why'd you have to ruin it?*

I don't know what I'm about to say to my friend Abby. For years I shouted words to her down shooting falls. The language of recrimination would hook on to the pluming cascades and gush into the earth below. The discharge would satisfy me for a time. It's not that I hadn't known that Abby had a crush on Ryan. He had that kindness about him. He always knew the right things to say. "Abby, that color looks good on you. Abby, come with us to Beech for the weekend. It'll be fun."

The three of us shared a lot at Davidson. So when I reminisced about college days, there was very little to remember without feeling cheated. The memory of the two of them stripped most of the good away. Some slipped through the current that flowed inside of me: Abby singing at the top of her lungs in the shower, Abby playing April Fool's jokes on our friends, Abby reading to me from a study guide before an exam because I forgot to pick up a new supply of contact lenses and lost my glasses.

Ryan and I never submitted to Abby's tantrums and pessimism. *Crabby Abby.* That's not to say we weren't sympathetic and aware of her fragility. By treating her as the adult she almost was, we thought we were giving her the skills she needed to grow up. Just like the rest of us.

She is waiting for me in the solarium. It is a brightly lit room enclosed in glass with long-range views from all angles. She is curled up on a cream-colored sofa with her legs tucked underneath. How I wish for clouds up above, something to refract the sun's glow from our faces. Every blemish and flaw is captured in the light. We are bare and exposed and unable to hide what we know is about to brim to the surface.

I don't bend over to greet her. There are no phony hugs to bridge the depth and distance of the betrayal. I notice at once that her hair has grown long and the bangs that once framed her forehead now brush against her face, revealing a softer look. Gone are the pounds of makeup she used to bury herself in, leaving a noticeable weightlessness. Her whole aura has transformed. But I know Abby better than anyone. Beneath the new facade, she is a mess inside. I can see it in her posture, how the worry cracks her eyes open. She's not sure if she should smile or grit her teeth.

I fling my coat on the chair beside her and take a seat on the other side of the couch. There are residents and guests milling around the campus. Trees sway, birds squawk, but in our secluded bubble there is silence. My eyes fix on her so she has trouble turning away. I won't make that mistake again.

Hers immediately brim with tears. "Lauren . . ."

It is jarring to see her after all these years. How sad for us that we will never experience a nostalgia-laced reunion. In a hushed voice, she asks if she can begin. I nod my head. I haven't prepared a speech, and I can't pluck the paragraphs from the falls. Seeing her makes me seethe inside, and it feels awful to kick her when she's down.

"My counselor and I discussed your visit," she begins, her hands knotted together, and her words flat and rehearsed. "There were dozens of layers to peel. I'm ready for this. It's something I have to face and work through.

"The first few months were the worst. I saw you at every turn. I couldn't move forward because you were always there pulling me back. The suspense, the doubts . . ." The wistful look in her eyes halts her words. She tries to find the strength to continue in the folds of her fingers but gives up, finding my eyes again. "We were so not grounded. He was waiting for you with a heavy heart. I was waiting for you to cut through mine."

For years, I had imagined saying three words to her. Three words that would never undo the damage but would hold her accountable for what she'd done. I straighten my back and beat her first with my stare and then with my words. "How could you?"

She doesn't back down. Maybe it is some form of self-punishment. She's controlled when she asks, "Which part?" while everything else about her appears to crumble. I notice her fingernails are chewed to the quick. I let the pity wash over me until it emerges as rage.

Her lower lip trembles and she is half-crying, half-pleading. "I didn't plan for that night to happen. You were gone. He was alone. God, he was distraught. None of us could reach you." Her throat sounds clogged with regret.

"We drank . . ." she pushes on. "I'd never seen him so torn up inside . . . It was like we were on equal ground . . . Does that make sense? It's not an excuse, but if you can see where I was coming from . . . Why I would do such a thing. I never got the attention you got. Not just from someone like Ryan. Anyone. The one guy I started to like killed himself!" Then she buries her face inside her hands before flapping them in the air.

"What I did was horrible," she says, her shoulders softening with remorse. The shaking subsides, replaced with defeat, and I can tell the withheld secret has been torturous for her. Her sobs collide into each other. "Imagine how awful I had to feel about myself to do that to my best friend. I wasn't thinking about that at the time. Ryan was paying attention to me. *Someone* was paying attention to me! There wasn't any way I could stop myself."

She reaches for the tissue box beside her and blows her nose into the feathery white. She is distraught, but she keeps on talking: "I didn't like myself back then. I don't like talking about that person. It was the last thing I shared with my counselors. You can't possibly imagine the circus that has taken residence in my head. It's much deeper than betrayal."

I was friends with Abby for a reason. When others questioned me about our kinship, I said that I overlooked her faults because I knew how to find her strengths. Seeing her unravel now is tough to watch.

I hover between reaching for her hand that has the Kleenex fisted in a ball, and slapping her.

And then I remember how much we meant to each other. How we laughed at the same stupid jokes and got what others could never understand. Abby never pretended to be someone she wasn't. She had a great sense of humor. She didn't require effort or excuses. When I needed her, she was the first one there. Even though her life was an encyclopedia of chaos, open for all to see, I missed having a friend like that. It is this insight that reaches down my throat and pulls out these words: "I can forgive you for that night."

She is quiet, not sure how to trust what I'm saying, and I continue: "I can understand why it happened . . . the weaknesses in both of you. But I will never understand the other betrayal."

She begins to cry, and my compassion is eating away at the tougher, useless feelings.

I was in Uganda shooting the Murchison Falls when the first message reached my cell. It was over a week old, and I was so shaken up that I dropped my phone into the water. It took three days to secure tickets, find my passport, and get to the States via South Africa, New York, and eventually Charlotte.

How could I have known that one month into my journey Ryan's father would go to sleep and not wake up? They called it a heart attack. Blockages and carotid arteries aside, I knew better: the muscle was weakened by years without his wife. Living without someone you love. That's a broken heart.

I should have left a message at his dad's house. I should have kept calling until someone answered the phone, though, at the time, it seemed more important that I get to him. He had to feel my arms across the miles. He had to know I would have done anything to get to him.

I arrived at his parents' house, fatigued and unshowered. Standing in front of the old colonial, the summer sun beating against my back, I had thought long and hard about the journey I had taken and decided that I wouldn't go back: the program, the traveling, the waterfalls—all would have to wait. Ryan could come with me, or I could shoot falls in the United States. Somehow we would make it work. I already had a ring, so we would be together forever.

I quietly let myself in.

What greeted me was this: Abby and Ryan having sex on the family room couch. I was standing in the doorway, wearing the same clothes I'd traveled in for seventy-two hours. My hair was a mess, my eyes puffy from crying, and my best friend was on top of my boyfriend.

It was the back of his head. I could tell by the skin on the nape of his neck. He was thrust against the sofa and I blinked. *No, this can't be.* I could have easily tiptoed out of there unnoticed by the two of them. Except I felt like I was going to be sick. My feet were frozen to the floor. Abby looked up and our eyes locked.

She didn't stop. She didn't get up. Were my eyes playing tricks on me? Opening and closing them again, I reached for my glasses, though they couldn't help, not when I already had my contacts in. Abby was still glaring at me, her expression telling me what words could not. I ran out the door without bothering to close it. I ran and ran and ran with what little strength I had left in my body, eventually escaping to my mom and dad's house on Beech.

For two people who could always sense each other's presence, I was shattered that Ryan had no idea of what had just happened. The promise of forever dissipated at the snap of a finger.

"You saw me there," I whisper, holding back the emotion that had gripped me for years.

Regret spills down her cheeks while her body hunches downward. She is racked with defeat when she mouths, "I know."

"Why didn't you stop?" I cry out. "Why didn't you tell him?"

She wrestles with this. She cowers. Her cheeks explode in red. "I was scared! I was scared I'd lose him!"

"You didn't have him, Abby! You let him believe I didn't love him, that I handed him over to you!"

"You could have done something," she shot back. "You had every opportunity to contact him, to tell him you were there. Do you know what your silence did to him?"

My remorse turns me inward. I can't face her or the accusation, so I focus my attention toward the stretch of open field behind her head. The velvety grass blankets the earth, and soon it will be covered in powdery white. The shuffling seasons never bothered me before, the winter's frost, spring's renewal, the blistering heat of summer, the shades of fall. Human temperament is much harder to follow.

"Lauren," she says, with her arms reaching for me, "I'm so sorry I hurt you. I was wrong. So wrong. Please find it in your heart to forgive me. I'm begging you . . ."

I don't know what I had expected. A fight? Denial? Abby's culpability was something new, something I hadn't prepared for. Did she expect me to her embrace her? "Do you realize what would've happened if you had told him?"

"I know exactly what would've happened," she says, her arms falling away. "I would've been raising Juliana on my own."

"He's always been pretty old-fashioned," I hear myself say, as though I could pretend all of this didn't kill me inside.

"He loved you," she relents. "Nobody came close."

"And now he loves you," I say.

But she is shaking her head. "I'm not sure about that. I'm not sure about much anymore. Being here is like turning back the clock. I'm visiting places in my head I've been too afraid to inspect. There's a lot I don't like. I'm sure he sees it too."

Her honesty is too much for me. I silence the part of me that wishes things could be different. "It's good you're getting the help you need."

"Why didn't you tell him?" she asks, untucking her legs from beneath her and tilting her head in question. "Why did you let him think you'd vanished?"

I had vanished. There were parts of me I would never find again. "I was stubborn," I begin, my voice moving through a deep well of pain and landing on despair. "I thought you would tell him. But when word got back to me in London about the baby, I knew there was no point in contacting him, when we both knew Ryan would never abandon his child. Whether you told him or not, he had a baby on the way. I would've never forced him to choose. I not only lost the love of my life, Abby. I lost my best friend and the city I loved." This part is awful to share with her. My emotions are teetering and I know she will see me cry. "Do you know how hard it is to cut a chunk of your life from memory and pretend it never happened? I thought our friendship mattered to you, that I mattered to you. And I sure as hell thought you cared about him enough to relieve him from all the unanswered questions, to explain my absence."

"I lived with your absence every day," she whimpers. "We pranced around it for years, like some big vacuous hole we were going to fall through. I know what I lost when I betrayed you. Ryan and I never worked without you. I don't work without you."

I had hated Abby for years. I had hated her with a flaming venom I could not tame. I hated knowing what she was capable of and how she had taken my future into her hands and balled it up like wastepaper. Hating someone you once loved is far worse than bitter dislike. The betrayal strips you of memories you once trusted. A snapshot of what used to be becomes a lie. And the anger mixes with the hurt. I will never forget the look in her eyes when she saw me. Those eyes haunted me all over the world.

Today she reminds me of the characters in my books, and I'm sure some of the more evil ones were created with her mind. I observe Abby like I might one of my creations. It's all too easy to make an assessment and an assumption without facts. Girl sleeps with best friend's boy-friend: tramp, whore. Don't I owe Abby the same courtesy I owe my fictional characters? I had grown to love these folks as though they were extensions of my family, my closest friends. I had breathed life into them. How could I not afford Abby the same regard?

I ask her this: "Do you love him?"

"You know I love him," she says, her cheeks flushing. "I always loved him."

"I'm not talking college crush, Abby. I'm talking about pure, unself-ish love—telling him I showed up, telling him I was there. So when I ask, 'Do you love him?' can you put his needs before your own?"

Her body straightens, and she taps her nervous foot against the floor. "You didn't put his needs before yours. You were the selfish one. If you had loved him, you would've never left him alone."

"Abby, tell him the truth. Tell him I was there, on that day."

My character is human and flawed. Her imperfections band together and, at times, eclipse her strengths. Like any of us. I feel bad for Abby. I am angry at Abby. But I am able to see all of Abby. I say to her before turning to leave, "When you love someone, Abby, really love someone, there's nothing worse than secrets."

CHAPTER TWENTY-FOUR

ABBY

I am free floating. Falling. The picture is fuzzy. Grainy. Somewhere between back then and now. We were all getting high on the roof of the fraternity house. Lauren and Ryan were beside me, laughing and smiling at each other, cocooned in their impenetrable fog of bliss. I didn't like smoking pot, but everyone was doing it, and I figured it might take the edge off the anxiety. It was dark and the rooftop was packed with kids. The music was loud, and I could feel the vibration beneath my feet. The drop was a dangerous distance. I puffed on the joint that had been passed back and forth, then covered my mouth from the flaming cough.

Ryan noticed first. "You all right, Abs?"

Elbows and shoulders and bodies were bumping into us, swaying to the deafening music. I think that's what he said, though I knew by the way he wrapped an arm around my shoulder that's what he meant. His eyes were concerned. If they were water, I would have drowned in their faded green. I handed the blunt to him and he finished it off. At once I was insulated from very bad things. I closed my eyes and imagined scenarios I wasn't allowed: Ryan's arm remained around me, his lips reaching mine.

From out of nowhere emerged Lauren. She hustled her way under Ryan's other arm and the one that draped around me fell to his side as he leaned into her. My heart began to race. I was feeling dizzy. I couldn't discern whether I was on the merry-go-round or whether my surroundings were moving. I tried to swallow, but my throat was too dry. The frigid wave passed through my chest and left me on the verge of something awful.

They were kissing each other and swaying softly to the music. The blanket he momentarily wrapped me in had slipped away.

The railing came into view and the distant sky merged with the dark ground. In one seismic rush of adrenaline, I was compelled to jump. The music faded, and all I could hear was the quickening of my breaths. I was rooted to the floor, fighting the urge to break free and leap. I had to get out of there. I had to get off that roof. My legs were my enemy. Could I will them to walk in the opposite direction or would they betray me and carry me toward death?

Usually when I am having a dream steeped in terror, I can force myself to wake up. I can separate myself from the action and become acutely aware that what feels real is not. Rose's silky voice is wrapping around my head. She is jostling me awake because I am crying out and shaking. What she doesn't understand is that I am not asleep. This is no nightmare.

After Lauren left, I was plagued with guilt and a long list of memories. Jeannie was the one who found me slumped against the cushions in the solarium.

"Tell me in words," she said.

I was hysterical, wishing for curtains or blinds to hide the shame. "Can't we just talk about this like two people?" I attack. "Can't I just vent and not be psychoanalyzed? I'm scared. And I'm so incredibly sad."

"Let's begin with the fear. What are you afraid of?"

My body is trembling and the words shake out of me: "He's going to leave me."

"What else?"

"What else? What could be worse than that?"

I am now strewn across the sofa so my hysteria is hidden from the outside world. Jeannie has stood up to lock the door for privacy. If this is going to happen here and now, this is where it has to be. I am crying into my hands, the tears filling my palms and making it impossible for me to stop. My defense mechanisms did a fine job. They erased Lauren from my life so I could build a crafty lie to keep my husband. Full disclosure returned her to my heart. I had never properly mourned the end of our friendship, and the wound was deep. I choke on the words as they fall from my mind and edge down my throat: "She won't forgive me . . . How can I live like this? This is no life . . . Running from the truth has only exhausted and hardened me." I search Jeannie's face for the answer, for the *how to do this* prompt. But what I see staring back is my own solution. "Jeannie, I'm not willing to live the lie anymore," I tell her.

By allowing myself permission to feel the feelings, Jeannie said I was learning to curtail the expression of anxiety. "Acknowledging that you fear you will lose your husband or that you have betrayed someone you loved is acknowledging an actual threat. Anxiety occurs from threats of the subconscious. Own the real threat. Share it. If you step on them or push them down, they will manifest in some other way."

"Please stop," I tell her. "I know I'm on the couch, but I don't want to be on the couch right now. I just need to cry. I just need to get this sadness out of me. If I don't, I don't know what will happen to me." I've never spoken to Jeannie like this before. Always full of surprises, she doesn't flinch. Instead she says, "I'm proud of you," which after thirteen tissues begins to make sense.

After I calm down, we go for a stroll around the facility.

The day is undecided, like me. Earlier the sun had blinded me in its brilliance, until it became a blink, then all but vanished behind the clouds. You couldn't see the wind whipping the bare trees, but I could feel it wrapping my arms tighter around me. Jeannie has warned me about crossing my arms when we are in therapy. She says it suggests a guardedness about me. Cagey. It's my internal security system, the way I protect myself from lurking doom. I do as she says and loosen my arms from my chest and let them fall by my sides. I have grown fond of the land surrounding Cold Creek. Maybe I am appreciating the world around me with renewed interest because my eyes are open outward instead of in.

"You're making great progress," she says. "It took a long time for you to get to those emotions, but you did it. And you felt them. And you didn't resort to the old familiar patterns to work through them. You didn't panic, and you didn't die."

I thank her, but the compliment comes with a price. I am emotionally and physically exhausted. "I'm going to tell him."

She doesn't hesitate: "That's a wise decision."

<hr>

"Abby, are you sleeping?" Rose persists, tugging at my sleeve and inching closer to my face, plucking me away from the chilling thoughts of Ryan abandoning me. I look her straight in the eyes and say, "Yes, I'm sound asleep."

She laughs and elbows me. I laugh back.

I have found an unexpected complacency to my days here. While I have had some gritty issues to work through, the pieces of my internal puzzle are slowly making their way toward one another. Things hurt. I'm afraid. But it's remarkable how I've managed to handle the stressors. I know there's no finish line, that this never ends. I'm learning how to fall, dust myself off, and take the next step. I'm also weeks into a really good antidepressant and a mild antianxiety medication. They definitely help. I will probably remain on these drugs for the rest of my life.

Stigma is a terrible word in the world of quiet sufferers. Cold Creek, and its staff of professionals, has worked closely with patients and families to relieve them of the shame associated with mental illness. When a patient presents with symptoms of diabetes or heart disease, and the treatment is lifelong, the general population accepts the diagnosis as a matter of physical health. Unfortunately, diseases of the brain are classified and perceived differently than diseases of the body. Your brain forms your personality. Your behavior is the result of the disease, of the brain misfiring. It's easier to separate blame and fault from an impaired kidney or a damaged aorta than from an obsessive, compulsive, phobic person.

In here we talk regularly about normal, successful people with arsenals of hidden truths. I wish I didn't compare myself to the mothers at school—the capable, bright spots in the car-pool line, the shiny leaders of the community—but I do. I look at Rose and her nubile beauty; Sybil, and her enviable success in business. One of the most helpful moments for me with Jeannie was ridding myself of expectations and embracing acceptance. We're all part crazy inside. I know it was not a mistake to come here.

"Were you having a bad dream?" Rose asks.

"More like a bad awake," I tell her.

"Is there anything I can do?" she asks.

"Nope," I reply. "I got myself into this mess, and I'm going to get myself out of it."

Rose rests her head beside mine and wraps an arm around my shoulder. "We're here if you need us, Abigail," she whispers into my hair.

My name actually feels nice rolling off her tongue. It shows me how far I've come.

Abigail.

CHAPTER TWENTY-FIVE

RYAN

It's our final week of practice before the championship game. We have had to adapt to E.J.'s absence and fill the gaps where needed. I do my best to steer the boys away from the press. They unknowingly give me the initiative to fight my inner battle.

Juliana is in the stands waiting for me. I notice how she uses her jacket to shield herself from more than the cold. She's been unusually skittish lately, and instead of going home after school, she has been driving over to Pine Ridge to watch practices. Sometimes we grab a bite before heading home. Other times she follows me as we take the short drive home. As her father, I was the last to know she and E.J. broke up.

We are in the locker room, and the boys are goofing around when I overhear one of them talking about Jules. They say she's waiting for E.J. to show up. They say she's been stalking him for days. And here I thought my girl was feeling the impact of her mama being gone, and wanting some time with her daddy. She's waiting outside, and I go to her.

The night sky is deep purple. Juliana is bundled up. The cold air pinches her skin, and she shivers. I wrap my arm around her as we walk to our cars. I didn't want to get Juliana a car, afraid of accidents and how foolhardy kids can be, so she got her own—worked for three straight summers at the Y as a camp counselor and filled in at that bra store whenever they needed her. She earned enough to put a down payment on a used Jetta. She calls it Heisman, after the trophy.

She leans in to me with her eyes locked on the ground.

"Jules?" I ask, without really asking.

The parking lot is empty, and the temperature has dropped too many degrees. She tells me very matter-of-factly, "E.J. and I broke up." I act surprised. Until she adds, "I wanted to have sex with him and he dumped me."

I'm not sure what she's more upset about: the refusal or the breakup. She doesn't cry. She just stands there, waiting for my reaction.

Juliana hasn't had the most normal of upbringings. Early on, I knew much of the responsibility of rearing her would fall on my shoulders. And I didn't mind. If I do one thing right in the world, it will be to make sure she grows up knowing she is loved.

Our house was always teeming with boys from the field. Conversations, while inappropriate for a young girl, often centered on the rough and tumble of male companionship. "Gorilla speak," I called it. Nothing surprised me when these boys were together. Jules was always at ease in their presence, and they treated her like their kid sister. Until she blossomed into someone they saw differently. Then the game of cat and mouse began, and with it, my heart escaped my chest.

"You're too young for sex," I tell her.

"I'm *sixteen!*" she shouts back in this ticked off, haughty way that makes her sound much older.

"*This* is what's bothering you? Of all the crap that's landed on our doorstep, this is what you're focusing on?"

"I have needs," she says.

I laugh out loud.

"I love E.J. He loves me."

"Yeah, well, that kind of stupid love makes babies and problems you're too young to deal with."

"You taught me to be careful. All my life, Daddy. I know about protecting myself."

"Right now? We're going to have this conversation right now?" I am pacing back and forth.

"It's different today than when you were growing up. No one has relationships anymore. Everyone just hooks up. At least I'm in a relationship."

"Is that supposed to make me feel better? Do you know how ridiculous you sound? Sex is about love. Love is about respect. Without that, you got nothing. I don't care what those hormones are telling you. Your generation sounds like a pack of fools."

"Marlee's mom said she'll take me to the gynecologist . . ."

I may lose it on Marlee's mom. "Why are we even having this conversation when you two have broken up?"

This quiets her down. The last of the players leaves the parking lot, and it's just me and my girl. I shake my head back and forth. "You don't really think having sex with him is gonna make him come back?"

Juliana is tapping her right foot ever so casually while her hands rest on her hips. It is a pose I have come to associate with most every teenage girl. I can infer annoyance and expectation in that one adolescent stance. I'm not sure how I've gotten so lucky with E.J. He actually turned this beautiful creature down. I'm relieved he's out of my house, and if he were nearby, I would pat him on the back.

A lone car enters the gates of the parking lot. It could be one of the players who left something behind, but it's not. It's Devon and Ellis. I bark out at Juliana, "Get inside!" but my headstrong daughter retreats, instead, to my side.

Ellis is a tall, burly man whose eyes are full of mean. Devon is a few inches shorter and wider. The older man is angry, and he's going to threaten everything I love. "Coach Holden," he begins.

"Ellis. Devon." I extend my hand, not letting them see me flinch.

The older man ignores my reach. Devon avoids my eyes, but his hand finds mine.

"Coach, where's my son?" Ellis asks.

"That's a good question. Shouldn't you know where your son is?"

Evil ricochets from Ellis's eyes. "He owes me money." Then he turns to Juliana and fear shoots through me.

"Don't you dare eye my daughter."

Juliana is shifting beside me. I hear her trying to quiet her breaths and the effort propels me into motion. I have had run-ins with fathers like Ellis Whittaker before, career criminals whose sons I have raised in their father's absence, but none as dangerous as Ellis. Worse than their crimes is the legacy they leave behind.

Devon is staring at his shoes. The boy was always a conflicted player. He wears his struggle on his face. I understand at once how E.J. gets pulled into the boy's indecision. "Devon," I begin, "do you remember when you played for me?"

Devon looks me squarely in the eye. I know I only have a short while before I lose his attention. I've seen him straddle this fence before. It's why he gave up after a year on my team.

"Do you remember the night you intercepted on Edgewater? You ran for sixty-five yards. A touchdown. Biggest one of your career. Do you remember what I said?"

Ellis interrupts, "Boy, this man ain't your friend. Get your mind out of them football dreams of yours."

Devon is watching me, unsure of what to do.

"I said, 'You can do this. Just reach deep inside and pull out your best effort. Do you remember that day? Do you remember what you were able to do when you gave it your all? What the hell you doin' wasting your life like this?"

Ellis is ready to attack. He is closing in on me and Juliana is screaming for him to back off. I shield her as best as I can with my arms, and my pulse is shooting through me.

Devon searches my eyes. He wants to speak up. He's my player again, and like most players, he needs a firm hand to guide him.

Ellis's breath is all over my face. It stinks of booze and cigarettes. He's a formidable man, and although he is terrorizing me and my daughter, I do my best to mask my fear. "This ain't no football game, Coach," he rasps.

I take a step closer to him. Our faces are almost touching, and I am breathing in his awful odor. "Don't you dare threaten me again," I say. "I will destroy you."

That's when I feel the gun against my belly and things take a chilling turn.

Devon stammers, "Pop, leave him alone."

Ellis flinches. "Boy, what'd you say?"

This is the first time I have had a gun pressed against me, and adrenaline runs up my chest and seizes rational thought. I am shaking inside, but I'm fairly certain I haven't imagined Devon's words. Until he says them again: "Leave him alone."

"You fallin' for this hero worship?" he says, swatting Devon in the head with the side of the gun. "You think you're some football star because he says so?"

It is quiet around us, but for Ellis's nasty voice and the beats of my heart. I am watching as Devon deteriorates under his father's fists. "You ain't got no future in football, son. You never did. Tell him, Coach. Tell him he ain't ever as good as Evan James. Tell him he ain't got no shot being good at anything. Pigheaded fool."

I focus on Devon, drawing courage from the young boy's indecision. "Do you remember what else I said to you that night?"

He doesn't nod his head or speak. His eyes lock on to mine, and I know.

You may never understand how proud I am of you. It's remarkable to witness the revitalization of someone who has been beaten and burned, ridiculed and bullied. Everything about them changes. Their face, their eyes, their posture. That night Devon had drunk up my words. If only he could have held on to those words longer.

Ellis is royally pissed and turns again to me. He waves the gun in the air like some prize and wields his power in our faces. I am no longer breathing. I am acting, protecting, stuffing fear away until it's replaced with guts. "Don't make me pull this trigger, boy," he says.

"Devon," I begin, steadying my voice. "You don't need to do this. It's not too late to set things straight. To tell the truth about that night. You gotta come forward. It's the only way I can help you."

The boy is breaking before my eyes.

"If you love your brother at all, you gotta man up. Don't let him go down for this. I know why you did it. There's something to be said for that. There's leniency."

My words infuriate Ellis Whittaker. I don't see the punch to my face coming until the sting sears my skin, and I am flayed on the floor. Juliana is shouting at him, calling him an animal, and I bark at her to stop, to clear out of there, but she resists. My fingers find my nose, and the wet liquid stains my fingers. I get to my feet and see that Devon is wrestling the gun away from his father. Ellis shouts obscenities in the air, threats that sound like bullets. I scream at Juliana to get behind me. "Juliana! Now!" I have to shield her from this madness.

Devon is no match for his father. They are wrestling on the ground, and the gun falls by my feet. With Juliana cowering behind me, I race to pick it up. Blood drips from my nose, but I am a man with everything to lose. Fear grips me, a trembling that burrows deep in my chest. The flight-or-flight response kicks in and I take action.

Devon is saying something. I think he is swearing, trying to tell his father what he plans to do. "I've gotta go to the police," he says.

His father disagrees, pinning his son to the ground and grabbing his neck with his large, spiny fingers. "Over my dead body, son."

And a shot is fired.

CHAPTER TWENTY-SIX

JULIANA

I clamp my eyes shut to avoid seeing the blood. My legs have given out, and I am heaped on the ground in a puddle beside my daddy's gray sweatpants. If I open my eyes, everything will have changed. Someone will be hurt, or worse.

"It's okay," my father says, but I don't trust words right now. Daddy may be all right, but someone else isn't.

The firing of the weapon startles the two on the ground. No one is yelling anymore. There is silence, except for the wind that rattles the fence around the parking lot. I hear their voices: Ellis and Devon. My eyelids slowly trust the night sky, opening and closing until they are convinced that we are safe. And there is no more blood. Slowly, relief washes over me in fits of nervous tears. I had bottled them up until they came gushing out. A single streetlight illuminates the enclosed area. I clamp my eyes shut and pray for E.J. to be here. I pray for him to talk some sense into his crazy family.

Daddy's holding the gun in his hand, aiming the pistol at the dark sky before turning it on Ellis. There's hatred in his eyes, someone I don't immediately recognize. I want to shout at him to stop, this madman with a gun, but I can't. I'm terrified. And the gun in Daddy's hand is the way it has to be. He's firm when he tells them to get off his field. "You don't belong here," he says.

When Devon repeats, "I'm going to turn myself in," Ellis bows his head and keeps his wicked thoughts to himself. Now that Daddy has the gun and it's pointing right his way, Ellis is a lot quieter.

I study E.J.'s father, wondering how it is possible that I could love someone who came from such evil. I shiver inside. "I'll do it," Devon says again, this time directed at my dad.

"Ellis, you hear that? Your boy's going to do the honorable thing. I'm thinking I might call Buford over here right now. Sure he'd enjoy this little party." Daddy sounds rational and calm, but I know there's fear licking the tips of his words. Until Ellis disappears, Daddy will pretend for me. That's what he does.

Ellis slowly backs away. He wipes at his pants and shirt, as though erasing evil were that simple. "Keep hearing what you want, Coach. You ain't gonna fix this. You might be the local hero around here, coaching them boys and all, but you ain't gonna sink your vampire teeth into my sons."

"Go to hell!" I hear myself shout at Ellis Whittaker.

Daddy takes my arm and pulls me close to him. I'm ready to punch Ellis in the face and tell him what a disgrace he is as a father.

Ellis stands less tall, and his eyes are raging mad with defeat. "You got a fiery one over there, Coach. Better get her under control."

"Think you'd better worry about your own kid."

"Devon don't know what he's talkin' about. He ain't turnin' himself in. No speech from a tired coach is going to change that." Devon eyes Daddy with defeat. Ellis continues, "Now get up, boy. We're going to find your brother, and we're gonna mess with him good."

I beg my father to stop them. He is holding me back with his stare and an outstretched arm. I scream at Ellis with no shame. One thing spending hours on the football field has taught me is how to swear like a boy.

"Let 'em go," he whispers to me. "They're not worth it."

"They're going to hurt E.J."

"No, they're not. They can't. Ellis needs E.J."

We watch as the two men drive off into the dark. Daddy still has the gun in his hand, and he unloads the chamber and throws the bullets into a nearby trash can. I am too frightened to ask how he knows to do that. There's a lake behind the field, and I watch him walk out to the fringes and toss the gun far into the center of the water. In its absence, we both begin to breathe a little easier. He refuses to let me drive home alone, so we leave my car at the school and get into his.

Neither of us speaks as we head toward home. I shield my eyes from the blood that drips from his nose.

"This isn't what I wanted for you."

"Daddy . . ."

"Don't interrupt me." He grips the wheel. "I never wanted the hatred of this world touching you. Seems your mama and I haven't done a very good job protecting you from much." He looks at me, taking his concerned eyes off the road to make sure I understand. I'm a strong person, but every once in a while it's nice to have someone take my hand and tell me that everything is going to be all right. That's what my Daddy does. He takes his hand off the wheel and reaches across to find mine. "I promise you this will all work out. It'll be all right. I know you miss your mama. I know you miss E.J."

"It's not your fault, Daddy. You couldn't help Mama. You did everything you could. We both did. She just needs to figure it out on her own. Isn't that what you told me? And how you help those boys every day, how they look up to you. Do you know how proud I am of you? Do you know what it feels like to hear them say you changed their lives?"

He is squeezing my hand tighter: "It's you who changed my life."

Sleep comes so deeply that night that I am unsure if the banging is something exploding in my head or the grumbling of dreams. I awake with a start, and the clock says it's two in the morning. Daddy's shouting down the hall for me to stay in my room. My body is stiff with fear, and I'm not sure I could move if I tried. Someone is hammering at our door. The persistence can mean only bad things.

I hear a shuffling down the hall and the opening and closing of doors. Voices permeate the house. They are loud and frantic. "E.J.," I shout, heading for the hallway and the voice I think I know.

"Get back in your room," my dad screams. "Now!"

The house is dark but for the exterior lights casting a glow through the windows. A familiar car is parked in the street, and I can make out the shape of a figure slumped against the front foyer. Usually the area is covered in boots and jackets and somebody's keys. Tonight it's covered with limbs and legs and that person is crying out something awful. The face is covered, but I recognize the black parka and scuffed shoes. It's Devon.

I tiptoe back to my room, and by instinct I dial E.J. I need to hear his voice. He needs to be okay. The call goes right to voice mail, and I feel the bile rising in my throat. I sit at the doorway with my head pressed to the frame. My father is coaxing Devon out of a stupor. I hear things like "talk to me" and "tell me what happened," but Devon doesn't respond. He is writhing and moaning in a way that sounds like death.

Then I hear Daddy dialing someone, and I know things are really dire because he says, "A boy has been badly beaten." And he gives them our address.

"Juliana!" he shouts, and at once he is father and coach. "Get me something to stop the bleeding." I spring from my room toward the linen closet and grab a handful of towels. I do not turn on the light. The grunting sounds of the part boy, part animal by the front door guide me in his direction. Daddy knows this, too, and spares me from having to see the damage to Devon Whittaker. I don't need a light on to know the boy is in bad shape.

"Who did this to you?"

I drop the towels by his side and see the whites of Devon's eyes glaring at me. A jumble of pain and regret is staring back at me.

"Go grab some ice."

I follow Daddy's instructions and return with a foamy pack from the freezer. He is tending to wounds and bumps in a darkened haze, all the while calming Devon with his voice. I escape to the opposite side of the room, my eyes clamped shut.

"Devon, you gotta tell me what happened."

"I shot him," he weeps. "My dad. I shot him."

The blaring sounds of the sirens approaching our house combine with my relief.

"He's gone," he adds.

I am ashamed to be relieved that someone has died.

"He came after me," he pants. "He said I betrayed him. The gun went off . . . he was dead. I had to get away . . . his car." He stops to catch his breath. "He would've killed me. He was ready to shoot."

Daddy is listening to all this, trying to stay calm. "You did right," he says. "You were protecting yourself, son. He won't hurt you anymore."

Devon succumbs to his injuries and falls out of consciousness. I'm not really sure where his wounds are, though I know what it feels like when a parent disappoints you. The EMTs are in the house, crawling along the dark space surrounding Devon. When they turn the lights on, I have to leave the room. I don't walk. I run toward the hallway and kick my door open. I dial E.J. again, just to hear his voice on the message. I hang up and call again and again and again.

Hours later we—me and my dad—are back in CMC-Mercy sitting in Devon's room. People like Devon don't get many visitors. Ruby's boss wouldn't let her leave her job to come visit. The way he sees it, he can't let his employees leave whenever one of their kids gets into trouble. The other visitor is a detective with the local police. He had spoken with E.J. earlier in the day, and now it's Devon's turn to corroborate the story.

Devon has several broken ribs, a broken arm, a mild concussion, and multiple stitches along his cheek and back. There is some internal bleeding from where Ellis kicked him in the stomach with his work boots. His face is badly bruised and his top lip, a scary shade of purple.

It hurts for him to talk, but he opens his eyes to confess. The detective informs him that a surveillance video at the burglarized home had a clear picture of Devon's face. Because the jewelry was returned and E.J. explained the circumstances surrounding Devon's plight, the couple who lived in the house decided not to press charges. They took a liking to E.J. and the graceful way he protected his brother. Besides, they got their jewelry back. They figured it was best to put the event behind them. E.J. would have gone on lying to protect his brother forever. That's the boy I fell in love with.

I can tell the minute he walks into the hospital room that he wonders why I'm there. Why does this boy have to be so darn pigheaded? With Ellis and his threats gone, there is no reason for us to be apart. He disagrees. But he's seen what one incident in his family's life can do to us. That's why he argued with me that people like us need to know when it's time to let go. I didn't want to let go. And I think he will soften over time. He is just feeling spooked. Doesn't he know I will never give up on him?

"You're lucky Mama's not here to see you," he says to his brother, taking a seat beside his bed. Devon is in a half sleep, caught between painkillers and wanting to crack a smile. He doesn't say much, though he knows we are all there.

E.J.'s wearing a black Lees-McRae College sweatshirt that I think Daddy gave to him. His sweatpants are neon yellow, the same ones I sat on a few weeks ago, long before everything went crazy. And there is his scent, traveling through my nose to my mind and to the secret parts of me that only he can inflame. He looks in my direction and nods.

I wish I could go to him. I am not sure that my heart will listen to the stampeding denials of my brain. Daddy sees me eyeing E.J. as he takes hold of his brother's hand. E.J. has beautiful hands, rich brown with long, long fingers. I must radiate thirst, because Daddy tells me to go to the cafeteria and grab him a diet Coke.

When I return, I hand Daddy a regular Coke instead. "Aspartame will kill you," I say.

Usually this would get a laugh out of E.J. Not anymore. E.J. is distant. He talks to my dad as though I'm not in the room. It feels like I have intruded on something, and the exclusion hurts.

Angry and confused, I escape into the hallway and slump to the linoleum-covered floor. Their voices drift through the hallway and into my ears. I shut my eyes and listen.

"I wish I could give you some wise fatherly advice right now, like how to deal with grief. There's no quick fix. Time. That's about it. One day at a time."

E.J. says he's all right. "Ellis was never my daddy. My mama raised me. She was the one who made sacrifices."

Then Daddy starts talking to him about football and his future. E.J. says, "You saved my brother."

"Devon saved himself."

"You believed in him."

"I believe in all my boys. They need to trust what's inside of them. It's been inside Devon all along. I told you, son, when you love something, you have to learn to protect it. You fight for it. For them. You don't let them go."

I am certain Daddy is referring to me, and I feel the blush across my cheeks. But when he says what he says next, the blood drains from my face.

"Football. Football is going to take you out of here. When you love something this much, it'll love you back. I know you've been battling stuff. We all got battles. Some we win and some we lose. What matters is how you handle those battles. Win with integrity. Lose without losing yourself. Stay faithful to who you are, E.J., and you'll always be a winner."

E.J. mumbles something, and Daddy tells him he expects him on the field tomorrow. "And Devon, as soon as you're back on your feet, you can come too. It might not be much to start, but you'll help me with operations. Maybe I'll even let you assist my defensive line coach. One caveat: you keep your nose clean. I won't protect you again."

"I don't know how to thank you, Coach," E.J. says.

"Yes, you do. You both do."

CHAPTER TWENTY-SEVEN

RYAN

The drive to Cold Creek feels longer than usual. I would have skipped Ellis's funeral if not for E.J. The boy feigned control, but I knew he was about to break. We decided as a team we would show our support for one of our own. Devon was there, a shade healthier than the days before, and beside him was Ruby, impossibly elegant in her bright purple dress and matching hat. The woman has a heart as big as her floor-length black jacket. No matter how awful Ellis had become, Ruby was there for her children when they needed her.

I don't particularly care for cemeteries. They remind me of what I've lost, the two parents I've buried, and I don't like the feeling of vulnerability. My daughter stood beside me. She dressed in black, which made her seem older than sixteen, more like a woman whose childhood leaked from her eyes. I saw how she yearned for E.J. to face her. I knew she wants so badly for things to be the way they once were. How easy to revert back to the familiar and unchanged.

I should have listened to the prayers, but I have never been one to pray openly or believe in God. I think we all have a higher power within us that we hold ourselves up to, and against, in times of need. To me, prayer is positive thought.

The reverend spoke a few words and the small number of guests and family members tipped their hats to the stricken Whittakers. The sturdy casket was draped with a single bouquet, a token provided by the funeral home. It was a cold November, and the forecasters had predicted an early storm that would frost the stark trees. A cloud from his breath filled the sky when he spoke, forming a misty veil above his head. I was convinced the cold was Ellis's spirit collecting all the warmth from the air. Just as he stripped those around him of life, he could transform the air into thick, unbreathable swells.

Looking down at the casket, I imagined how days earlier I was standing across from Ellis while he antagonized me and my daughter. Then in a sliver of night sky, only hours later, he was gone. *Poof!* Like that. Senseless crimes rock me to the very core, and even though Ellis's demise was by no means a surprise to anyone in our town, the finality of his death sent ripples throughout the community.

The sadness snuck inside my jacket and grabbed hold of my throat. It would not let go.

I pulled at my tie, thinking I could breathe more easily without the confining fabric around my neck. The tie was my favorite, or Abby's, because what was best for her quickly became best for me. I always attributed that to being a guy who didn't care about what he wore, though it was probably more than that.

The ring of the phone is shrill, echoing through the truck's speaker system. My cell is in the glove compartment. It's there whenever I drive, so I'm not tempted to peek. ESPN and MaxPreps send me notifications daily. After I had made a few too many risky moves behind the wheel—checking my texts—I learned to tuck it away. Now I hit "send" on the screen next to the wheel and the phone connects. Her voice is so close, her breath is on my cheeks.

"Ryan, I'm sorry to bother you," she says.

If I weren't driving, I'd shut my eyes and let her soft voice take me somewhere far away. Somewhere I might rest my head and sleep. Somewhere I might imagine what could've been, what might've been, had she not left. A haven free of criminal parents and a wife who is sick.

"Ryan?" she says my name again.

"I'm here."

"Can we talk?"

Something about Lauren has always loosened me, weakened my ability to control myself. I clear my throat, ignoring her request. "Do you ever wonder what would've happened?" I ask.

She is silent, and I imagine her draped across the couch that's overlooking the mountains. I think about how my words are wearing away at the walls we put up.

"If you hadn't left," I repeat, "do you ever wonder what would've happened to us?"

She whispers, "I'm not sure what you mean."

"Come on, Laur, I know you. Every inch of you. Don't tell me you haven't thought about it."

I should tell her I love her. That I never stopped loving her. Her face and her eyes followed me around for years, staying with me long after we first said good-bye. It takes all my strength to keep my thoughts to myself.

"I'll be driving through Charlotte this week on the way to shoot the last of the falls. Can we grab coffee?"

"Didn't we say everything we had to say at the house?"

"No," she says, "we didn't."

As I pass through the stone entryway, the private drive tugs me away from Lauren and hoists me toward my wife. "I'm pulling into Cold Creek," I say.

"I need to see you."

Hearing Lauren, the person I have quietly loved my entire life, tell me that she needs to see me feels like rain as I stand in a desert. My whole body awakens. But just as swiftly as the raindrops cover me, they evaporate.

"The café at the bookstore? Say, three o'clock?"

"I moved on, Lauren. Isn't that what you wanted me to do?"

The quiet space between us edges us close and then apart.

"I'll be there," she says. "If you change your mind."

She hangs up, and I'm not sure if she said good-bye. The media screen on the dashboard reads, "Call ended." The finality of it all cuts me every time. Good-byes always confuse me.

I wrap my coat around my shoulders and head toward Cold Creek's visitor center. The afternoon is as depressing as my mood: dark and mean. Abby waits for me where she always sits when she knows I'm coming, beside the fireplace, sipping some herbal tea that helps her sleep. She stands up to greet me, and even though we both try to find each other's lips, we instead greet each other warmly on the cheek. Her hair is pulled back off her face in an orange strip of fabric, and her lips have a pink shine. She looks twenty-one again in her tight jeans and sweater.

We walk hand in hand outside. This is what we do. Despite being alienated from the monotony of our marriage, we have found a way to make our separation as predictable and comfortable as home. Abby takes me outside to one of the many trails on the grounds, and we walk and talk. The cold bites at our fingers and feet. I ask her if she's warm enough, and she tells me she is. "I've grown used to having another layer around me," and I know at once she doesn't mean a jacket. It's what they're teaching her in here. I'm getting pretty used to the insights that pop out of Abby's mouth—she calls them "balance-enhancing phrases" that keep her whole. What the heck do I know? I'm a football coach.

We set out along the perimeter trail, a walking path that runs parallel to a stream. The water is scarce this time of year, and the trickle helps me relax. I tell her about E.J. and Ellis, and she apologizes for her absence. "Juliana needs me."

"She's a good girl. She knows this is the best thing for all of us."

"I miss her," she says, turning to me.

I know I should hug her. That is the cue for one of us to make the gesture toward the other. Instead, we stare into each other's eyes until one of us turns away. Abby is very different from when I last visited. She has lost something, but she has gained something too. I don't know what it is, but it's the reason I keep my distance, and probably the reason she keeps hers.

When neither of us initiates contact, we resume our walk and forgo our usual seat in the garden. Abby talks with her hands. Today they are darting out in front of her. She's distracted. Something big is on her mind. "Why are we doing this?" she asks.

"I'm not sure I understand."

"We're pretending everything is normal when it's not. It's freezing frickin' cold out here, and we walk the same path every time we meet even though it doesn't take us anywhere."

"I thought you liked walking. You said you liked when things are orderly and predictable."

She sighs. It's a big one.

"What's wrong?" I ask.

She waves her fingers in the air, and I see that Sybil has painted her nails a new dark color, to match her eyes. "You just don't get it." Then she turns from me and heads inside.

I follow her through the doorway of her room. Sybil and Rose don't even try to get me to play games with them. Despite how much better my wife looks, the girls are eyeing me, signaling for me to be cautious as they file from the room.

I throw myself across her twin bed with the frilly yellow comforter and sheets, arms folded behind my head. She's in the nearby rocker, which she's dragged to the side of the bed. The room feels too small for us, for all our problems. I begin by saying, "I thought you were doing better. What do the doctors say?"

The hands come to life again. "They say I've made significant progress, though it would be nice if you noticed the change so I didn't have to point it out."

I look at my wife, and I am trapped in a maze of helplessness. I bow my head and she goes into more detail about her therapy and what she calls the "masterful web that had her brain on fire." It's unsettling, heavy stuff, and my mind can't immediately wrap itself around the conclusions she's drawing, or adjust to the degrees of complexity that, at times, make my wife a stranger.

"I've learned a lot—I know this is gibberish to you—a lot of self-reflection and how to let go of blame and anger. To accept others, and myself." She is hardly talking to me. Her eyes are focused on something on the wall, and she's brushing her fingers through her hair. "Some stuff's been easier to look at than the other."

Then I remember, and before I can rope the words in, they charge from my mouth.

"She was here, wasn't she?"

"How did you know?" she asks, the accusation lining her face.

"I had a feeling this would happen."

"You knew? You knew she was back in town?"

I should sit up, but I am pretending this information doesn't unnerve me. I'm not sure why I have failed to mention that I saw her and that her voice was in my ears only moments ago. Her presence is all around us, beginning with the picture Abby found in my drawer, proof that it was impossible for the three of us to fully separate. The stop and go of my heart is almost as distracting. Lauren is the puppeteer, masterfully pulling on our strings.

Abby blinks. Her hands fall to the sides of the chair. "I can't believe this." And I wait for her attack, but it doesn't come. "Look at us, look at us keeping things from each other . . . It can't work like this. Seeing her was hard, but she was right . . . I failed her, and you, and I can live with that, but not with the goddamn secrets."

I don't know what to say. Talking about Lauren hurts. I sit up and try to rid myself of the feelings. "I think we failed her together."

"No," she starts, and then stops herself. I watch her finger the arms of the rocking chair. The chair tips close to the bed and then slowly away. She looks serious and scared.

Abby continues: "This is when I'm supposed to tell you how she destroyed you when she abandoned you. How she didn't bother calling or showing up. She didn't care about either one of us, but mostly she didn't care about you. Always you. That's what you want to hear, right?"

I'm confused, though I say what I believe she wants me to say: "It doesn't matter, Abs. It was a long time ago. We were young. Things happened the way they were supposed to happen."

"If I say those things, you'll feel better about that night. You'll feel less guilty, right? It'll help for a few minutes, until the next time. We've been so good at relieving ourselves of our guilt because it's been so easy to blame Lauren." I'm not sure where she's going with this, and I feel her bracing herself for something big. She is watching my reactions like a hawk. I feel naked under her stare. She breaks the silence: "How much do you love me, Ryan?"

I feel like this is a trick question. My body tenses and I finger the band around my left ring finger. "You know how I feel about you, Abby."

"That's not really an answer," she says, and I notice a cloudiness to her eyes. They are about to cry. "Did you ever love me the way you once loved her?"

I search the comforter for the answer, anything to avoid looking at those tears. Of course I love Abby, but it's different from my love for Lauren. How could I compare the level of love I've felt for any two people? Feelings are too complicated. She leans forward and takes my hand in one of hers while the other grabs hold of my chin. She does this so I can't turn away. She looks frightened and determined all at once.

The seriousness of her face matches the gravity of her words. She speaks slowly, deliberately: "If I told you that Lauren had shown up, that she hadn't abandoned you, that she was there for you, would we be together today?"

"What does it matter?" I say, shaking my head, pushing the possibility away. "She wasn't there."

She settles back in the chair, grabbing the handles. Her hair falls against her shoulders, and the words fall off her tongue as though she had practiced them for years: "She was there, Ryan. I saw her. She saw me."

It takes me a minute to put together what she's saying. The force of the blow knocks the air out of me, and I feel myself moving away from her. "What are you talking about?"

"Lauren. She came for you."

I am sure she is joking or testing me or playing some twisted hoax. I even let out a laugh. "Lauren wasn't there. I would've known. She would've let me know."

"I was on top of you, Ryan. Do I need to remind you? She was there." The rest of it comes out from a distant place inside of her I don't even recognize. Her face is emotionless. "I can't say why she didn't call out, but I saw her standing there in the doorway."

I drop my head in my hands and turn away from her. She is talking to me, and I hear bits of what's coming from her mouth, but it's muffled by the sounds of my denials. My shoulders hunch forward. I don't want to hear this. I don't want to hear how Abby has manipulated the truth.

"Before I could say anything, she was gone."

"It's not possible," I hear myself say. My fingers run through my hair in disbelief. *No. It can't be!* If she were there, everything would be different. What happened that day was wrong, but it had made sense because Lauren wasn't there. It was her absence that had let us act without reason.

"It's possible," she whispers.

Her words seep inside me, where they mix with an assortment of misgivings weighing me down. Years of my life have been stolen. Possibilities have been burned to the ground. They fight with one another to come out. I am disciplined enough to keep them from the surface. "You saw her?"

"I did."

"And you didn't tell me?"

She rocks back and forth in the wooden chair. I want to grab hold of the chair's arms and shake it, shake her, toss them both across the room. The brown of her eyes is filled with tears. I can't even begin to process this information. There is no way to know how.

Lauren. She was there.

Lauren walked in on me having sex with her best friend.

It has been too long, but I know the number of years by heart. The betrayal shouldn't hit me as hard as it does. It feels like yesterday—the sting, raw and bubbly. Her eyes invade my memory. Her long legs, the orange wisps of hair. I built a future based on lies, on facts my wife chose to rearrange and misplace—it has crushed my lungs and the ability to breathe. I can't hear these confessions and bury them with my long-ago feelings. I can't do that. I feel cheated and pissed.

"How much do you love me now?" she asks again.

I stand up and force myself to sit back down. "How could you keep this from me?"

"You know why. Don't make me say it."

"For all these years!" I shout to her face. "Didn't I deserve the truth?"

"I had no idea she was going to leave, like, really leave! I thought she would confront me later. Confront you." She reaches for me, but I back up. It is a reflex I can't control. Her lower lip trembles when she says, "I just wanted that moment with you. I knew we would never be together. I knew you could never love me the way you loved her. I just wanted that night." She collapses into something small and cowardly. I feel achingly sorry for her.

"Days went by and I waited for her to show up. Every time the phone rang, I jumped. Every time you called me, I was on edge. Then I found out I was pregnant . . .

"By then I was convinced you cared. It was a lot easier to tell myself that she did this to us, that we didn't do this to her. *She* was selfish. *She* left. And she never called! How long were we expected to wait for her to show up?"

My wife crumbles into an unrecognizable mess. Whatever beauty had earlier lit up her face is now replaced with ugly shame. Her dark hair makes her scary. Her lips seem to wince.

"I know you're angry. I know you're disappointed in me. I've lived with this for far too long. It has eaten me alive. Knowing I was your second choice, knowing I lied to you for years—it has crippled me. If I lose you now, that's the price I pay. But being in here has forced me to face what I've never wanted to and to finally make things right."

I am furious. My words are stiff and calculated like her: "What the hell do you want me to say?"

"Say you forgive me."

"Jesus, Abby, you just dropped a bomb on me!"

"Ryan." My name falls from her tortured lips. Her eyes, rimmed in red, are pleading, "Please don't hate me. Please. I'm doing the best I can. This was no easy confession. I'm saying I'm sorry. What I did was wrong."

I have watched my wife struggle since I've known her. I have felt her whole body shiver in the heat of summer. I have heard her sobs when she thought no one was listening. I know firsthand how she's surrendered herself. I've been the one to pick her up off the floor, the one to intercept the phone calls from her parents and Juliana's school, the one to study the lines on her face, looking for the script of how I am supposed to act. Cold Creek was a huge step for her, for all of us. Did this effort matter when something this huge now pins us apart?

"I'm trying to fix this," she says. "I'm sorry that it hurts."

"I need to think about it." My eyes are stinging. Wiping them doesn't release the burn. She tries to stop me, though I am off the bed and walking toward the door.

"Where are you going?" she asks, getting up from the chair, too afraid to come any closer.

"I can't be here right now."

Her eyes beg for me to stay, and the plea shrouds her face in shame. "Ryan, please don't go, please don't do this . . . Please talk to me."

She is weak and desperate, crying and trembling. I think it's too late.

"I can't be here," I tell her again.

The door slams behind me and all I can think to myself is that I hate my wife.

CHAPTER TWENTY-EIGHT

ABBY

I have lived in fear much of my life, mostly of thoughts that were fighting to come out. For the first time, I am plagued with real danger.

It's over. He's going to leave me.

I can't breathe. I sink back into the rocker, and I wish for it to wash me down, taking the feelings along with it. But it won't. Instead, I have to face the panic, accept the feelings, and ride out the thick layer of emotions that curdle my insides and make me want to run. This is what Jeannie has been describing to me. This is the test of how far I have come. Jeannie's voice reminds me to experience the feelings. Anger can no longer be turned inward. Fear must thrive. Though the fury of the emotions makes my body tremble, and it feels like I'm dying, I cannot die from a feeling.

My eyelids close, and I find my inner balance. After a few satisfying breaths, I am able to guide my feet the few steps to the bed, where I collapse. I turn over and smell Ryan on the covers. The tears roll off my cheeks, and I quiet my brain from shushing them away. My mind once called me a coward for crying, so I am allowing myself to cry. My beating heart once told me I was crippled when its rapid speed paralyzed my arms and legs. So I tell my heart she is okay. She is just scared. I comfort her. My soul screams at me: "You are evil and bad for what you did, and no one will ever love you." So I whisper to her: "You are human. You make mistakes. You'll get through this."

CHAPTER TWENTY-NINE

LAUREN

I am in the parking lot of my favorite indie bookstore, and I don't expect Ryan to show up. I know his feelings for me are mingled with anger and regret. Besides, I've read in the paper that he's gearing up for the state championship.

One of the few things I missed while shooting the falls, far from city lights, was this bookstore. The bustling world moves at a frantic pace, but I slow down when stepping into the cozy space with pathways to the imagination. The rooms are filled with my closest friends, and the welcoming no longer eludes me. For years, I have disguised myself behind my work, my pen name a shield, the armor that protects me from critics' scrutiny. It has also distanced me from readers who have written letters to Quinci about how they've been touched.

I never set out to become a well-known author. Though I enjoy the process of spinning words into sentences that matter, it is carving out the story and intersecting characters' lives that moves me to sit at my desk each day. I've always said there are great writers and great storytellers. I'm no Wharton or Brontë, but I can tell a good tale.

Searching for the travel section, I pass a long line of books promising adventure. It's hard to feel alone when possibilities are summoning me to slip inside a book's pages.

I'm looking for a specific title. Quinci asked me to check out a book that claimed to have a similar premise as ours. My cell rings, and I know it is her. The woman has an antenna that stretches across time zones. "Did you find it?"

"What's it called again?"

"The *Mountain River* or *River Mountains*. Something like that."

My eyes catch sight of the shooting cascades of Iguazu on the cover. The book is half the size of ours and not nearly as dramatic. It feels flat and artificial. "I'm not worried, Q."

"Did you visit our friend, Ms. Sutherland?"

She knows I never visit my books. Once I have given birth to one, I see the book as no longer mine. Except today I can't squelch the curiosity.

"Go look!" she squeals, as only Quinci can.

As I turn the corner of travel and cross in to romance, he finds me.

"I've gotta go, Q." She keeps talking, but I have zapped her from the screen.

He's standing in front of me, and around me, the words from the pages seem to fill the aisle, shouting our names, screaming their versions of our story.

"Hey," he says.

I dressed casually for the day: jeans, Uggs, black sweater. My messenger bag is over my shoulder, and I drop my phone into the opening at the top. He is leaning against a shelf of Roberts, Steel, and me—Virginia Sutherland. His Giants sweat suit is gray and somber like his face. "Hi," I say to his clear green eyes.

"Do you remember when you had that horrible stomach virus and I read to you?" he asks.

I nod.

"You were always a sucker for a mystery."

He grabs my arm and leads me down another aisle. It is not the way I'd imagined him touching me again, angry and unkind. We pass John Green and Lauren Oliver when he says, "I'm the one who's been in the dark."

He looks tense and preoccupied, guiding me through more aisles and then the cafe. "She told you?" I ask.

"Do you really want to talk about this here?" he asks.

I thought the faces of my friends would shield us from any eruptions. I realize now what a mistake I've made. He knows the truth, and he is about to explode.

Neither of us speaks as we exit the double doors.

"My truck's over there. Let's go for a drive."

The truck is huge. There are large doors and windows, and it seems to go on for miles. Inside and out, the color is dark and masculine, almost mean. When it roars to life, I expect it to holler at me, too. I pull my jacket around me, and he instinctively turns up the heat. It feels wrong and unnatural being there in Abby's seat. Though she hadn't thought it was wrong to take mine.

We drive in silence before I ask about her.

"She's all right," he says.

"I used to be able to read you better."

He doesn't answer. He fingers his messy brown hair with one hand and grips the wheel with the other.

The lightly trafficked streets are leading us into the town of Davidson. As we enter the bucolic land of our youth, the memories resurface, tugging us back in time. We are quiet with our thoughts, revisiting a past that once had meaning. It's nearing Thanksgiving and already the trees and storefronts are decorated with holiday lights. Summit Coffee. Raeford's Barber Shop. The sprinkling bulbs spring life into a chilly, gray afternoon.

The thing about nostalgia is that it sneaks inside of you when you're not expecting it. When you get used to living without someone, you think you're immune to the emotions that grab you when they reappear.

I have lived a hundred lives without Ryan. I have immersed myself in the pages of my books, something he knows nothing about, and the cracks in the land—without him as my anchor. I have fallen in love. I have made love. And still I drive the streets where we began, and I am thrust through time, harnessed to his memory, tethered to his heart. The anger has lessened, replaced with a sentimental whiff that clouds my judgment. I'm not entirely sure if what I'm feeling for Ryan is real, or the memory of what used to be.

"This is what you meant when you said it was complicated. Were you going to tell me today?" he asks. "Is that why you called?"

"Yes. In part."

He finds a spot on Main Street and pulls the truck to a stop, turning to me: "I don't know if I can handle much more honesty." Then he opens the door and hops out. I take a deep inhale before following him.

We cross the street toward the campus. Davidson is a mere square mile, so it doesn't take us long to pass the main academic building with its impressive dome, the library, and the new science building. Around us, students are rushing to class to finish assignments and exams in time for the extended break. We had walked these pathways for four years. Now they feel haunted, as though our former selves had trickled into the brick and are fighting to come out. The buildings are more beautiful than I remember. I feel both safe and vulnerable here. The innocence of my youth is colliding with forbidden feelings.

We follow the stone path and pass Phi and Eu Halls, and the open porches where some of the greatest student debates were held across the lawn. The church pops up on our right, and we end up at the well. The trees are bare, jutting into a gray sky. Deep green ivy swaddles the brick arches. The last dying leaves are gathered on the floor in brown piles. They are a reminder of the fragility of life. I know that now. There is no in between.

He is agitated. He sits on the cold stone, then gets up again.

"This is where you told me you loved me for the first time," I say. "Right there." I am pointing at the stone benches that surround the arch and its pointed green crown. There is a streetlight behind us. It is flickering, caught between daytime and the shade of an early moon.

"Why didn't you tell me you were there? Didn't I deserve to know the truth?"

I begin, but the words won't come out. I have rehearsed them a million times, and now, seeing how much pain I have caused, I forget how to speak.

He raises his voice when he asks again, "Why?"

We are standing a few inches apart. His accusations crowd the air rising above us. I feel something damp flow down my face. His eyes burrowing into my own cause the pain. I gently ask, "How could you?" but I can't finish. His eyes stop me like a kiss, and words don't come.

I have to turn away or I will do something desperate and wrong. I gaze out at the place we first fell in love. Ryan sits again, with his head is in his hands, and waits.

My frustration gushes to the surface. I am a geyser, bursting with bottled-up emotion. "What did you expect from me? I was halfway around the world with no reception, and when I found a landline, no one answered the phone. Maybe I should've left a message, maybe I should've called a thousand more times, but I wasn't thinking. All that mattered was getting to you. When I walked in the door . . . She was . . . God, Ryan, what were you thinking? Do you have any idea what you did to me? I spent weeks in shock—which turned into years. So no, I didn't think to let you know I was there. It wouldn't have changed what I saw."

He can't look at me.

"Aren't you going to say anything?" I ask.

"What do you want me to say? I can't tell you my life with Abby hasn't meant anything. Or that I didn't think about you all these years, that I wished I would have married you. She's my wife, Lauren! I know what pain feels like. I lived with it when you left. I waited every day for a call. Anything to let me know you still cared. Everyone said I was a fool, but no one had what we had—no one."

I take the empty seat beside him on the bench. We aren't touching, though every part of him is so close I am sure we are joined somewhere inside. I don't look at him when I tell him I love him. "Not just back then, not all those years ago. Now," I say. "I still love you now."

Love and pain are so closely related, it hurts to tell him what I've longed to say. But when the words dissolve around us, I find his eyes and I know that true love does exist. I don't blink. I love Ryan with all of me and I know he feels it.

He doesn't answer. He's thinking about it, pressing it against him, pushing it away, this feeling that neither of us wants to carry into the present. Cars are honking around us, and a few students walk by. The only thing in life I'm sure of is that the world will go on as though my loss means nothing.

"Why are you telling me this? Why now? It would've meant a lot more if you had told me years ago."

I am sorry I hurt him with my silence, and I tell him so. My body shrinks beside him, letting him know that I'm not proud, that it was a mistake. "I was stupid to think I could leave and nothing would change. I should've told you I came back. I should've screamed at Abby and fought for you," I tell him. His silence is killing me, and I want this thing between us to make it impossible for him not to touch me, to forgive me. Slowly, my fingers find his hand. They stay there and he doesn't move them away. "I wasn't going to return to the program. When I walked in the door to your parents' house, I had already decided it was too hard to be away. I thought we were going to start our life together. But when I saw her . . . Something inside me snapped." We are connected. I feel every part of him sprouting through his palm. "All that bitterness, I stuffed it away. I wonder if we could have lessened the damage if the three of us weren't so darn stubborn."

He stares at me, and I wonder if my words are lost in his ears. We thought we had forgotten what touch could do to us. His hand on mine tells me more than he's willing to admit. He knows it and swiftly pulls away.

"I'm tired of running, Ryan. I should've told you how I felt sooner, but I didn't know how. And then I just kept running. But when I saw you, it all came back. It was as though I'd never left. There were too many secrets. You needed the truth, and all of it. Maybe being here to finish the book is the closure we've all needed."

I stand up from the bench. "I'll be leaving soon. A few more falls and then I'll go. This time it'll be for the right reasons. There's nothing keeping me here anymore. I need to get away from this place. From you."

"Where will you go?" he asks.

"I'm not sure. Maybe Atlanta, New York. That's the nice part—I can go anywhere I want."

"What about the house? You love it there."

"I do. And I've lived without it for this long. I can meet my parents there for a quick weekend whenever I want. I just can't live there full-time."

He nods as though we hadn't shared the greatest love of all time in those mountains. I want to shake him and kiss him, and I want him to grab me in his arms and insist that I stay. I hate who he's become. I hate what Abby has done to him. His composure stings.

"Just know that I love you," I say again. "I never stopped. I thought I might have. I thought I knew how to live without you. Being near you right now, I know that I don't. Everything reminds me of you, of us. I don't know how to fight it anymore. I don't think I can."

Either he moves away from me or it is his words that make me feel distant.

"I'm a married man, Lauren. I'm not free to love you. I was waiting for you. Always waiting for you. You chose to leave. You could've come to me. You could've called. Every second that went by was another betrayal. You let me believe you didn't care. You handed me over to somebody else. Now I have a family. I have a wife. What you're asking of me is wrong."

"I'm not asking you to do anything."

"Then why tell me you love me?"

"I thought I felt something between us."

"You let me go. I moved on. I did what you wanted. It's too late."

"You slept with my best friend."

He is getting angry. "I did. And it was wrong. I was suffering and she made me feel good, but I have a daughter from that night. Hurting you was a mistake, but creating Juliana wasn't."

"I just need you to know. I lost you once before because I didn't let you know. I won't make that mistake again. Take from it whatever you want."

He grabs my arm and he pulls me toward him. His face is so close I can smell his breath, the familiar taste of his lips. I fight myself to lean forward. I fight myself to feel those lips against my mouth. I want to make him want me again. "I would've done anything for you," he says. "Our love made me believe we were bigger and stronger than anything that tried to keep us apart. I'm sorry, Lauren. I'm sorry I hurt you. I loved you. Man, I loved you. Different from how I'll ever love anyone else." Then he takes my hands into his and squeezes. "You were the love of my life. I'm so sorry we didn't make it. I'm so sorry for what happened to us." And I know he means it because the regret that falls from his lips twists the words into a whisper.

I can barely breathe, and the tears are creeping down my face. The effort to pull away from him is bigger than both of us.

"You and Abby have fought long and hard. You should be happy. I want you both to finally be happy." Then I force myself to say: "I'll manage without you, Ryan. I promise. I did it once before."

And he touches my cheek with the back of his hand, and I let the warmth of his fingers fool me into thinking what I'm saying is true. I'll never manage without Ryan, but I love him too much to say otherwise.

CHAPTER THIRTY

RYAN

The drive back to Lauren's car is a quiet one. She doesn't wait for me to put the truck in park before she jumps out. She's a vision in black and orange.

She trips over something on the way to her car, and a man with his son helps her to her feet. I should have gotten out, but my legs wouldn't move. I watch the man search her eyes and appraise her, and I want to circle back and punch him.

I press on the gas a bit harder than I should, making the tires squeal, and I hightail it out of the parking lot, away from Lauren and everything I spent years trying to forget—the way she bounced when she walked, the way her lips pursed in a sulk when she was sad, how I felt when she whispered that she loved me. Normally I would snatch those three words from the sky. Today I let them go. I let her go. And it broke my heart to see the words trail off into nowhere.

"Damn it!" I shout at the steering wheel.

My watch tells me that practice has begun. I'll be late and my boys will worry. I slap the wheel again and again, barking at the traffic that clogs the road and my thoughts.

I am weaving in and out of lanes. If Abby were in the car with me, she'd grab at the door handle or the seat in front of her, petrified by my aggression. Abby. *What have we done?* I need to hear her voice. I need something stabilizing after what Lauren's words have done to me.

I should be able to speak her name out loud and have the woman who lives in my dashboard connect us, but I have not mastered the outgoing call commands on the phone. The traffic has slowed to a crawl, so I reach across the seats and snatch the phone from the glove compartment. When I press the number 1 on the screen, Abby's picture flashes across the glass. The call goes directly to voice mail. For an instant I forget she's not waiting for me at home with her cell phone.

Another pause in traffic allows me to dial the number of Cold Creek. After a short wait, they put me through to her room, and I toss the phone on the seat next to me as we talk over the speaker.

"Ryan? What's wrong?"

I am speechless.

"Ryan? Are you there?"

I pause, then: "We need to talk."

Her questions cease and quiet fills the car.

"Hello," I say.

"I'm here."

"I was with Lauren."

She pauses before she says anything. The silence is filled with uncertainty. Then she asks, "Are you okay?"

"What do you think? None of this makes any sense."

She sounds like she's getting teary and emotional. "What I did was selfish and wrong," she tells me.

"You're damn right."

I'm about to pull into the high school campus. The lights up ahead drag me away from the conversation. I see my boys running laps, a few of them talking to Wayne. There's Devon. He's banged up, but he's made every effort to show up and do what he can. I had told him to take it slow, but he's already running drills with my defensive line. The tight grip on my chest is beginning to loosen.

Abby asks if I can forgive her, if the life we've created is enough. "Haven't we proved what we mean to each other?"

I am shaking my head no, though she can't see that. I love someone else too. I never stopped.

"My God, Ryan. What are you thinking?"

I say, "You're my wife. We made vows. I'm committed to you. We're just going to have to work through this and everything else."

"I love you," she says.

"Yeah. I'm at the field now. I'll call you later."

The boys greet me with enthusiasm. Wayne shouts across the tired grass, "It'd better be worth it. First time you've ever been late to one of my practices."

It wasn't worth it, not at all.

We get through stretches and some offensive plays before E.J. lands beside me and asks if I'm all right. It's good to have him back on my field, but I don't tell him that. "Keep your mind on the ball!" I bark at him, before he turns away from me and makes a carry into the end zone. The boy is damn good. I congratulate him by pointing out that his right foot touched the line, out of bounds, at the ten: "That'll cost you the touchdown. Take a lap."

The energy has shifted on the field. I am being too hard and too short, and Wayne catches up to me with a snide remark: "Girl trouble?"

Wayne knows there's nothing that riles me up more than my girls.

The boys are feeling my push. Despite the frigid weather, they are flushed and out of breath. My coaching is wobbly and frenetic. A true leader never lets his players see his weaknesses. I tell them to take a ten-minute break, and they flee for the locker room.

Wayne holds a football in his thick fingers.

He chucks it at me. It bounces off my arm before I have a chance to catch it.

"What's got you all twisted?" he asks. "Which one of them girls?"

I think about how to answer.

"Son," he says, "whatever it is, we've got the biggest game of the season coming up."

"With all due respect, Wayne, I'm not up for a speech today."

"We can't afford to get sloppy. Not now. We've gotta be focused. Keep our eyes on the prize."

"I know all this."

"It's about timing, Ryan. Choices. Don't be wasting your time on things you can't control."

Before I realize it, I am in his face raising my voice. "I'm a married man, and I can't stop thinking about another woman."

His eyes widen. "Can you repeat that?"

"You heard me," I say, scrambling for the ball that he's dropped on the floor. I take a few steps back and fire it at him. Uncovering this truth makes me feel alive. "Lauren's in town. Damn woman told me she loves me."

Wayne laughs a loud, belly-shaking hoot.

"You keep on laughing there, old man," I say, while he drops my next two passes.

"You tell them boys all the time to go after what they love. You preach to them to be true to themselves."

There is no reason to spell it out for him. He understands my hesitation and says, "She hasn't been a wife for a long, long time. You're as stubborn as my wide receivers. I tell them to turn right, they go left. They don't see the whole field when they're lookin' left."

"She got me in the blind side," I say.

"You've held on to that girl for too long." And I have no idea which one of them he's referring to.

"Abby's coming home soon. We got a championship in sight. Besides, Lauren's leaving. Going off somewhere. Nothing for her here."

"That's the most pathetic line of crap I've heard. Boy, you're stubborn. And dumb."

"Abby and I don't have what you and June have. We never will. But I'm not about to leave her now. Not when she's hurting the way she is."

He tosses another bullet in my direction. This time I catch it in two hands. "What about what you want?"

"I'm just fine, Wayne. I've got everything I need."

The boys come in pairs back onto the field. I try to stay focused the remaining hour, but my thoughts keep drifting away. Our defense is solid. We'll have to go over a few drills with the offensive line tomorrow. The boys are tired and taking their cues from me, and I'm of no help to any of us.

The whistle blows, and Wayne follows the boys into the locker room. "Are you coming?" he asks.

I tell him I'll catch up with him in a few minutes. Instead, I take a seat in the middle of the field. I sit back against the turf and stare into the night sky. Vince Lombardi once said, "The difference between a successful person and others is not a lack of strength, not a lack of knowledge, but rather a lack of will." I had persevered on the field. Despite losses and setbacks, I had succeeded as an athlete and a coach. How had I failed to have this determination in my life off the field? When I got knocked down, I didn't get back up. It's no wonder Abby and I have spent the better part of our married years with me half alive, half a step behind.

I see Lauren in the air above me. She's telling me she loves me, and I'm ignoring her, hiding all that it is in my heart. It took every ounce of strength to turn away from her. Football is about the team. It's about loyalty. Isn't marriage supposed to be the same?

CHAPTER THIRTY-ONE

JULIANA

What the heck is my daddy doing?

I am steering my car through the student parking lot when I see a lone figure on the field. He looks like one of those snow angels with his arms and legs stretched across the green. Only there's no snow, and Daddy looks like he's dreaming.

Devon and E.J. are walking out of the locker room when I take my eyes off Daddy and smile up at E.J. "I'm going to keep stalking you until you answer my calls, E.J. Tell him I've got nothing to be afraid of, Devon."

The brothers are smiling. Devon elbows his brother. "You should be afraid of this one. Very afraid."

E.J. is softening, and I can tell how happy he is to see me. His angry face is gone, but it's fighting with his "I'm sorry, I was wrong" face.

"What's up with Coach?" I ask, and our three sets of eyes rest on the figure on the fifty-yard line.

"Something's got him acting all crazy," says E.J. "He was a bear at practice."

"Stay here. I'll be right back. I can drive you two home."

"Nah, Jules, we're gonna catch the bus. Or one of the guys will take us."

"Jules," I say to him. "You called me Jules."

E.J. blushes. The boy still loves me, and I'm giddy inside.

"Please just wait for me."

He dips his head down and tells me another time. This playing-hard-to-get crap is tiring.

I slip into the gated fence that leads to the field. The deserted space and its measured green are far more imposing in their stillness, but that all changes when I see my daddy sprawled across the center.

Today was "dress-down day" at school. Instead of our crusty khaki uniform bottoms, we were allowed to wear jeans, and I was sporting my favorite skinnies. We had to wear the uniform top, though—red with the school's logo. Over it, I have on E.J.'s sweatshirt. E.J. didn't see it under my coat, but I know it's there.

I kneel before my dad and flop in the grass beside him. It takes a minute for him to sense I'm nearby. He doesn't open his eyes. He just reaches for me with one outstretched arm and pulls me close.

"Whatcha lookin' at?" I ask.

"Everything," he says.

"You're gettin' a little spooky on me, Daddy."

"Sorry, sweetheart. I got a lot on my mind."

I nuzzle into him. "Mama's coming home soon."

"Yep."

He's brushing my hair with his fingertips. I can tell why he comes out here. It's quiet, and nobody else would bother to disturb him.

"E.J. said you were a bear at practice."

"Are you two back together? I didn't get the bulletin."

"Nah," I say, "But soon . . . I love that boy, Daddy."

He is quiet, then: "You girls today are too dramatic."

"Ellis can't hurt us anymore."

He opens his eyes and turns to me. "You see, Jules, that's just it. When you love someone, you get hurt."

"Not always."

"You're young. Why tie yourself down to one person?"

"Would you prefer I be like the other girls my age who think it's cool to hook up with three different guys in an hour?"

"They do that?" He looks surprised. "Do you do that?"

"Gosh, Daddy. You're so old school."

He takes my hand and squeezes it hard. "You're out here thinking about E.J. and love, and you know what he's thinking about? Girls, sports, and food. Like all boys his age."

"E.J.'s different, Daddy."

"I know, I know. E.J.'s different. It's only a matter of time before you two get caught up in whatever it is you kids today call it. He's not going to say no to you forever. And kids your age aren't ready for that type of responsibility."

I say it again: "I love him."

"Enough to be a mother?"

"Um, Daddy, we just went from not even dating to having a baby."

"That's how it begins. A blink of the eye and your whole life has changed. You don't know how being a parent changes everything."

"He won't even hardly talk to me," I say with a shrug. "The sex thing isn't an issue."

"I'm liking that boy more every day."

"It's not funny." I jab at him. "He thinks he can protect me from the world by letting me go." He pulls me closer, and I feel the grass nipping through my skinnies and creeping into my boots.

"He'll come around, honey. Losing a parent is tough; give him some time."

"I'm just about dying inside, Daddy . . ."

He's not listening. He's staring up at the sky with a serious gaze pinned onto his face.

"If you had one wish to make on that one star up there, what would it be?" he asks.

I say, "Three more wishes."

"My greedy girl."

"For Mama to be better, for E.J. to take me back, and for you to smile again."

"Reasonable wishes."

"And yours?"

Daddy doesn't immediately answer. He's thinking about it, and I wonder what makes him pause. "Of course your mama getting healthy. Then for E.J. to continue to turn you down. And for you to know your worth, every day of your life. To know how loved you are."

"That's four."

"I could go on," he says. I don't know why his wishes make him look and sound so sad. He keeps staring up at the sky as if it has all the answers.

Something about being there on the field with Daddy lessens the pang of E.J.'s absence.

"You've made your mama and me real proud."

"I know," I say with a smile. Then I ask, "You and Mama, how'd you know she was the one?"

He takes a moment before telling me it's a long story.

"I'm not a baby anymore. I was at your wedding, for gosh sakes."

"Your mama's a fiery woman," he says, forming a cloud of cold air above us. I try to grab it in my palm.

"Is that a nice way of saying she's messed up?"

"You've had to deal with the brunt of her disease. It shouldn't have been like that."

"What about you? You've taken care of Mama better than any of my friends' daddies could. She could appreciate it more."

"She does. In her own way. Your mama hasn't always had it so easy."

"Lots of people don't have it easy," picking at the grass. Feeling the cold blades in my fingers.

"She can help herself only up to a certain point. Her brain works differently than ours. But she's doing a lot better. If she stays on the right medication, she'll be on the right track."

"Is she going to come out someone different?" I ask.

"She'll be your mama. A better version of the one you've had. Give her a break. And be a lady."

I shrug.

"She loves you so much, Jules. You've always been everything to her."

I don't have the heart to tell him she disappointed me when I needed her most. Instead, I lean in closer and tell him how thankful I am for him.

"Look at you making your daddy blush," he says, and though I'm not facing him, I can feel his smile smeared across his face.

"Cross that wish off my list," I say. "I like it out here, Daddy. I can see why you do too."

"You girls in my life make my head spin. This is where I take a rest." He notices the time and sits himself up. "It's getting late. How 'bout we stop for ice cream on the way home?"

Daddy's arm finds my shoulders, and we walk off the field together.

"I love you, Jules," he whispers, as he kisses the top of my head.

CHAPTER THIRTY-TWO

ABBY

Today is the day I will begin again.

There is freshly fallen snow outside my window, and I am watching for Ryan's car to turn up the drive. My suitcase is packed, and I've said good-bye to the team of therapists, and finally to Rose and Sybil. They have written me beautiful cards, and Sybil has decorated my face for my unveiling into my new normal. This time, I tell her that I enjoy my ordinary face, and she need not overly paint me. Being capable of sharing my feelings is exhilarating. I am sure it's the reason my cheeks shine with barely any blush and my eyes light up without glitter.

I am going to miss the serenity of this place, the ease with which I could grab hold of the wheel and steer through the minefield of indecision. I have survived. I am energized by the notion that what weighed me down is the force now lifting me up.

The doctors told me I would feel different upon my departure. Not a lobotomy-sized change—a subtle tweak in the zaps spiking my brain. Cold Creek gave me a set of tools for navigating my never-ending problems and fears. The fear will still arise, but when it does, my responses will be different. The texture of daily life might not feel as smooth as it had under the watchful eye of professionals, but I know I am equipped to handle the bumps. "You're still the same," they said. "You'll still experience highs and lows, but your highs will be less high, the lows, less low." *Balanced*, they mean.

Ryan arrives, and he seems smaller to me, though I immediately chalk it up to my new lens on life. We don't hug. He takes my bag and kisses me on the cheek before I step into the backseat. He smells different, and I wonder whether my other senses have changed in my metamorphosis. He maneuvers the truck slowly, as if we have far more to be cautious about than icy conditions.

My last days at Cold Creek were extraordinarily painful. "And with great pain," says Jeannie, "comes great joy." Lauren's voice lingered in my ear. Ryan's disappointment was everywhere I looked. The individual threads that had frayed over time were finding their way back together. Ryan called less and visited just once. We sat in Jeannie's office, where our grievances spilled to her floor.

"I'm trying to process this," he said, "but it's a big one. It's pretty much altered everything I once thought to be true." I sat there silently, staring at my newly grown fingernails, refraining from taking a bite. "My wife lies to me. What am I supposed to do?"

"Ryan, you're allowed to feel hurt and betrayed."

"I'm not hurt. I'm outraged."

I never once felt as though he regretted what happened between us—I mean, I know he wasn't proud of it, but listening to him and seeing his fury was like a giant question mark, and Jeannie saw it too.

"Do you ever think about your role in the betrayal, Ryan?" she asked. "We talk a lot in here about issues with anger, different levels and manifestations, and often the emotions go hand in hand with guilt. I imagine you must have some feeling about what happened. Despite the outcome and having a wonderful daughter, there have to be real feelings there. It would help you to get to them."

Ryan squirmed in his chair, and I just knew he was asking me with his eyes why he had to do this. In here. With her. He wiped his eyes, and he was about to say something, but his mouth closed before a sound came out.

And then he stood up and walked out Jeannie's door, the words lost in the slam of the door.

The car ride home is full of awful pleasantries. The things we aren't saying are about to burst wide open, and neither one of us wants to fight. We pull up to the house as Juliana walks out the front door. She's carrying her backpack, and I ask where she's going. I didn't expect her to have balloons and a sign strung to the porch, but it would have been nice for her to have waited for me to come home before making plans. Her hair is in a braid down her back and she seems nervous to see me.

"Where are you going?" I come right out and ask, while Ryan carries my bags in to the house.

She tells me she's going to the twins' house. I ask her why.

"The new normal is going to shift your entire family dynamic, Abby," Jeannie had said. "Juliana and Ryan are used to you being one way. They're trained to react. It's going to be difficult for them those first few weeks to get used to the changes in you. Expect some friction."

Juliana, hand on her hip, replies, "Because it's Saturday."

I reach for her, brushing the bangs away from her eyes so we can make contact. "I thought we'd all have dinner together."

Juliana doesn't know what to make of this. Jeannie is right: I have never questioned where my daughter is going or the time she allots to me. It was always easier to let her go and enjoy herself so I could wallow in my misery.

"Mama, please," she says, and this sends a dagger through my heart, one that I deserve, but it doesn't make it any less painful.

I say, "Things are going to change around here, Jules." This forces her to look down at her shoes, Uggs that are worn and probably too small. I'll take her shopping. I can start by buying her new shoes. And I see my daughter as though for the very first time. The urge to hold her close overwhelms me, and I drop my purse to the floor and cradle my arms around her. "I want my daughter back," I whisper to her cheeks, her hair, her neck. She smells like resistance and Finesse shampoo, but when I hug her harder, she drops the backpack to the floor and hugs me back.

"This is hard for you, I know. You probably don't know if you can trust me again. I'm going to work with you to rebuild that trust in me. I told you when I left for Cold Creek that I promised you I'd be a better mother, and I will."

We stand like that for a few minutes and I hold back the tears clamoring to come out. They are reminders of what I've missed and lost in the years of emotional absence.

She says, "I want to love you again, Mama." And I inhale those words like they are my last breaths.

"You will, honey. I promise."

While I can tell Ryan is pleased to have me home, I know he is holding back. "I'm still digesting this, Abs. You held on to the truth for years. I think I'm entitled to sit with it for a while."

We make it through dinner with his beers and my club soda before I tell him I am tired and ready for bed. He has exhausted me with his talk of the team and playoffs, explaining the four quadrants to me—as though I have never followed football. The Giants have remained alive in their bracket, and the feat means they'll play in the state championship at Charlotte's Bank of America Stadium. When he asks me if I'm going to the game, I tell him yes, even though he's done well enough without me.

"Do you still believe in our superstition?" he asks.

I'm not really sure what I believe in anymore, but I don't say that. Instead I tell him that we can talk about it tomorrow.

He asks me what he can do for me, how he can make the transition home smoother. "I don't know what you want."

What he means is that he doesn't know how to sit across from me and pretend that everything hasn't changed, when it has.

The conversation explodes just after dinner when we are preparing for bed.

At first he is cordial and accommodating, passing me my face towel in the bathroom and making sure that being back there doesn't freak me out. Then he demands answers.

"I know you're fragile. I know you've worked hard to get to where you are. But goddamnit, Abby, how could you have lied to me? I trusted you."

I put down my toothbrush and let him come after me. I deserve it, and at least I have the skills to manage what he is throwing at me. I hear Jeannie whispering in my ear: *let him talk, don't interrupt, just listen*. I can do that, but what is eating away at me is the question that sits between us like a child: what would it have changed?

"You didn't give me a choice. How could I have known what I would've done?" He's sitting on the side of bathtub watching me get ready for bed. The swipe hurts.

"I deserve that."

"Look," he begins, "I want to understand why you'd do this. To me. To your best friend. We were pawns, players in your hands. For someone who hated the demons that controlled you, you saw nothing wrong with controlling all of us. I hurt her. Hell, yes. More than she deserved. She was someone I loved very deeply. But this, you can't expect me not to have strong feelings about it."

He eyes me cautiously and I take a swig of mouthwash. "And for her?" I ask.

"If we're going to lay it all out on the line here—yes, I have feelings for her. The same feelings I had for her when you seduced me all that time ago. And I still ended up with you. It didn't make a bit of difference."

My body stiffens as I search for a response "So I seduced you. Is that how it happened?"

"Didn't you? If we're being honest, can you at least admit you took advantage of me?"

I pull my bathrobe tighter around my waist. I wield my hairbrush dangerously close to Ryan's face. "You could've stopped me. There were two of us on that couch."

"I was inebriated, Abby. I'd just lost my father, and my girlfriend was overseas. Could you have picked a worse time to make your move?"

Jeannie's voice is bellowing in my ear: *He's hurt. Let him denounce the relationship. Give him time to heal. Do not, under any circumstances, throw Juliana in his face. He loves her. This is not about her.*

I bring the washcloth to my lips to wipe the invisible liquid off my mouth. I do this to hide the gulping sound when I swallow.

"If you can lie about this," he fumes, "what else can you lie about? How do we trust each other again?"

My voice turns into a wail: "Can't you see that I've learned from my mistake? Did you not see how it ruined me? I would *never* lie to you again."

He is staring at me in the mirror, our reflections trying to decipher each other. God damn he's hard to look at. Even when he's furious with me. Those delicate eyes are asking me all sorts of questions. "What?" I ask.

"Nothing," he says, shaking his head, getting up from his seat, and heading for the door.

My legs rush after him, my hand grabs his wrist, forcing him to look at me. "What happened to 'we took a vow and I'm committed to you'?" I plead. "And the part where you loved me?"

His face is devastatingly sad. "Abby, I do love you. I'll always love you. I just don't like you very much right now." Then he turns away from me.

And I fight my fist not to throw the brush across the room.

Later that night, our hands wrestle with the foamy white covers until we find our usual places under the quilt. He reaches across the bed, and I feel his palm land on my hip. My body stiffens. The surge is so strong that I am sure he can feel it through his fingers. His hands move gently down my stomach and thighs. All I can do to stop myself from crying is to turn from him and face the opposite direction.

He comes closer and curls around me.

I am saying no with my head, shaking it back and forth against his cheeks. "How do you do this? How do you find room inside to love me when there's so much hate? It's not normal."

I can feel him turn away from me. The room is dark, and I know he is talking to the ceiling. "You're mad at me for not being more mad at you? Am I missing something? 'Cause it sure as hell feels like you're pushing me away. Do you want me to leave? Is that it?"

"Sometimes I wish you'd just scream at me. Then I'd know you're human, that you're one of us."

"Abby, I'm trying."

"I don't think the therapists meant with sex."

He rolls over and I feel awful about the rejection. When he reaches for me again, I don't back away. I let him kiss my cheek, and I let him explore the places that had died while I was away, though it doesn't take long for me to know that something feels off. The doctors warned me of the side effects from the medications. I didn't expect the sacrifice would be dried-up female private parts.

But this feels like more than a side effect. I don't want him to touch me. And since I can't reject him twice, I tell myself I can do this. I can go through the motions, close my eyes, and give us what we both need. The idea spreads down my legs and cracks me open to let him inside. We begin to move, and it's awkward and uncomfortable. The clumsiness makes it clear: this is not a medication issue. I am dead down there. I can't go through with it. I don't want to go through with it. Ryan's poking at me and it hurts, but not as much as looking him in the eyes and telling him to stop.

CHAPTER THIRTY-THREE

RYAN

Everywhere I look I see Lauren.

She was in my truck when Abby stepped in, her perfume drifting through the air vents. On the long drive home, I only heard every other word coming from Abby's mouth. Thoughts of Lauren kept interrupting, taunting me. I was replaying our conversation of the other day. I was staring into her blue eyes when she'd said she still loved me. Instead of turning from her, my mind makes up a different ending. I face her and let her know I love her back. I'm selfishly not thinking about my recovering wife.

Over dinner, Abby played with her food while I talked about the game and the team because I couldn't bear to talk about the things that would drive me away from her. I wedged more space between us by perpetuating a string of lies.

I don't know what Lauren was thinking when she said those words to me. Could she have known there was a chance I still loved her back? That surviving without her all these years was essentially just coping?

That first night in our bed, I reached for Abby out of habit. I thought to myself, *If I can have sex with her, if we can join our bodies, then I can erase Lauren from my mind, just like I did all those years ago.*

She looked me in the eyes when I was on top of her, and I had to turn away. I was relieved when she said the medication had killed her libido and we had to stop. My motions were mechanical and detached. I had unknowingly fake-loved her for years, and now every memory of us together was marred by the thick swell of my deceit.

I asked myself, *How can I continue living this lie of a life?* The question released a slew of regret I'd locked away: why I didn't seek out Lauren, why I had let her slip through my fingers without a fight, why in God's name I had had sex with her best friend.

The husband in me says I can't leave my wife. The man in me says I deserve more. I struggle with the conflict as I have for many years, accepting what I thought was lost. Lauren is leaving again. The feelings will go away as they did before. I will pull the stinger from my skin, for the second time.

CHAPTER THIRTY-FOUR

JULIANA

Marlee, Sophie, and Nicole are sitting next to me in the Bank of America Stadium when E.J. takes the field. Daddy's out there, too, and he finds me and waves.

The stadium is packed, and the cold air drills through our bones. Marlee is complaining about the chill again, and we listen to her rant that she is moving to Florida when she graduates. "Nobody gets fat in Florida because the weather's so nice. Winter kills me," she says, throwing her gloved hands up in the air.

The stands are filled with Giants navy jerseys and the purple of the opposition, the Plymouth Vikings. The twins ask me about E.J., and I sigh, wishing I had something more to tell. He's been stuck in his stubborn head, and it's maddening. So when he emerges on the field behind Daddy and sees Daddy waving in my direction, I am certain he will wave too. Instead, he scans the stands for someone else. I spot her off to the side, a solitary figure—Ruby Whittaker. She wouldn't miss the championship game, no matter the cost. I watch her wave to her son. She draws something in the air with her finger, which he immediately understands. He taps on his heart with his gloved hand, and I feel my own heart skip a beat.

The crowd is loud and on its feet. The Friday-night lights are even brighter tonight, aglow with energy that fuels the players on the field as the Vikings kick off and the action begins.

Daddy's marching along the sidelines; Mama's back in her usual spot with June Harrow by her side. It's a different set of bleachers, but the same number of rows behind the bench. Marlee and Sophie and Nicole are checking out boys while I eye the only boy for me on the field. E.J. is a natural out there. Whatever hardship he's endured away from these beaming lights propels him across the grass. I swear that boy came outta his mama wearing those cleats.

I want to believe he's watching me when he's out there, though I know he isn't. He always said that no matter how loud the fans, he didn't hear a sound in his head except Coach's voice. The stands were a blur, and the only thing that he saw was the faces of his teammates. I used to tease him about the cheerleaders. All the dolled-up girls who would flirt and shake their pom-poms at him. He told me I was the only one: "There's no one for me but you, Juliana."

The scoreboard clock ticks away toward the end of the first half. The rival teams spin a wild tale of football. Just when we squeak ahead, they pull off another score. There is hardly room to exhale between touchdowns, and Daddy looks wicked cross on the sidelines. His hands are folded, and he's shouting something into the mouthpiece connected to his headphones.

"I don't understand your affinity for this game," says Nicole, who is posing in an inordinate number of selfies.

"You don't love it because you don't understand it."

At halftime, we hook up with a group of kids from school. Mama's talking to some of the other parents, and she doesn't look nervous or afraid. She smiles at me, and I can't help but smile back.

When we find our seats again, Plymouth has scored another touchdown on their first possession. By the end of the third quarter we are tied, and the skies open up with a steady sleet. Marlee, Sophie, and Nicole run for cover, but I remain rooted in my spot. The wet wind stymies the back and forth that had dictated the earlier quarters, and the fourth begins with frustration on both sides of the field.

With less than ten seconds left in the game, the Vikings are about to throw for the game-winning touchdown when one of our defensive ends comes out of nowhere and pops the Vikings quarterback. The ball floats through the air. I have watched miracles before. Daddy's always reminded me of the power of perseverance. There is a shuffling on the field. It happens so fast that no one knows where the ball lands, until out of the storm shoots E.J.

My young stud mostly plays offense, until those pivotal games that require a talented cornerback. The ball is in his hands, and with eighty yards ahead of him, a few seconds on the clock, and an entire Plymouth team charging toward him, he takes off. The sleet is slapping the field, and players are losing their footing. First he speeds past one man, then breaks a tackle, before breaking out into his full, unstoppable pace. The last player in his wake doesn't have a prayer of catching him. Before the clock runs down and the last whistle blows, E.J. has crossed the threshold to victory. The stands go wild. The fans storm onto the field. The Pine Ridge Giants are the state champs. And the sleet turns into a steady rain that no one seems to notice.

There's not a dry eye in the stadium when the team lifts E.J. on their shoulders and hands him the game-winning ball. I am so proud of him that I can't even move. The tears fall down his face, and mine. The crowd around him is layers deep. People want to touch him, take pictures with him. A flock of reporters wait by the sidelines for an interview.

I am alone in the stadium, feeling the distance, drenched in the wet rain that has mixed with my tears. I don't know how long I stay seated. The fans have cleared out, and there is a handful of press and a few rowdy fans lingering by the end zone. My cell phone is vibrating in my pocket, and I text the girls to say they can go on without me. "I'll hitch a ride with my mom," I write. I begin to shiver, and in my soaked jeans I go down the steps to where my mama waits. Back before crazy, we would drive to school and wait for the buses to return with the players. Joined by friends, families, and girlfriends, we were an elite group of caregivers. Chosen ones.

"You're soaked!" she cries out at me. "You can't go to the parking lot like that. You'll freeze to death."

"Mama, I'm going."

We drive in silence. There's a stillness between us. I've had one parent for so long it makes sense that we argue and fight when she tries to mother me again. We're sitting side by side like two strangers. She tries to talk to me. It feels unnatural and weird.

"Are you sure you don't want to stop and get a change of clothes?"

"I'm sure. I don't want to miss the bus."

We arrive among the throngs of people ready to celebrate the state champions. The rain has stopped, replaced by a gentle snow. I am no longer cold. I am ready for E.J.

"You shouldn't throw yourself at him," she says, before getting out of the car.

Maybe it's the cold, maybe the water lodged inside my head, replacing logic with cruelty, but before I can ignore what she just said, I spew sass: "You have no right to give me advice about E.J."

"Don't you dare speak to me like that," she says, startling me with her firmness.

I stare out the window when I tell her, "You haven't been my mama in a long time."

She unbuckles the seat belt and says, "That's not fair, Juliana."

I turn to face her. "It's not fair that we've cleaned up your messes and now you're all whole and healthy, and we're supposed to forget years of living with crazy."

She rests her hands on the steering wheel and seems to be counting to ten. When she's done, she says very softly, "I'm going to make it up to you."

"Whatever," I say, slamming the car door, and walking away.

The wait for the bus is endless. When I finally see it round the corner, I have forgotten how rotten I was to my mom. She is hovering nearby, not talking to anyone, and I feel sorry for her in her aloneness.

The boys file out and I see Daddy. He's got a towel thrown over his head from when they gave him a Gatorade shower. Daddy doesn't notice the snow or the cold, he's so happy.

His eyes are searching for someone, and she emerges from the crowd and stands in front of him. Her face is partially covered by the hooded fur of her parka. Her hands are tucked in her pockets, though he pulls her close. She leans in to him and kisses his cheek. It's not an illusion; my parents look like two normal people, except I can't help thinking their movements are tense and clumsy. Daddy puts his arm out for me to join them, but I spot E.J. stepping off the bus. I stay where I am and wait to see what he will do.

E.J.'s teammates are surrounding him. They are all commotion and chaos, as though they have had too much beer. Once he would have found me no matter where I was standing. He would have walked over to me, and I'd sink into him, not even minding the sweat and the smell. I allow this memory to cushion me. The earlier rains turn into a gentle snow. Flakes drizzle down my face and force my eyes closed. I swear I can taste the salt of his lips.

I feel him before I see him. His fingertips brush the crystals from my lashes. My eyes open, and I don't turn away from his stare. His are bluer, his hands softer. The longing that had filled my heart disperses around us, caught in the flurries.

"I knew you'd come."

"Yeah," he laughs, "how'd you know that?"

"Stalker habit."

I smile and congratulate him on the win. He's holding his helmet in his hand, and the game ball is tucked inside.

"The win felt good," he says. "You being here . . . even better."

"I would've waited a long time."

"Don't go saying stuff you can't make good on."

"I'm not the one who left."

His lips come down on mine with an urgency I've been waiting for. The helmet crashes to the floor, and he scoops me up into his arms. E.J. doesn't like gratuitous displays of affection, but I kiss him back. Long and hard, as though this will seal us for life.

The team is surrounding us with cheers and jeers. The hoots and howls pull his lips away, but we stay close. They are calling his name. He doesn't seem to notice when he bends down to whisper in my ear. Despite the noise coming off the crowd, I can hear his every word. Like the air around us, I breathe them in one at a time.

"You get inside my head, Jules. You get in so deep I can't think. I had to protect you."

"Ellis is dead, E.J. I don't need saving."

"I was scared, baby. And stupid. If I let you go, then I'd never have to know what good-bye feels like."

He kisses the top of my head, and I'm smiling inside when he whispers one more thing: "Next time, I'm not gonna be saying no to you."

CHAPTER THIRTY-FIVE

ABBY

I waded through the months waiting for a relapse. As the earth transformed from the numbing freeze of winter to the lively birth of spring, I expected my calm to thaw within me. Flowers bloomed from seedlings, and I, too, sprouted tiny vessels of life. At first my steps were awkward and shaky. Then with the cushion of the fresh grass beneath my feet, I stepped on land with secure footing.

You'll experience the anxious feelings again, I reminded myself regularly. I didn't want to manage them better than before. I wanted them gone forever. *That's wishing yourself away. Don't wish yourself away,* I'd tell myself. I was encouraged by Jeannie to continue talk therapy. *It's more important than the meds,* I'd think. And soon Babs was out of retirement, and I was back on her couch.

Babs—the woman meant more to me than I would ever admit. It's why it was so easy to walk out of her office and, years later, walk back in. I flourished beneath her tough-love tutelage. She was someone I could trust. We went over ways that I could make myself feel better, plans that would ensure my stabilization. Without the constant state of anxiety and the fear of scary thoughts, I was getting to know myself, possibly for the first time ever.

Part of the recovery was healing relationships in my first family. My mother was genuinely surprised and happy to hear my voice. It wasn't an obligatory birthday call or anniversary wish. It would take time to rebuild these relationships, but without them, parts of me would be incomplete, and other parts wouldn't work at all.

Juliana and I dueled most of the time. She wasn't accustomed to my return, physically or mentally, and coupled with teenage melodrama, we faced some obvious challenges. Babs told me her daughter was born with PMS, and this gave me a good laugh.

Ryan was slowly coming back to me. There were moments we'd be enjoying each other's company, laughing about something, when I'd notice him get quiet. I could tell his eyes and his mind were drifting somewhere else. I had learned to accept this about him. It's not impossible to love in different forms and lifetimes. What matters is the love we share today. It's an effort within each of us, and we are striving toward a deeper understanding.

One area we were working on intensively was our roles in the marriage. We had survived for years with the stigma of my illness as our center. All of our actions and reactions danced around my moods and needs. Finding our new roles became a balancing act.

Plans for the summer were underway. Ryan was offered a post at a youth football training camp at Appalachian State University. One of the coaches had a home on Beech, and when a family emergency took him to Virginia, he was willing to give us the house for the summer. There was meaning in it for all of us.

Juliana didn't want to leave E.J. Alabama was waiting for him, though. Their good-bye was inevitable. She insisted she needed more time and begged and pleaded for it.

"He'll come with me and work in the program at ASU," Ryan says to me. "Jules can get a job there. At least this way, we can watch over them." His little girl was not so little anymore. Much of it had to do with her turning seventeen, though I knew his worry had more to do with E.J.

"You forget what you were like when you were her age."

He doesn't agree with me or disagree. Instead, his eyes cloud up with something thick and misty, and he rests his chin in his hand.

We're sitting on the porch, enjoying the mild temperatures of a late spring. The grass is freshly cut, and the afternoon temperature is a balmy seventy-six. The trees shade the area, and we sip iced tea like a couple. I hold on to this notion when the leaves on the trees hiss in the wind.

I fiddle with the string on my left wrist. I have never liked wearing bracelets of any kind. My wrists are thick, and most jewelry looks bulky and out of place on my arms. This is a string I wear to remind myself of how far I have come. It is red, and Rose told me it wards off evil. When I start to feel unsure, I tug on it. It grounds me and brings me back to my center.

Ryan rises from the rattan chair and comes up behind me, placing two hands on my tense shoulders. "It'll be good for us to get away. You can read all those books you have piled up next to the bed. I can run interference with our horny teenage daughter."

I have no reason not to believe him, so we close our house in Charlotte and set off for the mountains.

Ryan's truck is packed with our things, and Devon finagles his way aboard. He has proven himself during the playoffs and state championships, and E.J. worries it's too soon to leave him unsupervised. Devon is eager to please and willing to work hard. Ryan feels a personal stake in his turnaround, so Devon, when pressed, agrees to the plan.

Once out of the city, the drive up 321 always bored me. Now I'm in the backseat, behind Ryan, where I always sit. Cold Creek had cured a lot, but I am working on this lingering fear. The lengthy highway stretches ahead of us for miles, surrounded by dry, barren fields and a smidgen of cows.

Further along, the roads begin to narrow as we start into the mountains. The first sign of nearing the Blue Ridge is the change in temperature. My forehead against the window tells me when we've reached a higher elevation, and the signal brings the windows down, and with it, a curl of clean, cooler air. Blowing Rock comes into view, and the asphalt twists with views from every angle. By the time we pass Canyons Restaurant and its unobstructed views of the Blue Ridge and Grandfather, I'm remembering Lauren and Ryan, and it leaves me to wonder whether we've made a mistake. That's the problem for me with long car trips: I can think and ponder too much.

I start to replay my most recent conversation with Babs.

"When I was in Cold Creek I had this recurring dream about the three of us on the roof at a frat party. Ryan's arm was around me, and every time Lauren came near us, he would take it off and drop it around Lauren. In the dream, I'd get so upset. I'd have these scary thoughts about jumping off the roof. And it made sense. For a while. But then the dream changed."

"How so?" She was wearing a red spandex bandana around her forehead that day, which made it kind of hard for me to share the seriousness of what I was telling her.

"Well, he would let me go and, same thing, wrap his arm around her, and the ledge would beckon me . . . and I'd feel the impulse to jump. But this time there was this something in the sky that made it less scary. The sky was brighter, and birds were flying around . . . I don't know . . . Forget it . . . This is stupid."

"Abigail, don't demean yourself. Our dreams tell us quite a bit about ourselves."

"This is going to sound weird, but I felt free."

"Meaning you weren't scared to jump? It was less of a threat?"

I nodded. And she replied, "What's stupid about that?"

"I don't know. It's been making me uncomfortable. More uncomfortable than the original dream when the ground was in sight. Shouldn't taking a leap be scary?"

"Not always. Dreams aren't that forthcoming. They're complex representations." She took her headband off and started twirling it around her fingers. "Sounds to me like this new dream is a positive sign."

"I don't know. It has to mean something."

"It's powerful stuff, Abigail. I understand why it's making you so uncomfortable."

"I don't get it."

"You will. Keep at it. Clarity comes to us in unusual ways."

Ryan takes a sharp turn and I am back in his truck. The dream has become my latest obsession, but instead of turning away from it, I explore what it means. I think about Ryan and me. I think about how long I have loved him. And I think about why we are together.

Rarely do we speak on the way up. The scenic vistas strip our mouths of words. And Devon, I don't think he has ever left Charlotte before. The mountain pulls at him, and he hangs his head out the window across from me, lapping up the view like a puppy. We pass through Boone and make the turn onto 105. I gaze out at the cropping of trees along the mountainside. They are thick and bountiful. If we dig deep through any forest, beneath the treetops, we find weak trunks and bent limbs. What is perceived as magnificent is one twig away from ruin.

Here the climb grows steeper, and we know we are close. Yellow hawkweed lines the sides of the roads, and sugar maples come into view. The color drains from my face when Ryan takes the sharp turns too fast. Carsickness has always been a problem for me on the winding roads. Combined with the altitude, my head is usually in my lap by the time we arrive at the summit of Beech.

Our house is on Shamrock. It is an impressive, modern structure perched on the side of the mountain. The spacious home boasts high beams and floor-to-ceiling windows framing the layered mountaintops of four states. Luxurious finishes blend naturally with rustic furnishings. The high altitude makes it unnecessary for air conditioning, and we fan out on two floors, staking claim to our individual bedrooms and opening up windows. Ryan has strategically placed the boys downstairs, and Juliana is upstairs with us.

She has perfected her eye roll by now.

After a few trips to the car, our bags are dispensed in what will be our rooms for the next six weeks, and Ryan heads into town—*town* is a stretch—to get some groceries. Fred's General Store is a stand-alone at the top of the mountain and embodies its motto: "If we don't have it, you don't need it." For all other necessities, you have to trek miles away to the nearest grocery store. I don't offer to join him. Time has become invaluable to me: time spent with Juliana, time to return to my summer reading. Grabbing the bag of books from the foyer floor, I step out onto the balcony and take a seat in the double rocker.

When I joined a book club in the new year, the ladies assigned me an inaugural read with the date for the next meeting. Reading on demand was a pressure I didn't need, which is why I had always avoided such clubs. And because of my limitations, I had only read mindless magazines that didn't require concentration. But with my newly quieted mind, books became a critical source of entertainment. Not only did I keep up with the required monthly reading, I read volumes I had missed while living in a wordless world.

January was *Cutting for Stone*. February, *The Kitchen House*. March,

Once We Were Brothers. April, *The Help.* May, *Me before You.* Book club is on hiatus for the summer, but the ladies provided me with a list of books to read that they had discussed and enjoyed. I'd already delved into *Point Blank,* followed by *Defending Jacob, The Kite Runner, The Other Boleyn Girl, She's Come Undone* (ha!), *The Time Traveler's Wife,* and even *Fifty Shades of Grey.*

So far, I'm engrossed in *Point Blank,* a beautifully written novel. The ladies say the author has a few other books I might enjoy, and this one is her first and possibly her best. She does a great job of capturing the tenderness of love and loss. I cannot put the book down, and when the kids find me on the balcony, I am crying a well of tears.

"This is what she does now that's she's happy," says my daughter, staring down at me, her hands on her denim shorts.

Devon adds, "Are you okay, Mrs. Holden?" And E.J. runs inside for some tissues.

"If you'd get your head out of your phone and read once in a while, you'd understand," I say to Juliana.

"Why would I want to cry?"

I tell her that crying is good. It's like resetting a computer, clearing out the hard drive.

"But I'm not sad."

Which silences me.

The honking of Ryan's horn blares through the house, and I instruct the boys to help him with the groceries. I stare too long at Juliana. She really is a remarkable young lady, even if every mother says the same about her child. Like most teenagers, she mistakes my stare to mean something else. "We're not having sex," she says.

I know what I want to say, though I am cautious about how I phrase it: "It would be okay if you were. As long as you're careful."

This lack of judgment warms her to me and soon she is next to me on the rocker and stretches her long legs across the footrest. Her toes are polished in powder blue.

"You're not going to lecture me about being responsible and waiting to get married?"

"I'm going to do all those things. For the rest of your life. That's my job, but I've read a lot of really good books about really bad parenting. Every child is different. What's good for one family may not be right for ours. You need to know you can always come to me. Judging is useless."

She moves in closer to me and rests her head on my shoulder. Her limbs melt into mine; they have a long memory. Relief washes over me as I come to understand that she has forgiven me. It is a second chance that not everyone gets. I can finally make up for the years I had failed her.

Ryan pokes out his head and asks if we want to go for a walk before dinner. He eyes us on the chair and smiles. "My girls," he says.

And Juliana whispers in my ear while the wind rustles the trees around us, "Up to no good."

Later in the day, Ryan and I explore Shamrock and its intersecting roads. The exercise is just what we need after the two-and-a-half-hour drive. We see a few deer, and Ryan brings along his bear whistle, just in case. There is laughter in our voices and he reaches for my hand and gives it a gentle squeeze.

Returning to the house, I organize our things and find solace in the quiet that envelops the mountain. Ryan grills steaks for dinner, and I help in the kitchen with a salad. For dessert, we hike down the side of the property to the fire pit, and roast marshmallows for s'mores. The kids sing silly songs, and we watch them sway back and forth along the wooden benches.

It all sounds very lovely, *Leave It to Beaver*-ish, but I am riddled with doubt. When you've lived inside your head for as long as I have, you wait for the snakes and spiders to slither into your safe spaces. I'm waiting for the thoughts to return. I'm waiting for the fears. I'm waiting for the enormity of my feelings to turn me inside out. I carry a round, yellow pill with me for extra security: a sub-therapeutic dose of a well-known antianxiety medication—my safety net. Only my safety net isn't prepared for the new batch of thoughts. They spool around me and crowd my magical thinking. They're not obsessions, and they're not guiding me toward compulsions. They are different, rational and calm, a keen awareness that sinks into my skin. An insight like this gets buried under the brain's internal rubble, or, perhaps, it was born when the bits of me became whole.

I wonder if this is how Ryan felt all those years when he mistook loyalty for love.

I am putting away dishes when I spot the Beech Mountain Club Bulletin on the countertop. Finding a seat on one of the bar stools, I begin to read about the upcoming events on the mountain and spot the name Virginia Sutherland. I double check the spine of *Point Blank*, which I have tossed on the tabletop, and see that it is her, the author of the book. The article says she will be speaking at the club's annual "meet the author" event. I grab my cell phone and email the book-club girls. Many of them have homes on Beech. Perhaps they might want to join.

Ms. Sutherland has never spoken publicly about her work. The article describes a recluse, living alone across the pond. She has chosen Beech Mountain as her first and only public appearance because it is her "favorite place in the world" and she wants to "give back to the Beech community." I study the picture of the middle-aged author, the vague photo that adorns the back cover of the book. I can't wait to meet her in person.

CHAPTER THIRTY-SIX

RYAN

My days on the mountain begin with a short walk along the windy roads. The fog tumbles off the mountain at that hour, and it is a tranquil time for reflection. Sometimes E.J. joins me, or I take off for a jog. The crunch of my sneakers on the pavement squelches the anger that sometimes still rises up—that Abby lied, that Lauren waited too long to come back. It's a lot easier to be angry at Lauren for abandoning me all those years ago than to be sad for what will never be.

Abby laughs more often, and a peacefulness has chased away her edginess. Her love is less claustrophobic and aggressive. We've fallen into a rhythm that feels a lot like the old days when we were good friends, minus the nervous agitation. Nighttime is when the changes are most noticeable. She gets in on her side of the bed and I get in mine. We don't even make excuses. We fall away from each other and into sleep.

"Did you boys call your mama this week?" We are driving down the mountain to ASU in Boone, and it's a special time for me to engage with E.J. and Devon.

E.J. tries to explain to me that there's no reception in the house.

The boys have learned to bring out the best in each other, but like most teenagers with their bodies hunched over cell phones, texting and playing mindless games, they have a dumb-and-dumber quality that endears them to me. "Have you considered using a landline?"

They laugh, which makes me feel old. "No one has a landline anymore."

The forty-minute drive goes by quickly. The boys listen to ESPN radio and I hear them discuss imaginary fantasy football lineups. Opening the car windows, I let the cool mountain air shake us awake before we hit the fields with temperatures in the eighties. Devon has shaved his head and looks less frightening. Something in his eyes had changed, and possibly, something in his soul. He loves to hang over the seat between E.J. and me. I have grown fond of him and the way he handles the kids in the program with their daily running and passing drills.

The chime of ESPN's breaking news hits all of our ears at once. "They finally ruled on the Bobcats' name," says E.J. "They're going back to the Hornets." The boys high-five each other and come up with names I can't repeat, which make our home team sound pathetic and small.

The kids are waiting when we pull into the parking lot behind the Mountaineers' stadium. E.J. is a hero in the state of North Carolina, and the boys enrolled in this summer program dream of following in his footsteps. They line up daily to watch him toss a ball, and they ask him the most important questions in the world, every day, multiple times a day. He doesn't mind, though. He always pretends it's the first time they're asking. He's the same way with them on the field. I know I've done my job right when he exhibits the patience to watch the boys make the same mistakes without a sign of frustration. He encourages them to get back up, to shake it off, to give it a perfect effort—all the lessons he learned on my field.

Witnessing players grow up and mature is one of the most gratifying parts of any coach's career, and today is especially satisfying for me. It's not only E.J., or the young boys we are working with. What's different is Devon. Devon comes alive around these kids. The pounding he received from Ellis turned him into a caring, sensitive instructor, and by day's end the boys are fighting one another for his attention. A few even ask him for the same advice they ask of E.J., and others climb on his shoulders for a ride on his back. I can't bear to think what might have happened to him had he not been given this second chance.

Sometimes I let her sneak up on me. It could be a sign along the road reminding me of how happy we once were, or I'll hear E.J. tell Juliana how pretty she looks, and he'll reach for her in a way that makes me know he loves her deeply. I remember that kind of love. How it can consume and control. Make you think that anything is possible.

A package came for me in the mail right before we left Charlotte. I was clearing out my office at the high school for the summer and someone had dropped it on my desk. I recognized her handwriting at once. I fingered the letters of my name, how she could spell with so much emotion around each letter. There was a tiny box with a short note: "I've held on to this for too long. You should take it back." I should have known what it was. Instead, I ripped through the cardboard until the last piece of us sprang from the box and landed on my desk. I picked it up. It was smaller and duller than I remembered it being. I held it in my hand for a long time and for a split second I thought about picking up the phone and telling her this is wrong, she can't leave, that I didn't have the answers, but we would figure it out. We'd have to figure it out.

I can't live without her, I told myself.

But I didn't do any of that. I called Abby instead.

And she sounded happy to hear from me when she said, "We're all packed up and ready to go. Let's get this adventure started!"

And I shoved the ring, and all the feelings that went along with it, back in its box.

You don't take back what you never let go of.

CHAPTER THIRTY-SEVEN

LAUREN

My things are packed, and I'm ready to go. As soon as the luncheon is over, my new life as Lauren Sheppard begins in New York City. After months of interviews, moving back and forth from the mountains to Manhattan, Chicago, and Atlanta, I accepted a position with Condé Nast and one of their travel magazines.

Q says she can't keep up with my multiple personalities. Author, photographer, wanderlust, recluse, and woman behind the alias. I have kept her on her toes.

"Why now?" she asks.

"It's something I have to do. I never liked that name anyway."

"You loved that name. It took you weeks to come up with it! Wait until you see what happens when word of this spreads."

"Those books aren't mine anymore. The pain is someone else's."

Through the phone line, I can hear Q's brain churning. "Your waterfall book will be an instant success when you announce that you're Virginia Sutherland."

"That's not why I'm doing it."

"I know. You want to connect with readers . . . Blah, blah, blah. I wish all my authors were as righteous as you."

When Ryan walked away from me, knowing the truth about what had happened, the need to keep my pen name disappeared. I had hidden behind the guise of Virginia Sutherland to keep us apart. He wasn't mine to love anymore, and my words were purely fiction, no longer a testament to us and the great love I held in my heart.

If Abby could shed her skin, so could I.

The morning starts out bright and crisp. After the evening rains, the temperature has dropped, and I take a fast walk around our block to charge myself up before the lunch. The ladies at the club are wonderful and accommodating. There will be no meddling publicists and no celebrity antics. The ladies have advertised the event while maintaining the integrity of the Beech community.

My parents arrive from their condo in Charleston shortly after I finish breakfast.

"It's about time," they say, speaking over each other. Then my mother adds, "We thought we'd never see the day you got the recognition you deserve."

I hug them to me. Mom whispers in my ear how she's so happy she can finally tell the mah-jongg girls that I have an honest career and I'm not just traveling around the world with my camera.

We laugh, and I explain to them that this coming out is not some marketing ploy to build traction for the new book. Like most things in life, it's about timing.

I help them carry their things to their room when Pop says, "What's this?"

Lake Coffey is hanging above their bed. After staring at it for months,

I decided I couldn't look at it anymore. Like my books, the colors seem to have faded and grown dull.

"The girl has red hair, Arthur!" says my mother to my father.

"It's from Woolly Worm. Meline Stapleton painted it."

My father tells me it's lovely, though I don't believe he means it by the crispness of his praise.

"That Meline's such a delightful one," chirps my mother. "I hope she's coming today."

I dress in a plain green sheath and brush my hair back into a ponytail. There's no mistaking that I am not the Virginia Sutherland that the group of women is coming to see. I coat my lips in red and then decide it's too much and opt for light pink. It won't matter. I eat my lipstick before I reach the door.

The club is bustling when we arrive. Dawn, the manager, greets us with a smile, her short, dark hair forming a knit cap on her head. "It's hard to believe that little Lauren Sheppard is the renowned Virginia Sutherland." She gives me a hug, and I thank her for her discretion and for ensuring the event runs smoothly.

A waiter hands us mimosas, and my mom swats my dad on the arm. "Arthur, the cardiologist told you no alcohol." I can't gulp mine down fast enough. And before I can savor the flavor, they spot some of their friends and are thrust into the snowbird conversation that everyone seems to have this time of year.

Members and guests fill the room; so many, that some have crossed over to the balcony. Friends greet me with cheerful hellos, and I almost wish Q were here to distract me. She's always so good at making noise.

There is a podium set up at the front of the room that's surrounded by large, round tables. The centerpieces are autographed books that will be given away in a raffle. I walk toward the bar, which had always been my favorite spot in the club. It is an intimate room, a fraction of the size of the dining hall with its aged wood panels and plush brown carpeting. There is a stone fireplace and a few small tables. Golf is always playing on the flat-screen TV, which stands high above the bar, but today the TV is off, and I step down the stairs and take in the views of the real golf course from the wooded balcony. The foliage on the mountains is lush and green, and the backdrop is magnificent. The pristine golf course looks as though someone painted across the lawn in long, sweeping strokes. A hedgehog dashes behind the bushes. His friend is not far behind. I spend time watching them romp across the field before I take another mimosa from a passing waiter. My mother finds me and says, "Mimosas have a lot of sugar, honey. Don't fill up."

A voice from behind us calls out my name, and Mom and I stiffen. "Lauren?"

Mom's mouth opens in sheer surprise: "If it isn't Ryan Holden's wife here in the flesh."

"Gail, charming as ever," says Abby with a smirk.

Mom clears a path between us before whispering in my ear, "Walk away, honey, she's not worth your time," and disappears through the club doors.

Abby and I size each other up until she asks what I'm doing here.

"I'm going to go out on a limb and say I'm here for the same reason as you, to hear Ms. Sutherland speak."

She looks confused. "Ryan said you moved."

"I'm leaving this weekend. You should be pleased."

"You have it all wrong, Lauren. I don't want to fight."

She looks good, Abby does. Her white dress shows off her tan, and her hair falls loosely down her shoulders. She looks serene and settled. Cold Creek has had a positive influence on her. I think about Jean-Pierre and how I should have married him when he asked. Then he'd be holding my hand right now, and I wouldn't be alone, facing the woman who betrayed me.

"Have you read her books?" she asks.

"Every one."

"You know I was never much of a reader."

"I remember," I say, nodding my head, while a rush of memories collides into me. "I'll see you inside," I add, surprised by my shortness. I need to get away from her.

Guests are filing in, descending the stairs and taking their seats. Others hover along the fringes of the room, whispering among themselves. The echoes increase in sound, a rumble bouncing off the upholstered walls: Ms. Sutherland is a no-show. Pat Stringer, the club manager, approaches the front of the room and requests that the ladies take their chairs. I am seated at a table near the front with my parents and some family friends.

Pat's thick accent unravels the mystery clouding Virginia Sutherland's absence. I prepared her speech, and the precise wording of each made-up fact is timed to keep the guests on the edge of their seats.

"As some of you have already guessed, Virginia Sutherland won't be joining us." The groans in the room are loud. "But the real author of these outstanding books is here with us today. The town of Beech Mountain couldn't be prouder to welcome our very own Lauren Sheppard, author of *Point Blank*, *If I Only Knew*, and *That Girl*."

The room gasps and the applause slowly mounts. I feel eyes on me, searching for what they hadn't seen before, the ordinary becoming extraordinary. As I take my place behind the podium, the smiles and praise remind me of how far I've traveled and what I've brought back to life. Everyone is standing, and as I begin to tell my story, I notice a blurry image toward the back of the room. I can't make out the face, though it is the one person who is still seated, the one who can't bring herself to applaud. And I know at once it is Abby.

I speak to the crowd for a full thirty minutes. The honesty is cathartic, and it opens up a thoughtful discussion.

When I'm finished, I sign books at a table in the bar area until there's no one left in line but Abby. I step away to kiss my parents on the cheek, thank Dawn for hosting the lovely event, and grab a vodka from the bar. When I return, she is still there, standing patiently in front of the table, thumbing through one of my books. I pack up my pens and sticky notes. "Are you waiting for an autograph?"

"Is this how you planned it all along? Did you think he was going to find you and profess his love to you?"

"I thought you didn't want to fight."

"What was it you said when that lady asked if your stories are about you? You said, and let me quote you, 'I write what I know.' Did you think if you wrote the fairy-tale ending you'd get it?"

Her accusations are wearing me down. They're the final straw in an already-tiring day. I plead with her to stop. "Abby, what do you want from me? Ryan loves you. He chose you."

"I read that book, Lauren."

"It's fiction. That's what sells."

"It's you and Ryan. You know it. I know it."

I'm finding the small space in the bar confining, so I cross over to the glass doorway that leads to the patio. Abby follows with a bottle of water in her hand. We are pretending to admire the late-afternoon sun as it soaks the field below in light. History tells me how Abby will stand with one hand on her hip while the other plays with her hair.

"I don't have five cats either," I say. "Seeing how you believe everything you read."

"Do you still love him?" she asks, in her soft voice. The one that tells me the tide is shifting.

"How can you ask me that question?"

"Do you?" she persists.

"It doesn't matter, Abby."

"It does," she says. "Did you tell him?"

I set the vodka on the ledge and steady myself for her reaction. "Yes," I say, "I did."

"Typical Ryan," she says, unusually composed. "We knew what he would do with that. Such a martyr. It's why he's so easy to love. I saw a lot of that in your book. It reminded me of the three of us."

"It's not real, Abby."

"Oh, but it is," she says. "We never loved that way. Not the way you loved him. Not the way he loved you. He'll always love you." Her eyes are welling up with tears. Her hand has fallen from her hair and takes the other one in its grasp. "After all the work I've done on myself, Ryan has paid the price."

"Abby, I'm not sure where you're going with this, but I need to leave."

Words tumble out of her. Whether for me or for herself, I'm not sure.

She says, "It's my fault, I'm owning it, but you made it a hell of a lot easier to cover up the mess and move on. If you had stayed, we could have figured this out. I used to think it would have killed me, but now I'm not so sure. Being in a crazy lie of a marriage is worse."

Inside I cringe when she talks about moving on. I thought I'd never move on. "Abby," I say again, "I need to go."

"Please don't," she says, taking hold of my arm. "We were supposed to be friends forever. We were supposed to know how to forgive each other. Nothing will feel right until I fix this."

There she is. The Abby I met on the first day of freshman year. Abby with the big brown eyes that suck me in. Abby who can get me to feel sorry for her even after she has betrayed me in the worst possible way. I am tossing the excuses around: *I did this. I left them. I didn't fight.*

Shoulder to shoulder we stare out at the mountains of Tennessee. A few golfers are driving by in their carts and wave up to us. "Abby, you don't need to do this. You don't need to explain anymore."

"I'm not asking for your forgiveness—well, I am. But I understand if you can't give it. Maybe you can try." She hesitates before reaching for my hand this time. "Please don't go."

Her body is melting into mine. I feel a tug in places I thought had banished Abby forever. "I have to go. It's time."

She's thinking about this, and I can tell her mind is working through something big. A beautiful white-breasted nuthatch lands on the railing beside us, though Abby doesn't notice. There's a lot going on in her, even now. Her eyes are darting back and forth as if she's just solved the world's problems. When the bird takes off in to the sky, its loud yammering takes Abby's eyes along with it. She's gazing up and over the mountains, following the tiny creature through the blue sky. The smile that spreads across her face is strange, but the rest of her looks free and light.

I have no more room in my heart to be cruel. "Abby, I don't mean to cut you off, but I have to make a flight."

She turns from the sky, her glowing face causing me to pause. "Is there nothing I can do to get you to stay?" she asks.

"I can't, Abby. Maybe some other time."

Her arms are coming around me and her words fill my ears. "You were my best friend. The two of you. I loved you both so much there was never any room to love myself. And still I never showed you what you meant to me. I can do that now. I can prove to you that I've changed." Then she whispers something so softly and so impossible, I, at first, think I am imagining it.

"Did you hear me?" she asks, backing away, her arms outstretched on my shoulders so we are facing each other.

Yes, I hear her. The crazy look in her eyes actually looks less crazy. I can't imagine why she's telling me this.

I have to move away from her or I will give in. I will remember sliding down falls with her, holding her hand as we skipped through Davidson, laughing ourselves to sleep. I will hear her telling me Ryan still loves me and I will wish for another chance. Abby. Her highs were always higher. Her lows always lower. The drama that surrounded her was hard to leave behind.

So I turn and walk away.

CHAPTER THIRTY-EIGHT

RYAN

The car ride home is always quieter than the ride down. The boys are worn out, and they put on headphones and drown out my compliments. At a traffic light, I reach behind me for one of Devon's earbuds, tugging it out of his ear. He tries to fight me at first, but I'm stronger than he is, and I tell him how proud he's made me, and I thank him. The grin covers his whole face, and he has to turn his head toward the window because it feels too good. If only I had the ability to fine-tune the women in my life as I have done these young men.

Solitude always brings her back to me, hard as I try to push her away. My mind wanders to what could've been, what would have happened if I had known Lauren was there. Instead of walking away without a fight, I run after her until I am out of breath. We fix the frayed edges until we are bound again. I shuffle in my seat and try to shake it out of me. And the feeling goes away, returning to a place I can't visit. And there is Abby. New and improved Abby. Mother of my child Abby. Thinking about her makes me wonder why we didn't have more kids, seeing how we made one that was so perfect. I'm reminded why: Abby's illness, the push and pull of her moods. And then I get angry and chase after Lauren all over again.

The club is up ahead, and we pull into the parking lot by the pool where Jules and Abby are tanning themselves. The home we are staying in includes membership and access to the club's amenities. E.J. is out of the car first, passing through the gate and diving into the water. Juliana, in an awfully small bathing suit, follows behind him.

I watch my daughter's eyes train on E.J., and I try to remember when she stopped looking at me with hero worship. She's growing up into a woman. We won't have these moments for long. E.J. is splashing her with one hand while the other tempts her with a plastic ball. "Tell me you love me," he keeps saying over and over again as she jumps for the ball, and he snatches it from her. I am thinking to myself, *I loved her first and best. Just remember that, buddy boy.*

Abby follows me into the water. She can still fill out a bathing suit, and I admire what I see. She doesn't lean in to me, and I don't wrap my arms around her, though her butt in the red bikini bottom is hot, and I give it a playful squeeze. She smiles, tells me her ass is fat, and snatches the ball from E.J.'s hand.

All these months of watching Abby improve, something deep inside of her has changed. Her eyes no longer sprout question marks; her lips seem to have found all the answers. The water rises and falls around us. Everything looks normal and as it should. Only, she is a few feet away from me, and there is an ocean between us.

At some point, she stops playing and swims toward me. Her strokes and her eyes are precise. When she reaches me, her smile is genuine.

"You'll never guess who I saw today."

CHAPTER THIRTY-NINE

ABBY

Ryan. Dear, sweet Ryan. He would stay with me no matter the price. Sweat and chlorine mix with his personal scent. He comes close to my ear and whispers, "I don't care who you saw today."

How long had I wished for this? How long had I wanted a clear conscience and a chance at a new beginning, to be able to feel tranquility from the moment I awoke in the morning?

Ryan is forcing me closer, and his hands tickle my neck. I feel as though I'm suffocating. The only thing that gets him to stop horsing around is when I say her name. His fingers lose their grip on my shoulders, and he turns away.

"She's here," I'm saying into the back of his head where the hair falls against his neck in the shape of a *V*. I am studying him. He is older, though he is the Ryan I fell in love with a hundred years ago. Our love was never predestined or otherworldly, but it has always been safe and reliable. He is safe and reliable. Good old Ryan. Everyone can count on him.

When he turns again to face me, I go on. "You know that book I devoured in a day last week? The one you said was the title of a Bruce Springsteen song?"

"I remember."

"Lauren wrote it. She moved to London after she found us and wrote novels for years, a string of love stories that became best sellers. It was the way she channeled her pain. She used a pen name. It's the name of two waterfalls she visited abroad. Virginia Sutherland. She strung them together and created a person to hide behind." I stop to take a breath. "Did you know any of this?"

The serious way in which he presses his lips together tells me he had no idea. "How could I?"

"She spoke at the club today. Seems everyone has a secret. She was the guest author I was dying to meet. Her big unveiling. I thought I was going to fall out of my chair. You really didn't know?" I ask again.

His hands break the water with a splash. The drops land on his cheeks and chest, and I think about wiping them off. "That my ex was a famous author? I'm pretty sure I would've mentioned it."

I walk toward the shallow end and step out of the pool.

"Are you mad?" he asks, coming after me.

I'm being elusive, though not for the reasons he thinks. Lauren's forgiveness, unearthing the truth—both mine and hers—has given me a gentle nudge toward true understanding. While I was hiding facts and hiding behind my disease, Lauren was hiding, too. We were both living fake lives.

We walk toward our chairs and grab our towels. Juliana is so immersed in E.J. that she barely notices we have left. Devon is nearby playing pickleball. The deck is hot, and we sit in our lounges. I am a bucket of nerves. One movement and I will tip over, and things will pour out that I just cannot stop.

I pull the string on my wrist. I take deep breaths. I can do this. I lie back on the chair and inhale, counting to three, exhale, counting to five. Ryan grabs hold of my hand because he senses I am struggling. It's like walking into a pitch-black room with no windows. Most people adjust to the dark, but I don't. And then I panic. *But not today. Today I'm going to hold it together.*

"Why don't we go back to the house," he says.

I suggest that we take a walk around the lake instead. Stepping into my shorts, I grab my jacket. It has a zipper in the front, and I pull it up as high as it will go. My bathing suit leaves a wet imprint across the front.

Ryan throws on a T-shirt. He looks nervous.

"It's all right," I tell him. "I think everything is finally going to be okay."

The short walk to Lake Coffey is made longer by my need to stretch out the moment. Clarity has come to me, like a stream. Like Jeannie said in our sessions, the work I had done would continue to reveal itself through "authentic interactions with those around me."

Lake Coffey is quiet and calm. A group of young boys is fishing at the new pier, and couples are walking their dogs around the circle. We start off to the right and follow the path around the water.

There is silence in our steps. The warning signs of anxiety that spiked my brain earlier are all but gone. What is left is the feel of my heartbeat as it awakens. We stop by the plank bridge and stare down into the shallow water. Ryan's reflection stares up at me. He is handsome and strong, the man I have loved for a lifetime.

"God damn you Southern boys," I finally say, "making us girls fall in love with you. All that sugary righteousness. None of us could have known it would tear the three of us apart."

He's staring at his hands, not our reflections below. He's been waiting for this all these months.

"When you really love someone, you want them to be happy. When you really love someone, you would rather die than hurt that person."

"Abby," he begins, to me, to the fishermen across the way.

"No. Let me finish. You don't need to do this anymore. You don't need to keep sacrificing yourself for me or anybody else. My head has never been clearer." I take a breath and whisper into the air, "I'm letting you go."

He turns away from me as though walking away will erase the words. "You're not making any sense, Abby."

I follow beside him and continue talking. "It would be a lot easier if this were one of those stories where everything broken got put back together, but it's not. I care about you too much to hold on to you any longer."

He stops walking and we are facing each other. He's confused, bringing his fingers to his forehead, and for the first time, I'm clear. He says, "Why are you doing this?"

My palm brushes his cheek, and he lets it rest against my hand. "Why are you fighting me?" I ask.

His eyes are filling with tears and his voice catches. "You're my wife."

I'm shaking my head. The gentle winds spill around us and the fresh air promises us hope. "We don't love each other the way two people in love should."

He takes a step back and swipes at his eyes. "We've been together a lot of years, Abby. Marriage changes people."

"We were never in love. I didn't even know you. I barely knew myself."

He stops at the footbridge and his hands grip the frame. "That's it? You get to decide? You go all *Eat, Pray, Love* on me, and we're supposed to forget the years we had together? We break our daughter's heart?"

"C'mon, Ry. You deserve more. So does she."

"You're not thinking rationally," he says.

He is holding everything inside. The fingers I once desired on my body run through his hair, only the strokes are angry and troubled, and those hands are no longer for me.

"I always thought you'd leave me for her. I spent most of our marriage waiting for that day to come."

"Is that what this is? You think I want Lauren?"

"She told you she loves you. You walked away from her because of me. You need to find her. You have to fight for her this time."

He takes a step back from me, his wife and this life. He is staring into my damp eyes as though to stop the words from pouring from my mouth. His eyes are wet too.

It's a subtle movement, a burst of glowing orange, but I feel her all around us. I take my eyes off his and scan the lake and its surroundings until I find her there. He has no idea what I've done for him. They were reckless, unplanned words, and she listened. And she is here. His eyes follow my gaze, turning in the direction they know best. When he sees her, coming up from alongside the brush, his entire body weakens.

I am crying because I know what this means.

"You need to tell her."

He doesn't look my way when he says, "She already knows."

We are watching her as she hesitates, standing beside a lengthy tree that makes her look small and unsure.

"She needs to hear it from you."

The winds whip the lake and the ripples creep into the banks. The voices of the children fishing sprinkle laughter in our ears. The sun flashes through the trees, as I take Ryan's hand and lead him along the wooden planks and around the circle. He doesn't speak. We stroll in silence. Dogs bark. I close my eyes and feel the warm air hug my cheeks and lick my tears. Just as we are nearing the bend to where she stands, I let go of his fingers. "Go ahead," I tell him. "I'm not afraid anymore. I can go down the falls by myself."

My face turns up toward the sun. There are a few stray clouds against a bright blue. The trees are larger, the flowers vivid, the leaves more brilliant. Their rustling mimics a peaceful rain. And I turn away, stepping along the path that takes me away from him. I can't look at her as I pass by, and I'm certain she's not looking at me. They are fixed on each other, watching the years they lost start to return. They are remembering how completely they once loved, how old feelings never die.

As I cross the narrow path that leads back to the pool and my daughter, I turn to take one last look. They are facing each other, their hands fumbling as though they can't trust what is happening. She is looking up at him the way she once did long ago, and he finds me there with tears in his eyes. I nod in his direction: *it's okay.* And my heart tells him I will always love him, but he has to let me go, too.

When he pulls her toward him, it is a sudden movement. It's as though he had saved all that love for this moment, and his arms grab her in a deep embrace. It was the kind that stole time and returned promises. It was different from the ones I'd witnessed before. At once I am both free and tortured. The colliding of these emotions thrusts me into an alternate universe, one where love ends and begins, dreams fade and ignite. I must close my eyes from them while my face turns toward the sky I can't see but can feel. It hurts and it heals.

Babs was right. The dream made perfect sense. I would be okay without Ryan's arm around me. I had learned that in the past year. My eyes open and fix upward. I am ready to take a giant leap.

I hear Juliana's laughter coming from the direction of the pool. I am a few short steps away. When she sees me approaching, she gets out of the water and heads in my direction.

"Mama, I wasn't sure that was you walking up. Have you been crying?" she asks. I tell her what she's noticing is me, just lighter.

"Where were you? Where's Daddy?" she asks.

I tell her, "Daddy's where he needs to be." Then I take my daughter into my arms and tell her how much I love her. She doesn't squirm away. She actually hugs me back.

"Mama, you're acting weird."

Still I grip her tighter and love her through the pain and joy of what's to come.

And even though it is awful what we are about to go through as a family, I know for the first time that this is what true happiness feels like.

Imagining it any other way would be impossible.

BOOK CLUB QUESTIONS

1. Falling in love, falling out of love, falling apart—how do the individual characters fall into and away from each other? How does this work for them? How does it fail?

2. The author uses water throughout the story to emphasize themes and emotions. How did it connect Abby, Lauren, and Ryan?

3. Mental illness is real and affects millions of people. How has this affliction become so far-reaching and how can we, as a society, reduce the stigma attached to it?

4. Lauren's eyesight played a minor role in the novel. Do you believe we see only what we want to see? Why?

5. In some ways, Abby is a selfish, distant parent. At the same time, she has raised an independent, self-sufficient teenager. How did benign neglect benefit Juliana? Where is the right balance for raising children?

6. How did E.J. and Juliana's young love impact Abby and Ryan's adult marriage? What were some notable parallels between the two relationships?

7.   Platonic love is a love that is more ideal than romantic love. When Abby makes her final decision, is she proving this to be true?

8.   In seeing all of Abby, and her flaws, should Lauren forgive her friend? Is there someone in your life you need to see more clearly in order to understand him or her better?

9.   Why do you think Abby was able to make the choice she made at the end of the novel?

10. Imagine you are able to write another chapter of *Where We Fall*. Where do you see the various characters at the next stage of their lives?

ACKNOWLEDGMENTS

Authors will tell you how hard it is to capture every person who has touched them during the writing process. There are those who inspire, teach, support, critique, or simply provide a listening ear or the hook for the next book. So much goes into the creative process; it is a collaborative effort complete with hair-pulling, love, and commitment. I am grateful to the following individuals for their contribution to *Where We Fall*.

Adam Chromy, my agent, for believing in this story and hustling like a rock star to make it happen. Danielle Marshall and the team at Lake Union Publishing for welcoming me into their home and providing a seamless entry into the world of publishing. Tiffany Yates Martin for your brilliant developmental edit. While there were moments of pure frustration and teeth-clenching, you challenged me to create a better story while shaping, smoothing, and polishing. It was truly an honor working with you. Kathrine Faydash, thank you for your eagle-eye edits. Your attention to detail and ability to fine-tune a sentence have made the manuscript shine. Thank you for making me dig deep below the surface for the perfect line—every time. Martine Bellen and Jan Blanck, your input and careful editing were an integral part of the manuscript in its early stages.

Thank you to all my early readers, particularly those who shared their invaluable feedback with me and plodded through multiple drafts to ensure I was on the right track. Amy Berger, Mindy Blum, Jill Coleman, Sandi Cooper, and Merle Saferstein.

For those who shared their insights, knowledge and expertise with me. Coaches Jeff Bertani and Wayne Rullan of my alma mater, the North Miami Beach Chargers, Coach Joe Campodonico, Coach Judd Hayes, John Battle, Marge Bailey, Alan Weinstein, Patrick Montoya, Meline Markarian, Allison Mars, Brooke Goldberg, Ellen Helman, Judith Chestler, Mark Panunzio, Richie Stolar, and Amanda Zaron. For all those who anonymously shared their heartfelt experience with depression and anxiety, you are the strongest people I know.

Thank you to all the readers, fans, and fellow authors who have rooted me on from the very beginning of this journey. It is your cheers that I hear when I'm alone at my writing desk. You don't know how many times you have gotten me through a bad writing day.

Thank you to my family and all my wonderful friends who have shared their ongoing support, love, and kindness with me. I hold each of you close to my heart, and I profusely apologize for my shortness, absence, and sheer craziness while I worked on this novel.

Randi Berger, Rob Berger, and Ron Berger. My siblings. My squad. Your support and love are immeasurable. There would be no stories without all of you.

Brandon and Jordan Weinstein, you're the best of all my stories. As you go through life, make sure yours is full of smiles, laughter and love. And don't ever forget the Grammy rule. I will always love you *more*.

Steven Weinstein, I am sure there is a woman somewhere in the world who wants her money back. But thank you for your unwavering support and believing in me more than I could ever believe in myself. You fill my heart and home with the kind of love girls can only dream about. You and the boys are my world.

Finally, thank you to all the butterflies that have perched themselves on my window while I write. I know you can't be here, Mom, but because of those beautiful wings, I feel you all around me.

ABOUT THE AUTHOR

Photo © hester 2015

Born and raised in Miami, Florida, Rochelle B. Weinstein followed her love of the written word across the country. She moved north to attend the University of Maryland, earning a degree in journalism, and began her career in Los Angeles at the *LA Weekly*. After moving back to Miami, she enjoyed a stint in the entertainment industry, marrying her love of music with all things creative. When her twins arrived, she sat down one afternoon while they were napping and began to write. The resulting novel, the highly acclaimed *What We Leave Behind*, explores the poignancy of love and the human condition. Her second book, *The Mourning After*, is a moving story of hope and resiliency. To learn more about her, visit her website at www.rochelleweinstein.com.